Death at the Shipshape Bookshop

A Southeast Alaska Mystery • *Book 1*

GRETA MCKENNAN

Epicenter Press Inc.
Alaska Book Adventures™

Kenmore, WA

published by Epicenter Press

Epicenter Press
6524 NE 181st St. Suite 2
Kenmore, WA 98028.
www.Epicenterpress.com
www.Coffeetownpress.com
www.Camelpress.com

For more information go to: www.Epicenterpress.com
Author's website: www.gretamckennan.com

Death at the Shipshape Bookshop
Copyright © 2025 by Greta McKennan

ISBN: 9781684922406 (trade paper)
ISBN: 9781684922413 (ebook)

LOC: 2024940281

For Jamie, Laura, and Johnny:

Three beautiful children

Acknowledgments

Thanks to my editor, Jennifer McCord, and the folks at Epicenter Press for taking my story and making it into a beautiful book. Thanks to my agent, Jessica Faust, and the folks at BookEnds Literary Agency for taking care of business, so I can focus on writing. It takes a village to make a book, and I am grateful to all of you!

Thanks to the following people who were willing to read my story, make helpful suggestions, give computer assistance, or even just let me run on about my ideas: John Barnhill, Mike Barnhill, Dordie Carter, Jami Denison, Nancy Eiler, Freda Westman, and Betsy Williams.

Special thanks and love to Mike for giving me encouragement and support on my cozy mystery journey—I couldn't have done it without you! Love to Jamie, Laura, and Johnny.

Chapter One

It was a lovely summer morning in Southeast Alaska.

The mountainsides breathed a mist that rose softly as we slid past them. The boat made very little noise in the early morning light, with the drone of the engine muffled by the drizzle of rain. A fresh breeze on my cheek promised fair weather as the day continued to unfold. There was not the slightest hint of murder in the air.

I pulled my jacket close around me and scanned the stony shorelines, ever eager for a glimpse of wildlife. A steep creek meandered down the hillside to flow across the beach and into the channel, providing breakfast for a mama bear and her two cubs.

I clapped my hands together. "Evan, look, bears are out fishing at Color Creek."

Captain Evan just grunted, like he does. He wore his pilot's cap pulled low over his bald head, a visual reminder that he was in charge of both the boat and the conversation. As usual, he preferred silence. I sometimes wondered how he managed to tolerate the chattering of the children who swarmed the boat at every port, browsing the bookshelves under the watchful eyes of their aunties. Apparently unmoved by the joy that our books brought to the kids in the remote villages, Evan focused all his energy on the running and upkeep of the *Northern Dream*, like he had for the past forty years. He was the only one I would trust with the ancient boat, Southeast Alaska's only floating bookmobile.

Mama bear snagged a salmon in her jaws and flung it to the ground near her cubs. The little ones jostled each other in their rush to snatch up the carcass. I could faintly hear their happy growling as they munched.

"Good morning," I called out to them, leaning over the railing to wave as we motored by. One of the cubs looked up, startled by my voice. But the lure of the salmon was too strong. The cub returned to his breakfast, cuffing his sibling to claim his fair share of the feast.

I drew in a deep breath of the fresh, salty air, heedless of the fine rain falling on my face. I couldn't be happier to be back home, after too many years Outside. This summer of 2015 was my first chance to be on the water with the bookmobile, after taking over the business from my uncle this past November. Florida beaches were fine as far as they went, but they couldn't compete with my hometown paradise. I closed my eyes and let the small sounds of the channel wash over me. Suddenly, a loud voice broke the calm.

"Ahoy, Junetta!"

My eyes popped open. We were running close in to shore, close enough to smell the tangy scent of sourdough bread baking in the big oven up at the lodge and hear the voice of the woman waving from the end of a long pier. She wore jeans and brown rubber boots, Southeast Alaska's ubiquitous waterproof footwear. Her graying hair hung in a long braid down her back, and her eyes were shaded by a Seattle Mariners baseball cap. She stood on the pier as if she'd been there forever, like a strong tree in the forest, holding up an eagle's nest.

"Ahoy, Mom," I called back.

It was our biweekly routine. Mom knew my sailing schedule as intimately as she'd known my mercurial moods when I was a teenager. It was always a joy for me to see her, but it meant more than that to her. For Mom, the glimpse of me every other week was her reassurance that I was still alive, that I'd survived another sea voyage through the Inside Passage. It was something we didn't talk about much. She never tried to stop me, though I knew how much my trips on the *Northern Dream* cost her in terms of worry. If I had a magic wand to wave away her anxieties, I would have done so in a heartbeat. Since I was wandless, at least I could keep my schedule as predictable as possible. She stood on the dock and I stood on the deck, two times a month, waving our love to each other over the cold Alaska waters. As family traditions go, this one was pretty sweet.

"Mary Porter sends her greetings to you, Mom," I hollered as the boat slipped by. "She wants to know when you're going to send her your recipe for sourdough scones."

Mom just laughed. We both knew that she would never relinquish her signature recipe, the one that took pride of place on the menu at her remote inn, the Sourdough Lady Lodge. Mary Porter knew it too, which didn't stop her from asking every time I saw her. I smiled at the thought of that familiar conversation, playing out time and again. Another piece of the fabric of life that made Southeast Alaska such a comfortable, friendly place to live.

"I've got a wedding party coming in from Boston tomorrow," Mom called out. "Twenty-seven people who've never seen the Alaska wilderness before."

"They've got a treat waiting for them!" If anyone could show outsiders a glimpse of the real Alaska, it was Mom. I blew a few kisses across the water with a final wave goodbye and turned my head forward as the boat slipped into Havoc Strait and the town of Ptarmigan Port came into view. It was a colorful collection of houses and businesses, clinging to the sparse shoreline at the base of the tree-covered mountains. The vibrant colors of the buildings served to brighten up the dark, rainy days in this boreal rainforest. No roads connected the town to the rest of civilization—the only ways in and out were by sea or air. From the water I could see the Tongass Glacier towering above its valley. The muted sunlight intensified the blue of the ice. The glacier flowed out of the mountains until it melted at the face to become Seven Mile Creek. Its close proximity to town made it a major tourist attraction to the hordes of cruise ship tourists who flocked to the region in the summertime. As the owner of the Shipshape Bookshop in town, I loved seeing the tourists every summer. They bolstered my book business, making it possible for me to serve the remote villages with the bookmobile boat. More than that, I loved chatting with people from all over the world, hearing their stories and sharing my own. Like Uncle Vance liked to say, not all stories live inside books.

Captain Evan steered us skillfully past the shipwreck site, where the SS *Fortunate*, a passenger ship from the Klondike gold fields, had the misfortune to go down in 1915, one hundred years ago. The ship's remains lay submerged on the bottom of the fjord. Havoc Strait was aptly named.

We didn't have to pass the other shipwreck site, thank goodness.

We motored past the cruise ship dock downtown and made for Cornell Cove harbor south of town, named for the founder of Ptarmigan Port. Craig Cornell was a prospector who had discovered gold in a stream bed in 1902 and started a short-lived gold rush and an enduring town. His last living relation, Reba Cornell, director of the Ptarmigan Port Historical Society, worked hard to ensure that everyone in town appreciated her grandfather's influence on local history.

Captain Evan tied the *Northern Dream* up at the dock, refusing my offer to give him a hand. Seriously, I knew better than to offer, but sometimes impulsiveness would get the better of me. I played it off with my hundred-watt smile, and left Evan on the boat feeling like he was the only one in charge.

I'd left my car at the harbor, so it was only a matter of minutes before I was driving down Ptarmigan Port's two-block long business district. I passed a colorful conglomeration of businesses and tourist shops, each one painted in bright hues designed to chase the winter blues away. Two totem poles anchored either end of the street: the weathered one that had overlooked our town since the early 1900s, and the newly raised one, freshly painted in vibrant colors. Both poles told the same story, of Raven bringing daylight to the world. Old and new, they symbolized the celebration of Tlingit culture in our town.

My bookshop occupied two storefronts on this cheerful stretch, where it had stood ever since my great-grandmother, Betty Denton, had opened it in 1947. The window on the left displayed an array of Alaska books and maps, interspersed with the latest bestsellers as well as some colorful picture books. The window on the right showcased the Last Chance Café, run by my best friend Marcy George. It had been her idea to pair the café with the bookshop in the first place. She had worked on Uncle Vance for over a year before he budged far enough to allow coffee to occupy the same space as his beloved books.

I paused to admire the teal blue exterior with its bright purple accents that always lifted my spirits on a dreary day. Each front door was painted a cherry red designed to catch the eye. On Marcy's side, the formline art decorating the sign for the Last Chance Café highlighted her Tlingit heritage. On my side, a hanging wooden sign embellished with a striking line drawing of the *Northern Dream* proclaimed, "The Shipshape Bookshop." I loved every bit of it.

I circled around to park in the alley behind the bookshop. That's when I knew that something was wrong. An Alaska State Troopers' van was parked in the alley, and the back door to the bookshop was cordoned off with yellow crime scene tape. I threw my car into park and jumped out. I hustled around the building and charged through the front door to the cheery jangle of the bell. The sound was sadly out of place.

The sight that met my eyes was an independent bookstore owner's worst nightmare. Someone had trashed my bookshop! Shelves were toppled over, spilling books out onto the hardwood floor. My antique brass cash register had been thrown straight through the glass display counter at the front of the store. It lay amid a scattering of glass shards, with its drawer hanging open and empty. Framed pictures had been torn off the walls and smashed onto the floor in a whirl of glass. A poster advertising the upcoming Founders' Day picnic hung in shreds on the wall.

I spun around in a daze, to see that a small crowd had gathered at the front of the store. I registered the familiar faces. Uncle Vance leaned heavily on his richly carved walking stick, never to be confused with a cane. His thinning gray hair brushed his shoulders, and his overlong beard gave him a genuine sourdough aspect. His bushy eyebrows hooded his dark eyes in an impressive frown. As former owner of the Shipshape Bookshop, or "owner emeritus" as I liked to call him, this vandalism appeared to hit him personally. Several customers milled around, with Marcy trying her best to keep them from touching anything. She clutched a bar cloth in both hands. She didn't even notice the wisps of black hair escaping from her headband. She saw me and broke free from the crowd to lumber to my side, slowed by her pregnant belly.

"Junetta! Thank goodness you made it. It's awful! Blake…"

I cut across her exclamations. "Where are the troopers?"

She waved an unsteady hand. "Nels is in the back room with the body."

The nightmare just got worse.

"Body?" I could tell I was screeching, but I couldn't help it. "What body?" I charged toward the back room without waiting for an answer.

My young employee, Patrick, stopped me at the doorway. His face was pale, almost green, in contrast to his bright purple hair. His bony shoulders quivered in shock. He averted his eyes from the sight of the strapping trooper in the back room bending over something on the floor. "You can't go in," he whispered.

I brushed past him as if he were no more than a shoot of devil's club impeding my way on a hiking trail.

I stopped beside the trooper to stare at the body on the floor. It was a real dead body, lying crumpled up on the floor with a knife protruding from the chest. It looked like… "Blake Rivers? Why is Blake Rivers lying dead in my back room?"

The trooper turned to pin me with his steely gaze. "Welcome back from the villages, Sis."

I cringed at his sardonic tone. "What happened here, Nels?" I couldn't tear my eyes away from Blake's chest. There wasn't a lot of blood, with the knife still in the wound. I looked closer, holding my breath. The knife hilt was made of ivory, carved like scrimshaw. I made out the two curling vines twining around each other to encircle the beaver at the top of the hilt. It was all so familiar. I raised my eyes to Nels's face. He stood with both fists resting on his heavy belt in an intimidating power pose. He voiced the suspicion that was creeping into my numbed brain.

"That's Uncle Vance's knife."

Chapter Two

"I need to sit down." I could barely hear my own voice.

Nels grabbed my arm and pushed me down onto a step stool. He shoved my head down between my knees. "Keep it together, Junetta."

I struggled against his grip and flung up my head. "I'm not going to pass out!"

Nels knelt down and gripped me by both shoulders. "Has Uncle Vance been feuding with Blake lately? Could things have gotten so bad that he stabbed him?"

I shook my head, more to clear out the fog of shock than to express a negative opinion. We loved him dearly, but Nels and I both knew that Uncle Vance was a cantankerous old sourdough who carried on feuds and vendettas with numerous people in our town. I'd never known him to hurt anyone unless you count popping his buddy Davey Harper on the head with his walking stick. Davey kindly refrained from pressing charges, given the fact that the walking stick incident was immediately preceded by Davey slinging a pitcher of beer into Uncle Vance's face. Both men were escorted out of the Grizzly Bar, and that was the end of it. No troopers necessary.

Uncle Vance's feud with Blake Rivers was different. Blake was the owner of Saltwater Tours, which ran glass-bottom boat tours to view the shipwreck site of the SS *Fortunate*. A big man with an abrasive personality, Blake rubbed a sizeable percentage of our small population the wrong way. Several fishermen suspected him of raiding their crab pots, a cardinal sin in coastal Alaska. I'd heard vague rumors of an extortion scheme, but the gossip mill was short on details. Uncle Vance nurtured a personal hatred of the man. This past spring, he publicly accused Blake of attempting to poison his little dog, Cosmo, and banned him from setting foot in the bookshop. Blake seemed to take a perverse pleasure in this ban. He would come around and stand directly outside our front door, waggling a foot over the threshold and chanting, "Little pig, little pig, let me come in."

Well, he was in now.

I averted my eyes from the body. "I've been gone for a week, Nels. I can't speak to the current state of Uncle Vance's feud with Blake. I guess it's over now, though."

Nels's cheek twitched once, as if in another life he might have smiled at my comment. His eyes bored into mine. "Dr. Starling is on his way with the ambulance. The body will have to be sent to Juneau for an autopsy."

"It's pretty clear how he died." I shut my mouth abruptly. Nels didn't need me to remind him of the near certainty that it was Uncle Vance who had stabbed Blake.

Nels led me out of the back room with a quick word to Patrick, "Don't let anyone get past you." Patrick saluted as if Nels were a five-star general. The kid knew how to get on the right side of the law.

The scene of destruction had not magically disappeared in the time that I'd spent in the back room. The crowd had dispersed, however. I looked around in a panic, to see that Marcy had shuffled them all into the café and was serving coffee and pastries as if this was a routine Sunday morning.

The Last Chance Café matched the cozy vibe of the bookshop, with a Tlingit flare. The front counter displayed tempting pastries, with a different kind of muffin every day. A pair of beautifully carved cedar paddles flanked the chalkboard menu behind the counter. The red and black formline art on their blades depicted an orca on one and a humpback whale on the other. On the wall, a wooden plaque with a carving of the story of Raven stealing the sun highlighted Marcy's identity in the Raven moiety. Coasters featuring her clan crest sat on several small tables which were scattered throughout the café. The only thing out of place was the trooper standing at attention at the door to prevent anyone from leaving. He was wasting his time. A robbery and murder were such a novelty in our small town that no one would dream of wandering off and missing out on all the excitement. The trooper's main job would be to keep eager onlookers from coming into the building.

I scanned the faces of the customers. I noticed Marcy's grandmother, Annalisa Martin, a beloved Tlingit elder. She sat quietly, her dark eyes watchful. There was Reba Cornell, director of the Ptarmigan Port Historical Society, who always wanted to know absolutely everything that happened in town for historical purposes. She was dressed for business in a navy skirt and blazer with her gray hair twined into a respectable bun, despite the prevailing casualness of our small fishing town. Then there was a young man with curly dark hair who I didn't recognize. Uncle Vance sat at a table by himself, nursing a cup of coffee. He shook his head when Marcy offered him cream for his coffee. "I can't drink the stuff anymore. Doctor says I've developed lactose intolerance in my old age," he grumbled. "That's just another way of saying that he's the one who decides what I do these days."

I went to join Uncle Vance, but Marcy headed me off.

She took my arm and led me to one of her small tables, shoving me into a chair. She snagged a super-sized coffee mug and poured me a whopping cup of fresh coffee mixed with warm milk the way I liked it. She dropped a blueberry muffin in front of me and sat down to face me. "Eat," she said.

I glanced over at Uncle Vance. He didn't look like he was going anywhere. I took a bite of muffin and a long swallow. The hot coffee jolted me out of my stupor. "Are you okay, Marcy? Did you discover the body?" I hated to talk about Blake Rivers in those terms, as if he had left behind a horrible inconvenience.

"I got here before Vance, like I always do. Folks were lined up on the sidewalk waiting to get in. As soon as I opened the door, I knew something was wrong. I guess I lost my head. I should have shooed everyone back out the door, but I just let them all in to follow me around and see what damage was done. Reba called the troopers and the rest of us just wandered around. I think it was Patrick who went into the storeroom first. Poor kid, he looked like he was going to lose it." She wiped the table in front of her with her bar rag, over and over in a circular motion that had nothing to do with cleanliness.

I reached out to lay a hand over hers. "This can't be good for Baby Rain," I said, using the name she and Rob gave their unborn baby. They didn't want to know the baby's gender, opting instead for a "secret baby." I could barely stand the suspense, but Marcy was content to wait for Baby Rain to make an appearance in the baby's own time.

She took a deep, slow breath and laid a protective hand on her belly. "No dead body is going to mess with my baby."

"You got that right!"

Now that we'd settled the most important thing, I pointed to the stranger. He had bright brown eyes under a shock of tumbled brown curls, and his brand-new rain slicker identified him as a tourist. He sipped his coffee with a relaxed air that was belied by his intent watchfulness. "Who is that guy?"

Marcy shrugged. "He came in with the rest. He's obviously a tourist. Come on, Junetta, you can figure out everything about him."

I couldn't resist a small smile. I did like speculating on people's backstories, and sometimes I actually got it right. I leaned my chin on my hands and studied the man in question.

He looked to be in his late twenties, roughly my age. He was left-handed, or at least he picked up his coffee cup with his left hand. Underneath his pristine rain jacket, he wore a Columbia University sweatshirt; he was an academic, and clearly not from Alaska. He wasn't scrolling through his phone or reading the newspaper or anything. Rather, he was taking in the scene in the café and the ransacked bookshop with avid attention. Could he be a reporter or private investigator or something?

He caught me looking and nodded in my direction. I picked up my coffee and scooted my chair over to his table and held out my hand. "I'm Junetta Beale, owner of the Shipshape Bookshop."

He took my hand in a firm grip. "Angus Montgomery. I'm visiting from New York." He spoke with a broad accent that didn't sound like the slight nasal twang that I associated with native New Yorkers. "I'm doing some research for my dissertation. I'm an historian." He said it with an infinitesimal pause, as if it were a new occupation for him, or perhaps a false one? Between that and the discrepancy between his accent and his place of origin, I didn't quite know what to make of him.

I didn't have much time to think things over. Nels shouldered his way through the groovy beaded curtain separating the café from the bookshop. "I need to get statements from everyone who witnessed the discovery of Blake Rivers's body. I'll start with you, Marcy. I want the rest of you to spread out throughout the café, one at each table, and refrain from talking to one another."

He led Marcy to the children's section of the bookshop, where a couple beanbag chairs and a child-sized couch made a cozy corner for reading. Marcy took the couch while Nels pulled up a wooden stool. Neither one looked comfortable as the questioning began.

I could hardly stand the suspense. No, make that, I could not stand the suspense. I slurped down the last of my coffee and abandoned Angus Montgomery for later. Trying not to call attention to myself, I sidled through the beaded curtain. I surveyed the mess, trying not to look like I was eavesdropping. I heard Marcy mention 7:00 a.m. and saw Nels noting her words down in his notebook, and that was where my surveillance ended. The utter destruction surrounding me captured all my attention.

I gingerly reached into the shattered glass case to extricate my antique brass cash register. I hadn't bargained on how heavy it was. I managed to lift it about six inches, and then gravity took over. The fool thing crashed back into the case with the sound of a shot. Nels leapt up from his stool, his pistol drawn in a flash. Marcy ducked instinctively. Patrick yelped, Reba gasped, and Uncle Vance spun around in his chair so fast that he dropped his walking stick with a clatter.

"Sorry," I called out. I could feel my face flaming in embarrassment. "Just trying to start in on the cleanup."

Nels holstered his pistol while advancing on me. "Don't touch anything until the crime scene has been processed." His glare dared me to argue with him.

He was my brother. We were born to argue. "I want to take a look to see if anything is missing," I brushed a few stray bits of glass off my hands, noting a couple of nicks. I'd need gloves before I got serious about this cleanup.

Nels grabbed me by the arm to escort me back to the café. I was disappointed in him that he resorted to physical persuasion, which he could only use on me because I was his sister. This wasn't the moment to resolve any sibling issues between us, however. I suffered myself to be led back to the café under the watchful eyes of all my customers. I paused in the doorway to scan the ransacked bookshop one last time, and in that moment, I saw what was missing.

Photographs of the *Northern Dream* on her maiden voyage in 1932 and of the Tongass Glacier stretching wide at the terminus in 1947 had been ripped from the wall and thrown in a heap on the floor. My framed business license hung askew, clearly not important enough for the vandal to bother with. One frame was missing.

I wrenched my arm out of Nels's grip and hustled back to the pile. Before he could redirect me, I shifted the mess until I was sure.

"The Pastor's Confession Map is missing!"

Chapter Three

Nels froze in the act of reaching for my arm. I had the fleeting impression that all eyes were riveted on me as all conversation ceased. From the children's corner, Marcy looked on in dismay.

If I was a detective in a mystery novel, I would have closely watched each face for reactions in that moment. Would I have seen guilt on someone's face, or anger at the theft of our town's history, or simple ignorance of the magnitude of this loss? As it was, I saw none of those things, because I wasn't watching. I was simply staring at the wall, my mind whirling, trying to make sense of why someone would trash my bookshop and murder a man to make off with a framed treasure map dating back to 1915.

Angus Montgomery spoke up. "Map? What kind of a map?" He leaned forward with interest.

Before Nels could stop her, Reba Cornell launched into a lecture. If Angus wanted to know about local history, he'd come to the right place. As head of the Ptarmigan Port Historical Society, Reba kept our local history alive. She collected dusty books and letters, cataloguing them in innumerable bookshelves and deep drawers in a storefront three doors down from the Shipshape Bookshop. The walls of the Historical Society were covered with framed photographs of a bygone era. Really, the Pastor's Confession Map belonged in the Historical Society rather than in my bookshop, but neither Uncle Vance nor I had ever felt the urge to hand it over, despite Reba's repeated requests. Now it was missing.

I pushed that thought to the back of my mind, back where I'd shoved the sight of the first murdered man I'd ever seen, and dragged my attention back to Reba's story.

"The Pastor's Confession Map is one of the most prized historical artifacts of our town," she recited in a singsong voice. She settled more comfortably in her café chair. We were all in for a detailed lecture about the history behind the missing map, despite Nels's instructions to refrain from talking amongst ourselves. At least we had plenty of time, while he picked us off one by one for questioning.

"It's actually only half of a map, torn right down the middle. It was found in the effects of Reverend Raymond Denton, pastor of the Presbyterian church in Ptarmigan Port from its early days since the town's founding in 1902. Interestingly, the first Presbyterian church built on the shorelines was a log cabin that could hold no more than twenty-six worshippers seated on wooden pews hewed out of yellow cedar with an adze."

Okay, maybe we didn't have enough time for Reba to tell the story of the map.

"Raymond Denton was an ancestor of mine," I chimed in. "He had a boat ministry to the outlying villages in the 1930s and '40s. He would preach at each village church at least once a month, like the circuit riders down south. I follow his routes in his very same boat, the *Northern Dream*, which I use as a floating bookmobile to bring books to the village children."

Angus nodded. "I've heard of this concept. There were a number of these boats connecting the Native villages. They called it the 'Presbyterian Navy,' right?"

"That's right," I said, delighted that this local story was known back east. "Rev. Denton's daughter, Betty, opened the Shipshape Bookshop in 1947, after the war. She was my great-grandmother. When her father, the pastor, died and Betty went through his things, she found an envelope with a letter and a map inside. The letter said that the map came to him during a confessional, hence the name."

"You might find it interesting that the pastor was holding confessional," Reba broke in, seizing back control of the narrative, "given that he was a Presbyterian minister. As the only spiritual leader in the area, he had to meet the needs of all the people. So, he accepted the map from an unknown supplicant, put it in an envelope with the notation, "Mr. A. Mont." on the front, slipped it into a drawer and it was never seen again until after his death in 1952."

"That's enough!" Nels frowned around at the entire group of us gathered in the café. "No more talking!"

Nels returned to questioning Marcy in the bookshop, as a reluctant silence fell in the café. I glanced over at Angus, who was contemplating Reba's story with shining eyes. I found myself staring at him, trying to figure out what this attractive man was doing in my bookshop on the morning of a murder.

Finally, Marcy ducked through the curtain to tell me it was my turn. She gave my hand a warm squeeze before Nels led me to the low couch and faced me. Even though he was my little brother, I found his intense attention to be intimidating. I'd never been questioned by the troopers before. I felt faintly like a criminal, even though I'd obviously done nothing wrong.

"Tell me about your morning, Junetta."

I took a deep, cleansing breath. "I came back from the villages on the *Northern Dream* this morning. I was gone a week, like always. The bookshop was fine when I left, and when I got back it was in a shambles and Blake was dead." I was still struggling to accept the reality of that last statement.

"Who was manning the shop in your absence?"

"Uncle Vance is always here, every day. You'd never know he sold the shop to me."

Nels nodded and wrote in his little notebook.

"Then Patrick comes in around 11:00 a.m. every day and stays until 4:00 p.m. He relieves Uncle Vance for lunch and then takes his own lunch in the early afternoon." I slapped my hands down on my knees. "It doesn't really matter who was running the shop. Someone broke in overnight, last night. Marcy discovered it this morning when she opened the café. Anybody could have broken in and killed Blake after trashing the bookshop."

Unfazed by my outburst, Nels plodded on. "Do you have surveillance cameras in the bookshop or the café?"

I stared at my brother. "No. This is Southeast Alaska, not New York City. Marcy and I don't spy on our customers."

"Maybe it's time to start." He gave me a strange look. "Do you have any witnesses as to your movements between 7:00 p.m. last night and this morning at 7:00 a.m. when Marcy opened the doors to the bookshop?"

I stared at my brother, open-mouthed. "You're asking me to provide an alibi? Your own sister?"

His neutral expression didn't falter. "For the record."

I glared at him, although I knew my exasperation wouldn't make it into the record. "For your information, I spent the night on the *Northern Dream*, like I always do when I go to the villages. Captain Evan slept onboard as well—and if you think you're going to make something of that, think again! I happen to know that he took sleeping pills last night, which he sometimes does when we're moored for the night. We left Mallory at 6:35 this morning to catch the tide. I waved to Mom at 7:45—you can ask her. We moored in Cornell Cove Harbor at 8:10, I got in my car, and came right here. You were here when I arrived." I huffed loudly, albeit still off the record. "Satisfied?"

A quirky smile appeared on Nels's face. "You're obviously not a suspect, Junetta. I just wanted to hear your whole rigamarole."

This flash of humor was so unexpected that I couldn't even get angry. It took my breath away, just for an instant, which was exactly how long it lasted. Without missing a beat, Nels went on to question me about the security features of my shop and the schedules of my employees. He wasn't impressed by my assurance that the doors were all protected by deadbolts, which we faithfully locked every night. In a small town where door locking was decidedly optional, I felt like I was doing the right thing. Nels obviously thought that a security system complete with surveillance cameras, motion detectors, and facial recognition technology was the way to go. Like so many aspects of our lives, we had to agree to disagree on this one.

"Tell me about Blake Rivers. Is there any particular reason why he would be visiting the bookshop after hours?"

I'd been asking myself that same question ever since I saw his lifeless form. Why was Blake Rivers in my back storeroom to meet his death after the bookshop closed? "It doesn't make any sense. He had no business being there at all. You know Uncle Vance banned him from setting foot in the bookshop. There's no reason why he should have been in the back room after closing."

"Maybe to meet with Uncle Vance?"

I shrugged. "You'll have to ask him. Good luck with that, though. Uncle Vance couldn't stand Blake on the best of days. But he's hardly likely to say so now that Blake is dead."

Nels grimaced. He knew I was right. No one could get Uncle Vance to say anything he didn't want to.

Quickly, before Nels dismissed me, I said, "How do you think the Pastor's Confession Map fits into all this? I feel like somebody ripped the heart out of our town—who would do that?"

Nels paused in his writing. He shot me the first glance of sympathy I'd gotten from him all day. "Uncle Vance looked pretty cut up about that one."

Evidently, Nels had watched the crowd closer than I had. "Yeah. He's always taken pride in that bit of local history." I wanted to prolong this moment of connection with my brother. "Remember when you swore you would be the one to find the gold and make us all rich? You spent all summer combing the woods with your notebook full of drawings of what the missing half of the map might look like."

"All summer…" Nels echoed. I watched the nostalgia wash over his face before it hardened again. "That was a long time ago, Junetta."

He was right. That summer was a lifetime ago, for all of us.

Finally, Nels sent me off to the café with instructions to send Reba in. I heaved a sigh of relief. I'd survived my first experience of being questioned by Trooper Nels, my little brother.

Even though he was done with me, I had to wait a long hour and a half while Nels picked off the rest of us, one by one, for questioning. In accordance with his instructions to not speak to one another or access our phones, all we could do was sit and stare. It was like a youth group game of Murder, each person staring into the eyes of everyone else in the circle in silence, waiting to catch the murderer winking before they winked at you. I couldn't help it—I winked at Marcy. She frowned back at me, as if to say, "this is a real murder, you idiot."

Uncle Vance was the last to go. Throughout the deadly silence he had sat without moving, staring at his hands folded on the table in front of him. He had a tremendous capacity for just being, but something was different today. I watched him closely, trying to figure out what had changed. He wore his usual faded flannel shirt, soft from many, many washings. His jaw worked slowly, grinding away at the wad of gum that replaced the chewing tobacco I remembered from my childhood. From the battered baseball cap on his head to his metal-tipped boots, everything about him seemed ordinary. Then I realized—it was his hands. His hands lay on the table, unmoving. In real life, those gnarled hands would be in motion, with a block of wood in one and a knife in the other. Uncle Vance spent all of his free time whittling. He had a collection of knives in different sizes to accommodate his latest project, depending on the intricacy of the carving.

The largest of these knives now resided in Blake Rivers's chest.

Uncle Vance made no objection when Nels came to lead him into the bookshop for questioning. Nels gave him his usual stool behind the counter, probably in deference to his age. Nels leaned on the counter and spoke in a low voice, pausing to listen to Uncle Vance's responses and write in his annoying little notebook. I couldn't make out any words.

Finally, it was all over. Nels came through the beaded curtain to announce, "I am taking Vance Peterman into custody. The rest of you are free to go. The bookshop and café will remain closed until the crime scene can be processed. Please make your way to the door."

Nels was arresting his own uncle for murder.

Chapter Four

I jumped up from the table and scooted past Reba and Annalisa to get to Nels. "What do you think you're doing?" He had no time for my protests. He closed his notebook with a snap and held out his arm in a shooing motion towards the door. "Out," was all he said.

So, I went out.

I grabbed Marcy by the arm and hustled her down the sidewalk toward the dock. She couldn't go very fast because of her bulk. I tried to be patient. "Nels just arrested Uncle Vance," I hissed, conscious of the possibility of causing a scene in front of a cruise shipload of tourists. "What are we going to do about it?"

Marcy gently extricated her arm from my grasp. She headed straight for a bench on the dockside overlooking the harbor. Easing herself down into a sitting position, she motioned for me to join her, heedless of the fine rain that continued to fall. "Did you see the knife, Junetta? Nels had no choice."

"That's ridiculous!" If I said it loud enough, maybe we would all believe it. "Anyone could have picked up one of Uncle Vance's knives. It's not like he keeps them safely stored away or anything."

Marcy heaved a sigh. "You weren't here yesterday."

My hands went cold. Here it comes. "Okay, what happened yesterday?"

"Blake came in for a cup of coffee in the morning. He called out to Vance that they had to talk. Vance growled at him, like he does, then the two of them went off to talk. They actually left the building, so it must have been something big that they didn't want other people to hear. After a while, Vance came back without Blake." She paused to watch a blue and white float plane land on the water with a roar of its engine that covered all other sounds.

When I could speak again, I asked, "Did you see Blake again after that?"

She looked at me, startled. "I'm not saying Vance took Blake out and stabbed him! But they were clearly having some kind of argument. Vance wouldn't talk about Blake again for the rest of the day. We all went out to the Grizzly Bar in the evening. I had a hankering for Kirk's famous salmon chips. Baby Rain loves any kind of fish these days." She rubbed the small of her back. "Blake was at the bar, and he and Vance got into a shouting match. I don't know what it was about, because I try to ignore drunken men getting into it with each other. It sounded like it had to do with money." She shrugged. "That's all I know."

I leaned back on the bench and closed my eyes, letting the rain fall softly on my face. The din of the float plane taking off again faded into the distance. Above the chatter of the people on the dock, I could hear the soft wash of the waves and the high-pitched call of an eagle soaring somewhere overhead. The savory scent of fry bread mingled with the fresh smell of gently moving water. I took a deep breath, trying to empty my mind to help me focus. The image of Blake's dead body invaded my thoughts, and my eyes snapped open. Marcy was watching me anxiously.

"I just don't see Uncle Vance as a murderer," I said. "I could totally see him bopping Blake on the head with his walking stick, but stabbing him with one of his own knives? That's not his way. You know he's a real sweetheart underneath that gruff exterior." I groaned a shade louder than necessary. "I have to get to the bottom of this."

Marcy grinned at me. "Do I see a sleuth sitting next to me? The Alaskan Nancy Drew or something?"

I couldn't help laughing, just for an instant. Then earnestness took over. "I came home to a dead body in my bookshop, and my brother just arrested my uncle for murder. Darn right, I'm going to look into it."

• • •

Marcy nodded, all kidding aside. We sat in silence for a moment, as the magnitude of my new quest sank in. But I'm not much of a one for silence.

"I'm sure I'm not going to be able to talk to Uncle Vance right away." I mimicked my brother's voice, "Out." I grimaced. "I hope Uncle Vance is giving Nels a hard time for taking him in."

Marcy smiled at the thought. "Your uncle can hold his own against Nels any day."

"Marcy, who else was at the Grizzly Bar yesterday? Maybe somebody else paid more attention to the rantings of a couple of drunk men."

"Sorry, I didn't know I was going to be called as a witness to murder. I would have done a better job of eavesdropping." She shifted in discomfort on the bench. "Your best bet is to talk to Kirk. Bartenders are supposed to know everything about their customers, right?"

I heaved a sigh, trying to ignore Marcy's sly glance. I wasn't a regular patron of the Grizzly Bar for the sole reason that I didn't want to talk to Kirk. As ex-boyfriends go, he was surprisingly persistent. We dated in high school, over ten years ago now, and he still thought we were going to end up in some happily-ever-after tale one day. He wasn't even fazed by my former engagement to Liam in Florida. Somehow, he must have known that I'd come back to Ptarmigan Port without Liam.

I assumed a singsong tone, "What a great day this is. A dead body shows up in my storeroom, my bookshop is trashed, and I get to go have a heart-to-heart chat with Kirk Dunbar. I can't say which is worse."

Marcy poked me encouragingly, matching my facetious tone. "It'll be fine. He probably won't propose to you today."

I grinned ruefully. "Fourteenth time's the charm? I don't think so." I stood up. "No time like the present."

Marcy waved after me. "I'll keep an eye out for that wedding invitation."

I waggled my finger at her, even though I knew that didn't count as having the last word.

• • •

The Grizzly Bar was only a few doors down from the Shipshape Bookshop. The contrast in style couldn't be more dramatic. While my bookshop exuded cozy, the Grizzly Bar lived up to its rugged name. Upon entering through the heavy swinging saloon doors, the first thing in sight was a glass case displaying a nine-foot-tall brown bear, Alaska's supersized version of a grizzly. With claws extended and mouth open in a roar, the bear would terrify patrons who'd had one too many. The glass case had a few nicks and even a bullet hole from drunks looking to protect life and property. The bar floor was coarse boards, and the wooden walls were decorated with a hodgepodge of expired hunting and fishing licenses dating back to the early days of statehood. A moose head with a magnificent rack hung over the bar, and fish nets and buoys dangled from the ceiling. The overall impression was that all you needed to be successful in the hunt was a few beers at the Grizzly. A sizeable percentage of our population subscribed to this notion.

In the early afternoon, the bar was quiet. I noticed a couple of diehard patrons huddled over their mugs in one corner. Uncle Vance's buddy, Davey, waved to me before turning his attention back to his beer. The only other customer was none other than Angus Montgomery, ostensibly an academic here in Ptarmigan Port to do research. The Grizzly Bar seemed a strange place for this.

But I wasn't here to talk to Angus. I gave him a quick nod and turned to speak to Kirk behind the bar.

Kirk greeted me with an enthusiastic grin. "Junetta Beale! I haven't seen you in here since last Fourth of July. You were wearing that red skirt that I love, and a dark blue sweater. Red, white, and blue for the Fourth of July!"

"Gotta love the Fourth of July, Kirk." I slid onto a bar stool and leaned both elbows on the bar. "I hear Uncle Vance was having a fight with Blake Rivers in here yesterday. What happened?"

Kirk drew me a beer unasked, sliding it along the bar as if he worked in Vegas instead of the small fishing town of Ptarmigan

Port. "How are you, babe? I heard you came home to a mess this morning."

Of course, Kirk knew all about the break-in and the murder. I doubted if anyone in our small town was ignorant of recent events, but as bartender, Kirk usually got the news faster than anyone else.

I took a swallow, grateful for the cool alcohol. I accepted the bowl of pretzels Kirk handed me. "It was pretty horrible. I'm sure you heard that Nels arrested Uncle Vance for murdering Blake Rivers. I'm trying to piece together what they'd been arguing about yesterday, to try to understand what happened."

Kirk leaned on the bar in an intimate, confidential pose. "Yeah, Vance and Blake were going at it last night. Blake had a skinful, and your uncle wasn't far behind. They didn't come in together, but they ended up playing a game of darts together. There were accusations of cheating, of course. Usually are with darts. I'm always ready to step in, in case someone wants to use their opponent as the dart board." Kirk chuckled to himself for a few minutes over this joke.

"Who accused whom of cheating?"

"Doesn't really matter. They were both pretty loud about the cheating thing. Probably both of them were cheating. Vance yelled at Blake that he didn't have anything on him, and Blake said he'd see him in hell. Vance said he'd be happy to escort Blake there at any time." Kirk chuckled some more. "Your uncle sure is quick with the comeback."

"Yeah, Uncle Vance is a hoot." I glanced over at Angus Montgomery, who was nursing his drink, apparently all ears. What did he care about this altercation between my uncle and Blake Rivers?

I leaned in a little closer to Kirk and lowered my voice. "Marcy thought the two of them were arguing about money. Does that ring a bell?"

Kirk reached over and rang the ship's bell that hung over a tray of glasses on the end of the bar. "Ding!"

I couldn't help laughing. "Yeah, just like that. Did you hear Uncle Vance and Blake arguing about money?"

Kirk rang the bell a second time for good measure, before leaning in again. "I did hear some yelling about bank accounts and the value of your bookshop. Sounded like Blake wanted to know if his investment was worth it. Poor fella—his bank balance doesn't mean a thing to him anymore."

I took another drink, as a moment of silence for Blake. I hadn't liked the man, because of his perverse attempts to get a rise out of Uncle Vance over the bookshop ban. My only interactions with him had been to shoo him away from our front door. I couldn't think of anyone in town who would call Blake Rivers a good friend. Still, no one deserved to die from a knife in the chest in the back room of my bookshop.

"Why would Uncle Vance and Blake argue about the bookshop? We've never sold shares to investors."

Kirk shrugged the expressive shrug of the bartender who honors the code of the bar confessional. "Who knows? It got so loud that I had to step in before your uncle started swinging his stick around. I got Blake out the door while Davey Harper started quizzing Vance on the benefits of wild salmon versus farmed." He chuckled again. "Your uncle has an opinion on just about everything!"

"Yeah, and he's not shy about sharing it." I took another swallow before setting my mug down with a thump. "Thanks, Kirk. Put it on my tab."

He waved a dismissive hand. "There's no tab for you here, Junetta. Stop back by any time." He winked at me as I made my way to the door. "I'm always here for you!"

I waved with a bright smile and hustled out the door before he took the sentiment any further. Another proposal was the last thing I could handle today.

I could feel Angus's eyes follow me out the door. I didn't know what part he played in the unfolding mystery, but I was sure he had some role. I resolved to keep an eye on him. It shouldn't be hard—what could be more conspicuous than an outsider in a small town, especially this small town where you can't even drive in or out? There's no such thing as anonymity.

For now, I left Angus Montgomery to his own devices, knowing that he couldn't go anywhere without my knowledge.

I considered my next move. Uncle Vance and Blake had had an altercation at the Grizzly Bar last night. I couldn't say if it was a routine dustup or if this one was especially violent. Could it have led to murder?

I paused on the dock to gaze out seaward. The light drizzle continued to fall unabated. It felt like such a long time ago that I had cruised into the harbor on the *Northern Dream*, thinking only of a nice cup of coffee and a pleasant day of greeting tourists and selling books. Nothing about this day was turning out as I'd imagined.

I made my way back to the Shipshape Bookshop, which was still blocked off with crime scene tape telling me that it was off limits. So much for the cozy Alaska atmosphere I tried to portray in my shop. This was more of a murder mystery vibe, and not in a good way.

I fingered the slick yellow tape. Nels rarely if ever got a chance to use it. I wondered how he was holding up with the first murder case of his three-year career. Would he even answer if I asked him about the investigation? I guess I was about to find out.

Chapter Five

I headed down the sidewalk to the public safety building. Even if Nels wouldn't talk to me, I had to get to Uncle Vance before it was too late. Our little town could accommodate someone in custody for a few hours only. If Nels chose to formally arrest him, he would have to send Uncle Vance to the Lemon Creek Correctional Center in Juneau. I needed to have a heart-to-heart talk with Uncle Vance before then.

The public safety building was on the edge of downtown within walking distance of the main drag, tucked away so that it didn't intrude on our picturesque fishing town. The gray wood facade and corrugated metal roof of the building looked like an invitation for the drunk and disorderly crowd which made up most of its visitors to sober up and behave. If only it were that simple. The building housed the Ptarmigan Port Police Department, the Alaska State Troopers, the Volunteer Fire Department, and Animal Control. All of these necessary functions boiled down to a couple of desks and a shared dispatcher, and a big garage to house our one fire truck and provide an amazing field trip for school children. The police dealt with most of the crime we encountered, while the troopers had jurisdiction over all felonies, including murder. Like it or not, Nels was in charge of investigating Blake Rivers's death.

He wasn't in when I popped into the building. A quick word with Stella Turner, the dispatcher, and I was on my way to the holding cell to chat with Uncle Vance.

He sat on a long bench, arms folded across his chest in a huffy pose of defiance. They'd taken away his walking stick and parked it in a coat stand by the front door. He looked vulnerable without it.

"Have you come to get me out of here?" he barked at me, not bothering to shift his position. He must have known the answer was no.

I grasped the bars of the cell and leaned in toward him. "I wish I could. What happened back there, Uncle Vance?"

He scowled at me. "Your fool brother decided to haul me in to make an example of me. Just because he couldn't figure out who the killer is, he decided to pin the crime on his old uncle."

I rolled my eyes at him. "'Old uncle,' my eye. You're just as capable of killing Blake Rivers as the next man. What I want to know is, did you kill him?"

Uncle Vance huffed loudly. "You've known me your entire life, and you have to ask me that question? Do you take me for a murderer, Junetta?"

I leaned my head on the cold metal bars. "I'd rather not, that's for sure. The thing is, Uncle Vance, you do have a bad temper, and you don't like Blake Rivers. You could have caught him ransacking the bookshop and stabbed him."

"I never stuck a knife into Blake Rivers." My uncle's scowl never changed, but I could tell he was shaken. If I, his only niece, his dearest family member in Ptarmigan Port, was questioning if he was a murderer, then things were very bad indeed.

"Okay, where were you last night? If you have an alibi, Nels will have to let you go."

Uncle Vance glowered at me. "It's nobody's business where I was last night. I have the right to remain silent. I'm invoking that right." He turned his face away.

Right or no right, I wasn't going to let him get away with this. "Kirk at the Grizzly Bar says you and Blake were arguing last night. He says you were shouting about the value of the bookshop, among other things."

Uncle Vance turned back to me, his face impassive. "What other things?"

"Other things like being happy to escort Blake to hell, for one. What was that fight about?"

If Uncle Vance could have possibly become more obstinate than he already was, now was the time. I watched as he transformed from a curmudgeonly old man to an immovable force to be reckoned with…and I was the one to do the reckoning. "Kirk has no business telling you what Blake and I were discussing at the bar. Doesn't he know anything about the sanctity of the bartender/customer relationship?"

I folded my arms across my chest in a parody of his defiant posture. "We live in a small town, Uncle Vance. If you have a shouting match in public, people are going to hear all the details, regardless of the 'sanctity' of the bartender relationship. I'd prefer to hear the details from you rather than through the grapevine. What did Blake care what the valuation of the bookshop was?" As the words came out of my mouth, a chill ran down my back. "Does Blake have something to do with the Shipshape Bookshop's finances?"

"Blake Rivers is dead."

The stark statement shook me for a moment. "Okay, I should have said, 'Did Blake have something to do with the bookshop's finances?'" I hugged my arms to my chest, hoping that he would give me a straight answer instead of a fight.

Uncle Vance just shrugged, like he was brushing a mosquito off his shoulder. "Blake Rivers was a boat captain. He knew nothing about books. Why should he concern himself with the finances of the local bookshop?"

"All right." I pinched my lips together in frustration. "But I am the owner of the Shipshape Bookshop, and I am concerned with our finances. If we're in trouble, you can tell me straight up, or I can go over the books myself, and all will become clear." I sounded like I was his mom or something—maybe the effect of those metal bars keeping him in. "Up to you."

Uncle Vance glowered at me. "You're not a policeman. I don't have to answer questions from you."

I scowled right back. "I'm your boss, believe it or not. I've trusted you to keep our finances straight, but if there's a problem there, now's the time to tell me about it."

Uncle Vance broke his intense eye contact with me to look over my left shoulder. I swung around to see Nels leaning on the doorjamb, silently taking in our conversation.

"Finances?" he said.

I swung back around to see that I had lost Uncle Vance. He leaned back on the bench, arms still folded across his chest, but now in a posture of nonchalance. Clearly, he had nothing more to say on the subject.

I sighed in frustration and addressed my brother. "So, you're going to arrest Uncle Vance and send him off to jail?"

Nels gave a slight shrug. "Maybe I should just hold him here for a bit and let you interrogate him. I might find out everything I want to know."

I bit back my annoyance at his sarcasm and threw on my hundred-watt smile. "We could question him together. Between the two of us I'm sure we could get down to the truth."

My smile never did work on Nels. "There's no 'two of us' working together. There's the trooper, me, and the shopkeeper, you. Head on back to your shop and leave Uncle Vance to me."

I was about to fire off a witty comeback when the import of his words hit me. "Can I get back into the bookshop now? Is the crime scene cleared enough for me to clean up the mess?"

Nels nodded, and then added, "We've arranged for the blood to be cleaned up in the back, so you don't have to worry about that. You might want to steer clear of that area for a bit."

I was touched. I didn't know if cleaning up the blood after a crime was the responsibility of law enforcement, but I certainly appreciated it. Of course, it could have been a ploy to keep me on Nels's good side. I was fine with that—if he felt the need to appease me, that meant that I hadn't lost my big sister influence over him. I'd give him the win on this one.

I turned back to Uncle Vance. "I guess you're headed to Juneau. Anything you need before Nels carts you off?"

"Can you take care of Cosmo? He's currently in my car behind the bookshop." He pressed his lips together. "I want him to stay with someone he knows."

"I'm your woman. I love that little dog. Anything else? Do you have an attorney?"

"What makes you think I need an attorney? I'm not guilty of anything." He glared at Nels. "The sooner you get that through your head, the happier we'll all be."

Nels ignored the gibe. "You have the right to an attorney, Uncle Vance. I can hook you up with Jeff Stevens."

Uncle Vance snorted. "Stevens couldn't tell the difference between innocent and guilty if you hit him over the head with it."

He had a point. Jeff Stevens was the only lawyer practicing in Ptarmigan Port. An earnest man nearing retirement age, he focused exclusively on wills and property issues. He worked out of a tiny office in his home, unless he was at the Grizzly Bar surrounded by an avalanche of papers strewn across a table. The people of Ptarmigan Port relied on him to resolve issues with their neighbors that couldn't be solved over a pint of beer. Murder was far outside his area of expertise.

"What about Mom's friend, Scott? Isn't he a lawyer?" It was my turn to glare at Nels. "You did call Mom to tell her you arrested her big brother, right?"

He cleared his throat, avoiding my gaze. "I haven't had a chance. Maybe you could call her."

"Don't you have a duty to notify close relatives?" I narrowed my eyes at him. "You're nervous about calling Mom. You're afraid she might expect you to justify your actions."

Before Nels could respond to this big sister accusation, Uncle Vance cut in with a growl. "Nobody's calling your mom. Got it? Not to ask for recommendations for friends who might be hotshot lawyers, and not to get her to take sides between her lawman son and her brother who is obviously innocent of murder. Your mom has nothing to do with any of this. Leave her alone."

Nels and I both stared at Uncle Vance, shocked out of our sibling squabbling by his impassioned speech.

He stared right back, daring us to argue with him.

It wasn't worth it. Chalk one up for Uncle Vance.

"Okay, no lawyer, no call to Mom. You're doing this on your own. Do you need anything else, Uncle Vance?"

Nels shook his head, a small smile on his lips. "He doesn't need anything else, Junetta. You can't take books or whittling sticks into jail with you."

It was an offhand remark, but it hit hard. We both knew that Uncle Vance was rarely to be seen without a knife in one hand and a bit of wood in the other. He had learned from the master carvers in the Tlingit community and took great pride in his work. The little figurines and bits of whimsey he'd given me over the years served to decorate my entire house. In the stressful atmosphere of jail, a bit of a hobby would definitely be soothing. Too bad Uncle Vance's hobby relied on knives, one of which was currently in custody as a murder weapon.

Chapter Six

A raucous cawing and high-pitched twittering greeted me as I walked back to my bookshop. I looked up to see a couple of ravens harassing a bald eagle in flight. The ravens scolded and pecked, swooping around the eagle until they drove it off into the woods. Then they returned triumphantly to their treetops, clucking and cawing in the multitude of voices that make ravens so interesting. In Tlingit culture, Raven is the trickster, the bringer of light to the world. Whenever I heard the chattering of a raven, I expected mischief. I was rarely disappointed.

I peeped in on Cosmo in Uncle Vance's car before going inside. The little white dog lay curled up on a bright red dog bed in the back seat. It was a peaceful sight, until Cosmo noticed I was peeking in on him. Then he exploded into a whirling fur ball of energy, zooming around inside the car as if he lived in a pinball game.

I spied a leash draped over the gearshift and managed to clip it onto Cosmo's collar before he could escape from the car. We set off for a brisk walk along the dock and back, circling around the bookshop to view it from the sidewalk. From the outside, there was no hint of the destruction inside. I opened the front door, to be hit by the sheer magnitude of the vandalism which washed over me like a tsunami. Almost every single book was thrown on the floor amid broken glass from the display case and splinters from a shattered bookcase. I groaned. What were the chances of selling any of them in this state?

There was no way I could bring Cosmo into this scene of devastation. I walked him back to the alley and cajoled him to return to his cozy bed. I refilled the water dish on the floor of the car and resolved to check on him every few hours.

Once inside the shop, I peeked into the back room, afraid of what I might see. The cleaners weren't finished yet, so I ducked back out before they saw me. I gritted my teeth and got to work, smoothing bent book covers and arranging crumpled pages. Like most people who work with books, I am a true bibliophile. I handle books with a kind of reverence, enjoying the sensual experience of beautiful paper or the way a book falls open in my hands. I love to breathe in the smell of a new book. It seemed like a sacrilege to chuck them about with such violence.

I caught myself with an audible gasp. How much more of a sacrilege was it for me to carry on about a bunch of books when a man had violently lost his life in my back storeroom? I set down the pile of books I was gathering up and sank down on my knees to put my head in my hands. What a horrible day!

A knock on the front door roused me from my introspection. Grateful for the interruption, I got up from the floor and peeked through the front window, and then threw the door open to Patrick. Too late, I noticed that he wasn't alone. Before I could stop her, Reba Cornell pushed past Patrick to enter the bookshop.

Patrick's face had regained a little color since I'd last seen him. His hands plucked nervously at his jeans as his eyes darted about the bookshop, looking everywhere except at the open door to the storeroom, where the sounds of cleaning could still be heard. "I came by to see if I could help cleaning up." The sight of the toppled bookshelves steadied him, somehow. He dived into the cleanup, setting bookshelves upright and starting to pile up the scattered books. He gave no explanation for the presence of Reba Cornell. He probably knew she would speak for herself.

"Such a tragedy this morning," Reba began, as she strolled about the bookshop, her sharp eyes taking in every bit of the destruction. "How are you ever going to be able to bear the cost of this vandalism?"

I pulled on some rubber gloves to tackle the shattered glass display case at the front of the shop. "We've got insurance, of course." I reached in with both hands to pull up the heavy cash register. This time I was prepared for its weight and managed to get it out without mishap. "It's a big hassle, but the bookshop won't go under or anything." I sidled past Reba to set the cash register down on the floor and started dusting off all the glass splinters. She made no move to lend a hand.

"Have you found anything else missing besides the Pastor's Confession Map?" she asked, stirring a pile of fallen books with her foot.

I sucked in a feeling of annoyance. "We're just getting started." I abandoned the cash register and inspected the glassed-in cabinet that held my few old books and first editions. Miraculously, the cabinet hadn't sustained any damage whatsoever. It stood solid as a lighthouse on a rock in the midst of heavy seas. I opened the doors to reveal the fragile books within. "My Robert Service editions are fine, and the Jack London first edition is here as well. No worries!" I threw Reba a glance of relief.

Patrick looked up from his work, his gaunt face streaked with dust. "It wasn't a very smart thief, then. That Jack London first edition could be worth $20,000."

I smoothed the covers of the old book. "I wish. If it was signed and in pristine condition, maybe. This one is merely a used first edition, worth around $500. Still, it wouldn't be hard to sell it online and collect a bit of cash. Clearly, the vandal wasn't looking for money."

Patrick's face fell. Evidently, he had nurtured high hopes of the bookstore getting rich off of first editions. "Why would anyone want to take the Pastor's Confession Map? It's not worth anything, is it?"

Reba was prowling along the perimeter of the room, stepping gingerly over fallen books. She appeared to be filing away the destruction in her mind as yet another chapter in the history of Ptarmigan Port. She spoke sharply over her shoulder, "The Pastor's Confession Map is an important historical document of our town. As such, it is priceless. It should have been housed safely in my archives at the Historical Society, instead of being on display here in the bookshop for gawkers and thieves to access it."

Patrick recoiled at her sharp tone, but I didn't rise to the bait. Reba had been having this argument with Uncle Vance for years, and when I took over the bookshop, I became the recipient of her alternating requests, appeals, and demands that we turn over the map to her stewardship. Evidently, we'd moved on to recriminations. I could hear in her tone, as clearly as if she'd shouted from the mountaintops, that the Pastor's Confession Map would be safe and Blake would still be alive if only I had given the map into her care.

I smiled sweetly at her, a gesture that was wasted since she was still turned away from me. "Reba, Patrick and I have a lot of work to do here. There's a broom in the back room if you want to help sweep up some of this glass. We'll be having a break-in sidewalk sale in the next few days. Until then, the bookshop is closed." By this time, she had turned around. I favored her with my brilliant smile again. "We appreciate your concern and well-wishes, but what we need right now is to muck out the mess." My eyes involuntarily turned toward the back room, and both Reba and Patrick followed my gaze. The three of us shuddered in unison.

Reba made a move toward the back room, as if she really was going to fetch a broom. I grabbed her by the arm. "No, really, don't go back there. They're not done cleaning up the blood." With my hand lightly on her elbow, I steered her to the front door. "Look for a sale in the next couple of days."

Reba paused in the doorway. "Your brother is wrong about Vance, you know."

I stood gaping at her for a moment. Then I pulled myself together and drew her back into the shop. With a quick glance over at Patrick, I said, "Do you know anything about what happened to Blake?" I kept a close watch on her face as I spoke.

A muscle in her jaw twitched. "I have no idea what happened in your back room. I do know that Blake Rivers was not well-liked in this town. Not at all."

I could see that Reba was ready to launch into full gossiping mode. I tried to refrain from rolling my eyes, which would have been my usual reaction. Gossip is a sleuth's best friend, right? I sought to encourage it. "I heard that he and Uncle Vance had a big argument at the Grizzly Bar yesterday evening. That's probably why Nels took him in."

Reba humphed. "As if Vance Peterman was the first person to engage in an argument with that man. If your brother was doing his job, he would see that there is a slew of people who have gotten themselves crosswise with Blake Rivers." She leaned close to me and lowered her voice. "You know he was blackmailing people, right?"

Her low voice and furtive manner gave me the willies. I glanced over my shoulder, almost expecting to see Nels and his little cop notebook looming behind me. All I saw was Patrick, bent over a heap of rumpled books. "Who was he blackmailing?" I whispered.

She tossed her head. "I don't know for certain. I have heard rumors that he's got a whole list of people that he's collecting money from. Suppose one of them got fed up with the shakedown and put an end to him."

I gripped my hands together, not sure how she would react to my next question. "Was he blackmailing you, Reba?"

"Me?" She recoiled. "Don't be ridiculous. Why on earth would he be blackmailing me?" She fixed me with a stern gaze. "Was he blackmailing you?"

I spread out my hands at a loss. "Not me, but what if he was blackmailing Uncle Vance?" I thought about Kirk's account of the argument at the bar, with Uncle Vance yelling at Blake that he didn't have anything on him. I didn't feel right about sharing that story with Reba.

Reba frowned. "I would have thought that ex-wife of his would have been a prime suspect. I imagine Blake would have plenty of ammunition for blackmail there."

Patrick looked up from the pile of devastation and threw me a beseeching look. I nodded at him. "Sorry, Reba, I need to help Patrick clean things up. Have you told Nels what you know or suspect about blackmailing?"

She pursed her lips. "He never asked me what I know about Blake. All he wanted to know was what I was up to last night. He got rather rude about it, in fact."

I bit the inside of my cheek to keep from blurting out something I would later regret. It wasn't my responsibility to answer for my brother's heavy-handed interrogation tactics. "I think you should tell him about this. If I passed it on to him, it would just be hearsay. I'm sure he wouldn't listen to me, but he would pay attention to you."

After some convincing, Reba finally agreed to go down to the station and tell Nels what she knew about blackmail. Small towns are famous for gossip, and Reba Cornell could hold her own with the best of them. If there was any truth to be found, Nels could sort it out. I opened the door to let her out.

"Bye, Reba!" I shut the door behind her and shot the deadbolt before she could change her mind. "Patrick, why on earth did you bring her with you?"

Patrick shook his head. "She came out of nowhere and followed me in. It was a classic case of tailgating. I'll bet she was the murderer, and she wanted to check on the scene of the crime. Maybe she was looking for her next victim, but she couldn't tackle both of us at once. If you hadn't been here, I might have been killed!"

I clasped Patrick's shoulders. "Get a grip, Patrick! Reba Cornell's not a murderer. She's a grouchy old woman who likes to make other people feel guilty. She's been trying that on me ever since I was twelve and picked nagoonberries in her special patch. It was public land along the beach, and she had no right to it whatsoever. That didn't stop her from calling me a sneak and a thief. My dad helped me to set her straight." I chuckled at the memory. Dad had marched me into the Historical Society with instructions to hold my head high and tell Reba that the Alaska constitution protected access to the water for all its citizens, and she had no right to impede me in any way. It was a tall order for a twelve-year-old who was intimidated by the stately Reba Cornell, but I loved my dad, and I knew he was right. I delivered his words with aplomb. It didn't stop Reba from making digs about the sanctity of her nagoonberry crop over the next fifteen years, but it taught me a valuable lesson: to hold my head high and speak the truth. "After that episode, I've never been intimidated by Reba again. You do make a good point, though. We should probably not be alone in the bookshop for the next few days, until Nels finds the right culprit." I noticed that both he and I naturally assumed that Uncle Vance was not that person. How I hoped we were right!

• • •

By the end of the day, Patrick and I had finished the cleanup. We had accumulated a large pile of books to put out on the sidewalk shelf at forty percent off for a break-in sale. It would attract a crowd of locals curious to gawk and gossip about the crime, as well as tourists who always liked to find something on sale. It would be a block party.

Ignoring my earlier advice, I shooed Patrick out the door. "No worries, Patrick, I'll lock up. I just want a few minutes alone in the space to feel if it's all good for tomorrow." It wasn't very articulate, but Patrick seemed to understand. He slipped out the door, leaving me alone.

After checking that all doors were locked, I ventured into the back room, which was finally cleaned of any traces of violent death. I closed my eyes, listening in the silence. All I could hear was my own breathing. The room smelled strongly of disinfectant. No other odors lingered. I opened my eyes and scanned the room, looking for anything out of place. I don't know why I bothered, since the police and the cleaners had thoroughly scoured the space. A stranger would never know that a violent death had occurred.

I abandoned my sensory experiment and went over to Uncle Vance's desk, which looked like it had not been touched by the vandal. As Owner Emeritus, Uncle Vance retained some important business functions for the bookshop, including keeping the financial accounts. I had instituted a computerized inventory system and was trying to get him to move all of our accounts to the computer, with no success. He was opinionated and old-school. A pile of paper ledgers stretching back to the middle of the last century bowed a bookshelf behind his desk. I scanned the pile, frowning when I didn't see what I expected. I checked each desk drawer in turn. The most recent ledger I found was dated July 1, 2003 – June 30, 2009. There was no sign of a current ledger.

Chapter Seven

A thorough search of the entire bookshop revealed that the current ledger was indeed missing. I sat at Uncle Vance's desk wondering what my next steps should be. Was this something to report to Nels or should I take it up with Uncle Vance? It was possible that he had simply taken the ledger home for some unknown reason, or it could have been taken in the break-in. Maybe it was the target all along, and the theft of the Pastor's Confession Map was a red herring to cover up the crime—and what connection did the ledger or the map have to do with the murder of Blake Rivers?

Suddenly, I felt overwhelmed with the desire to talk to Uncle Vance and hash out with him what was going on here. Without thinking, I snatched up my phone and dialed his number.

He may be old-school, but Uncle Vance had a state-of-the-art cell phone for his personal use. Nels and I had teamed up in an uncharacteristic moment of unity to get it for him after our uncle spent a cold night stuck in the woods when a heavy fog came down and he couldn't move for fear of falling into the creek he was hiking along. One simple mistake in Alaska's backcountry could mean the difference between life and death, and we all knew it. Uncle Vance grumbled about the phone, saying that his chances of being rescued were exactly the same as before and he wasn't about to rely on the internet to save his life. He suffered us to persuade him to keep it charged and carry it around in his pocket. I rarely saw him use it.

Nor did he use it tonight. I heard the phone ring three times, and then someone picked up. "Who's this?" a stern voice barked.

"Oh, hi, Nels. I was trying to reach Uncle Vance. Is he still in town, or have you sent him off to Juneau?"

An exasperated sigh whistled through the phone. "Did you want to read him a bedtime story?"

I bit my tongue to prevent myself from responding in kind. "I wanted to ask him a few questions about the business side of the bookshop. I've always relied on him to take care of the finances, and now that he'll be 'otherwise occupied,' I need to clear up a few things. Is he available to talk?"

"He's still here. We're flying out tomorrow. You can come by in the morning to ask him questions."

I breathed a sigh of relief that I hoped Nels couldn't hear. "Okay, will do. Tell Uncle Vance that you wouldn't let me wish him a good night and I'll talk to him tomorrow." I rang off before he could shoot back with a witty retort.

I tidied up a pile of papers I'd shuffled through and turned to leave Uncle Vance's desk. That's when I noticed the other thing out of place—or should I say, not in its place at all. It's hard to notice something that's not there, and I'm sure no one else would have ever missed it. It had been my gift to Uncle Vance, and its absence suddenly filled me with an overwhelming sense of loss. It was a simple thing—a god's eye made of popsicle sticks woven with purple, blue, and white yarn to make a cheerful hanging decoration. I'd made it in my second grade Sunday school class and given it to Uncle Vance for Christmas. He'd hung it up over his desk and there it had remained for the next twenty years—until today.

I searched through Uncle Vance's desk a second time, crawled around underneath, and even sifted through the trash, feeling increasingly frantic. I couldn't think why a murderer would want to steal something as homely as a child's craft, but the useless thing was gone. Finally, I flung myself down in his desk chair and burst into tears. It wasn't the god's eye at all—it was the capriciousness of the whole situation that didn't make sense. How could someone have come into my beautiful bookshop and defiled it with murder, while at the same time making off with a precious artifact like the

Pastor's Confession Map and a worthless but sentimental bauble like my handmade Christmas gift to my uncle? The world didn't make sense anymore!

I sobbed for a few minutes before pulling myself together. Some people feel refreshed after a good cry. Not me. I just felt congested. I wiped my face with a pile of tissues and abandoned Uncle Vance's desk to make my way out of the bookshop.

I felt better as soon as I stepped outside. Although it was nearly 9:00 p.m., we had almost an hour left before sunset due to the long days of Alaska summer. We were coming up on the summer solstice when we would get a whopping eighteen hours of daylight. I always loved the surplus of daylight. I circled around to the alley to liberate Cosmo from Uncle Vance's car. I could take him with me to the store to get some dog food before heading home.

Like most businesses in Ptarmigan Port, Green's Grocery was on the main drag within walking distance of everything. Outside, it was a small, whitewashed building with a sign on the door proclaiming, "Green's Grocery—in the family since 1957." I got a good chuckle every time I saw that. The Carter family had owned the grocery ever since Frank Carter chose the name Green in 1957 because it started with the same sound as Grocery. The current owners, Mike and Katie Carter, saw no reason to change the name. Katie figured that "green" was an endorsement for healthy living, even if the grocery did feature the biggest selection of doughnuts in Southeast Alaska.

Katie called out a hearty greeting when I jangled through the door, Cosmo in tow. "You got saddled with dog sitting duties, eh, Junetta? Your brother should know better than to haul away an old man and leave his poor dog stranded." She bustled out from behind the counter to scratch Cosmo behind his ears.

"I'm sure Uncle Vance would agree with you there." I shortened the leash to keep Cosmo from toppling the pyramid of salmon cans flanking the front door. "I'm in the market for dog food. What does Uncle Vance usually get for Cosmo?"

Katie helped me find Cosmo's preferred dog food and convinced me that he needed a few chew toys as well. With

Cosmo frisking about my ankles, I made sure to be as quick as I could. I was headed out when Uncle Vance's buddy, Davey Harper, came in.

Davey was a big man with a long white beard that delighted children every Christmas when he became Santa Claus. I could remember sitting on his lap and asking for a tea party set for my dolls. To this day, I considered him responsible for the package under my Christmas tree that year.

Davey waved to Katie and then bent down to give Cosmo's head a rub. "Evening, Katie. Hiya, Junetta. I want to thank you for taking in Cosmo. I was afraid Vance was going to twist my arm to get me to take him." He straightened up and said hurriedly, "Don't get me wrong, he's a great dog. Just a little too busy for my taste."

"You're right about that. I sometimes wonder how Uncle Vance can keep up with him."

Cosmo tugged on the leash, as if to say, "I know you're talking about me, and I'm ready to go, go, go."

"I think Nels is making a serious mistake sending Vance to Lemon Creek," Davey went on. "Vance will turn out to be innocent, and then he won't have any respect for his nephew ever again."

I sighed. "I hope you're right about the innocent part, Davey, and I hope you're wrong about the respect part. Uncle Vance is a hard man to please, that's for sure."

Katie clicked her tongue in sympathy. Her sharp eyes took in every bit of our conversation, as always. Between her and Kirk, everything that took place in Ptarmigan Port was common knowledge five minutes after it happened.

I lowered my voice to ask Davey, "Did Uncle Vance tell you anything? Specifically, did he mention anything about the bookshop's financial status? He's not telling me anything."

Davey shook his shaggy head. "Don't know nothing about that. Look, I gotta get going. I need to pick up some propane canisters. I'm headed out camping up Seven Mile Creek a ways." He moved off to snag a couple canisters and a few other items which he plopped onto the counter.

"How long do you plan to be out there?" Katie asked. "You don't want to miss the Founders' Day picnic on Saturday." She reached for his purchases to ring them up.

"Dunno. The weather's supposed to be good for the next week or so."

"Well, let us know what the moose situation is out there," Katie went on. "Some tourists said they'd seen a cow and her calf off to the west of the glacier. It didn't sound like their usual range to me."

Davey rubbed a gnarled finger on his nose. "I'll keep a sharp eye out. I'm not hunting on this trip, just going out to camp."

"You're not worried about that murderer, then?" Katie leaned forward on the counter, leaving her cash drawer hanging open. "We all know it's not Vance, but it is somebody. There's any number of people who would have liked to see Blake Rivers dead. Whoever did it has to make sure nobody ever finds out."

Heedless of Cosmo's energetic tugs on his leash, I lingered at the counter. "If not Uncle Vance, who do you think it could have been?"

Katie shook her head. "I heard there was a big argument down at the Grizzly Bar last night. Oh, wait, that was Vance and Blake arguing, wasn't it? You were there, right, Davey? What was it all about?"

Davey gathered up his purchases all in a bunch. He juggled the propane canisters in his arms, allowing them to take up all his focus. "I don't rightly know what happened," he murmured to a can of mosquito repellent. "One minute I was enjoying my beer and the next minute those two hotheads were shouting at each other. Kirk hustled Blake out the door, and I started jawing with Vance, and things cooled down from there. I didn't ask what the trouble was." He shifted his gaze to Cosmo, now contentedly gnawing on the edge of a shelf. "Better get that little dog out of here before he tears the place down." As if that were his cue to leave, he backed out of the store and hightailed it to his battered red pickup truck.

I twitched Cosmo's leash. "Katie, I'm sorry! He's really made a mess of this shelf here."

Katie ambled around the counter to peer at the chew marks. "Oh well, when this is all over, Vance can come and carve me a new shelf. It's his dog, after all. Don't give it a second thought, Junetta." She straightened up and watched Davey's truck rattle down the road. "Did Davey seem a bit off to you? That was the strangest conversation I've ever had with him."

I dropped one of the chew toys I'd just purchased, in the hopes of rechanneling Cosmo's energies for a few more minutes. "How do you mean?"

She dusted her hands on her jeans and resumed her place behind the counter. "Davey Harper is the most straightforward person I've ever known. He's got nothing to hide and never has. Until today. Did you see how he wouldn't look either of us in the eye? Too busy with his camping gear or with Cosmo. That's a classic sign of lying, or my name's not Katherine Carter."

My head shot up, entranced. "Your name's Katherine? I never knew that."

"You're missing the point here, Junetta. Why is Davey lying to us about a fight he wasn't even in?"

I scratched Cosmo's ears absentmindedly. "Or was he lying about going camping out at Seven Mile Creek?" I almost dropped Cosmo's leash as a horrid thought hit me. "Surely you don't think Davey's a murderer, Katie."

She finally pushed her cash drawer closed. "I don't know what to think. I never would have expected a body to show up in your bookshop. What if my grocery is next?" She reached under the counter and pulled out a handgun and smacked it down in front of her. "Anybody comes messing with us, they'll be sorry in the end." She stroked the gun's barrel. "Do you have protection at home, Junetta?"

I tore my eyes away from the gun, hoping that she never had to use it for self-defense. "I've got the best watchdog in Ptarmigan Port right here. Nobody's going to sneak up on me tonight." I gathered up all of Cosmo's food and toys and bade Katie a cheery goodbye.

"Come on Cosmo, time to go home."

It was only a five-minute drive in the summertime from the downtown flats to my house in the Hill neighborhood. Ptarmigan Port was a small strip of civilization clinging to the base of the mountains that came right down to the sea. A large part of the town was on the flats, as we called them, but my neighborhood snaked its way up the hillside with a series of houses built on either side of a zigzagging road. My house was along the final switchback, with a fantastic view of the ocean. It was a small log cabin built eighty years ago, and then added onto in the seventies when an enterprising landlord had bought up a mess of houses for rentals.

It was the nicest house. The original log cabin part of the house consisted of a tiny living room with a wood stove smack in the middle, and a long, narrow kitchen next to an equally long, narrow bathroom. A loft over the living room was the original bedroom, but I used it mostly for storage. The addition featured two large bedrooms and another, more spacious, bath. I loved the quirky nooks and crannies where the log cabin met the added-on parts. Lucky for me, the interior was finished with drywall, so I didn't have to dust log walls. In the winter, the cozy living room heated by the wood stove was my favorite place in town, and in the summer, the big windows overlooking the sea made me feel like I lived in a palace.

I found Cosmo a cozy spot for his bed next to the wood stove and set up his food and water bowls in the kitchen. He scampered throughout the house, nosing into one corner after another until he was satisfied with his temporary home. Then he circled around three times on his bed and dropped almost immediately into a sound sleep. I wished that I could do the same.

I tried to conjure up the feelings of serenity that my home usually gave me, but when I started to relax, all I could think of was Blake Rivers's dead body in my back room. When I closed my eyes to sleep, I could see his stone white face and the scrimshaw handle of Uncle Vance's best knife protruding from his chest.

I sprang out of bed and caught up my phone. I didn't care what Uncle Vance said, I wanted to talk to my mom. She would never forgive us if we left her in the dark about what was going on. I dialed her number.

Mom's remote lodge was far off the grid. The only way to reach her was on her radio phone. If she was in to answer it, the connection was often poor. Luckily, she picked up when I called. A wave of relief washed over me at the sound of her voice, despite the noticeable echo on the line.

"Junetta. Are you all right, sweetie? I heard what happened in the bookshop this morning. What a mess."

I sat for a moment, stunned. "How do you know about this already? Did Nels call you after all?"

"Oh, Nels is probably pretty busy right about now. Katie called me first thing. She keeps me informed on all the gossip, you know. I'm out of town but not out of touch, as they say."

"So, you know that Nels arrested Uncle Vance?"

"That's what Katie told me. Good luck to Nels with that. Vance will make his life miserable as long as he's locked up." I could almost see her shaking her head on the other end of the line.

"He says he doesn't want a lawyer. I was wondering if you might put him in touch with that friend of yours, Scott?"

I thought I heard a tsk from the other end of the line. "Vance is a big boy, Junetta. If he doesn't want a lawyer, there's no point in trying to saddle him with one. I'm betting that he didn't kill Blake Rivers, and he'll be set free in a day or two. He'll be fine until then, and he won't thank you for fussing over him. Just let him be."

She sounded exactly like her brother: "Leave her alone." That should be the mantra of the Petermans.

But I was a Beale. I wasn't about to leave things alone. I was on a mission to get to the bottom of Blake's murder and understand how it could have happened in my precious bookshop.

Mom and I chatted for a few more minutes about all the news from Ptarmigan Port, from the murder to the status of Marcy's pregnancy and everything in between. When she finally had to ring off to put the finishing touches on her preparations to welcome guests from Boston tomorrow, I felt a lot calmer.

Nothing like a good talk with Mom to chase the bogeyman away! I curled up on the couch with a lighthearted Fred Astaire movie and finally fell asleep to the toe-tapping tunes of the master tap dancer of all time.

Chapter Eight

I woke early the next morning, welcoming the light peeking through my blackout curtains, eager as always for a new day. Then it hit me—Uncle Vance was in jail and Blake Rivers was dead, and my bookshop was the epicenter of the crime scene. I ducked back under my fleece throw blanket for a moment. Then I was attacked by a wriggling white dog licking my face and frisking from my lap to the door and back again. I could see I was going to get my exercise in my new role as a dog sitter. I clipped on the leash and led Cosmo out into the light morning rain. "It's only for a few days, buddy, until I can figure this crime out and get Uncle Vance out of the hot seat. I know you're counting on me, and so is he."

I knew I couldn't take Cosmo into the bookshop, so I settled him in my house for the morning before heading out. I decided to get breakfast at the Last Chance Café, see how Marcy was doing, and then visit Uncle Vance at the public safety building before opening the Shipshape Bookshop at 10:00 a.m. to greet the first cruise ship in town.

The café was quiet when I went in through the beaded curtain from the bookshop. Only one table was occupied by Marcy and her grandmother, Annalisa Martin. Both women relaxed over a cup of coffee and a plate of muffins. I hated to disturb them, but Marcy saw me before I could duck back out. I waved both hands at her. "Don't get up, I can serve myself." I nipped behind the counter and snagged a coffee mug before she could object. I fiddled with heating milk in the microwave before adding the steaming coffee.

Marcy watched me with a critical eye. "What do you think, Grandma, should we hire her for the morning rush?"

Annalisa's eyes crinkled at the corners when she smiled, and her dark eyes twinkled. Annalisa was one of my favorite people in Ptarmigan Port. Wise in the old ways, she also possessed a keen sense of humor and a sunny way of looking at the world that never failed to lift my spirits. "I suppose you could, but then who would take care of all those books?"

I sat down next to Marcy. "Good point. Those books do require a close eye on them these days. Plus, I can't make a good hard-boiled egg to save my life." I glanced around the café, slow to take in the significance of the empty tables. "Why is it so quiet in here, Marcy? What's happened to all your regulars?"

She gave a start, slopping her coffee on the table in the process. "Did I unlock the front door? I must be losing my mind." She rose to her feet and bustled behind the counter.

I jumped up as well. "I guess you should hire me for the morning rush. You can pay me in cookies." I unlocked the door and switched the sign to "Open." A crowd was milling about on the sidewalk in the soft rain, looking for their cup of morning joe. I let them in and greeted them by name: Reba Cornell, back again; Stella Turner collecting coffee for the cops; Hank and Nancy Beckman, an older couple whose morning coffee excursion was the highlight of their day; and the newcomer, Angus Montgomery. I returned to my table, where Annalisa was gathering up her things. She leaned in close and whispered in my ear, "I'd better go before Marcy decides to recruit me for the morning rush." She blew a kiss to Marcy and slipped out the door.

I ordered an egg bagel to go with my coffee and waved a friendly hand to Angus.

"Come join me for breakfast. I didn't get a chance yesterday to properly welcome you to Ptarmigan Port. You should know that we haven't had a murder here in thirty years. Yesterday was not a typical day in town."

Angus picked up his coffee and croissant and sat down across from me. "Junetta," he said with a charming quirk of his mouth. "I don't remember your last name."

"Junetta Beale. I'm the owner of the Shipshape Bookshop, and the niece of the accused murderer, Vance Peterman."

I watched Angus carefully after delivering this casual shock remark. He paled a bit and covered it up with a deep swallow of coffee. "I'm sorry, this must be a terrible time for you."

"Yes, it must. My brother is the arresting officer, you see, so it's all in the family. But I don't think Uncle Vance is guilty." I leaned forward to pin him with my gaze. "Do you?"

He sputtered a bit. "I have no idea. I'm sure the troopers, er, your brother, had a reason to arrest him, especially if they're related." He toyed with his coffee stirrer, avoiding my intense gaze. "I don't want to intrude in your family's investigations."

"And yet, here you are, still in Ptarmigan Port a day later, still on site where the murder took place. Why are you here, Angus Montgomery?"

A pleased smile washed over his strained face. "You remembered my name."

I relaxed back in my chair. "Of course, I did. You're not from here, so you're automatically a celebrity." I shook myself back to my uncustomary sternness. Just because a man was endearingly charming didn't get him off the hook. "The fact that you're from out of town makes you suspicious. So, why are you here?"

Angus took another swallow of coffee, as if to steady his nerves. Or was he thinking up a story?

"As I told you yesterday, I'm an historian. I'm doing research on the sinking of the SS *Fortunate* in 1915. I've been in contact with Ms. Cornell from the Ptarmigan Port Historical Society in connection with this research."

Across the café, Reba's head went up like a shot. Not content to eavesdrop on our conversation, she picked up her cup and joined us at the table. "Did I hear my name being taken in vain?"

I tried to hide a smile at Angus's further confusion. "Not in vain, surely," I said. "Angus was just mentioning how you're helping him with his research."

I watched Reba swell in importance in front of my very eyes. If a person could blow up like a balloon, she did it. She straightened up in her chair, slapped both hands down on the table, and leaned in with a fierceness that spoke to her absolute passion for historical discovery. "Yes, Mr. Montgomery contacted me a few months back asking about the shipwreck of the SS *Fortunate*. I told him we have many fascinating records here at the Historical Society, which he is welcome to peruse at his convenience."

Angus turned back to me. "As this is such a small town, none of the records are available online. The only way I could see them was to actually come here. Not a bad excuse for an exotic vacation."

I wasn't sure whether to take offense at his patronizing assessment of our small town's capabilities, or to take pride in our special way of life. A big bite of bagel saved me from having to respond before Angus continued.

"I hoped to get a peek at the shipwreck itself," he said. "I was going to take a tour on Mr. Rivers's boat, but I don't know if that's an option anymore."

"I think the tours will still go on," Reba pronounced. "His nephew, Connor Fisk, is now the boat's captain, and with Blake gone, he stands to inherit the business. He'll need to keep the boat running to make ends meet. On a three-cruise-ship day with calm seas, he can't afford to observe a decorous time of mourning." She pushed her chair away from the table. "I must go say hello to Nancy. What time can I expect you at the Historical Society today, Mr. Montgomery?"

At the mention of time, I checked my watch and gulped down the rest of my coffee. I had just enough time to pop over to the public safety building to see Uncle Vance before opening the bookshop at 10:00 a.m. I heard Angus vacillating on his schedule for the day, trying to decide whether or not he would take Saltwater Tours' shipwreck sightseeing cruise. If I wanted to keep an eye on him, I would have to seek him out. Shouldn't be too hard in our quaint small town.

• • •

The public safety building was quiet—always a good sign. I

didn't see Nels about, but Stella was at her post at the desk. She waved me along to chat with Uncle Vance.

He sat on a bench in the same cell I'd seen him in last night. It was possible that he hadn't moved all night long.

"How's my favorite uncle?" I sang out, hoping to keep the atmosphere light—a tall order at any time with Uncle Vance.

He glared at me. "Last I checked, I was your only uncle. What do you want, coming here to butter me up with your carrying on? Don't even start with your questions about what I was doing the other night. I've got nothing to tell you."

I drew my brows down in a ferocious scowl. "Is this better?" Ignoring his eyeroll, I dropped the scowl, which hurt my face, and said, "I just came here to see how you were faring; see if Nels was taking care of you."

Uncle Vance snorted. "Only thing he's taking care of is his precious murder case. I'm collateral damage." He pierced me with his gaze. "Are you taking good care of Cosmo?"

"Yeah, he's great. I left him at home with plenty of food and water, and I'll zip home at lunchtime to walk him."

"Don't leave him alone too long, or you'll find your place torn up when you get back. He likes a lot of activity, that one."

I caught a brief bit of tenderness in his tone. I knew better than to comment on it. "Nels said you'll be headed to Juneau this morning."

"I'm on my way to a real jail, which might be an improvement on this hovel. At least I won't have to look at my little nephew who arrested me for murder."

I threw a glance over my shoulder, making sure that Nels wasn't standing behind me listening to our conversation. I could see that this case was going to strain his hard-won authority in Ptarmigan Port. A sizeable percentage of our townsfolk had watched Nels grow from a rebellious teenager to become the agent of law in our town. It wasn't surprising that he had to try harder than he would have if he'd gone to work in Anchorage or Juneau, or any other place in Alaska. He'd wanted to serve his hometown, with all the challenges that came with it. Arresting his uncle for murder was probably the farthest thing from his mind when he made that choice.

I heard the front door clang shut and realized that I had very little time left with Uncle Vance. "I have to ask you—I was looking for your ledgers, to figure out how to keep the books while you're in Juneau. I couldn't find the latest ledger."

"What, you think I'm going to be gone long enough to make a difference on our accounting?" He looked over my shoulder and mumbled a curse under his breath.

I checked behind me. Yep, it was Nels. He had his uniform jacket on and looked ready to hit the road, or in this case, the skies. Like Juneau, Alaska's inaccessible capital city to the north, Ptarmigan Port had no road leading in or out. All travel took place either by air or by boat.

"Hello, Junetta." That was all the attention Nels spared for me. "Gary's ready in the Otter. Time to go, Uncle Vance."

"Where can I find that ledger?" I persisted, even as Nels unlocked the barred door to usher Uncle Vance out. "Is it in the bookshop, or did you take it home for some reason? Or was it stolen in the break-in?"

Uncle Vance threw his hands up in an expressive shrug, and Nels tensed next to him. I don't know if he was expecting a jailbreak or what.

"Where's your keys, Uncle Vance? I can keep an eye on your place while you're gone."

"Ask your brother," he growled. "The troopers have probably been all over it by now."

I turned to Nels. "Have they? Did you come across a ledger for the Shipshape Bookshop? Do you have his keys so I can keep an eye on things?"

Nels brushed past me as if he hadn't heard a word. "Go sell some books, Junetta. I'll stop by later, if I get a chance." He led Uncle Vance out without another word.

I trailed after them, watching Nels lead Uncle Vance through the drizzle to the compact dock behind the building and load him into the blue and white floatplane bobbing at anchor. Gary

Fletcher's DeHavilland Otter provided most of the air traffic in and out of town. A hulking man with a bushy beard and a leather bomber jacket dating from the war with Iraq, Gary exuded Alaska ruggedness. But I knew he was really a sweetheart who named his Otter *Emmet* after the children's book that he loved to read to his grandkids every Christmas. I watched in silence while Gary revved his engines and *Emmet* taxied along the water leaving a churning wake behind before lifting into the air with a swoop like an eagle.

Uncle Vance was gone.

Chapter Nine

I checked my watch—9:35. I had a few minutes to spare before opening the Shipshape Bookshop for the day. I hustled back to my car and drove to the old neighborhood called Miner's Beach, where Uncle Vance lived.

A popular recreation spot with locals, Miner's Beach was the site of an early gold mine operation, the Seaside Mine, that had flourished in the years leading up to World War I. It was one of two abandoned gold mines, with the Lucky Mine being the other one located a couple miles away in the woods. When the miners abandoned their claim on the beach, they left behind a scattering of tiny miner's houses along the shoreline and an array of implements on the beach ranging from rusting vehicles to twisted railroad tracks. Kids liked to come here to look for treasures among the items strewn on the beach that were seen as "historical artifacts" by some, and "unsightly garbage" by others. I liked to walk along the dunes, imagining what the beach was like when the mine was in use.

Uncle Vance's house was the closest one to the beach. It had red clapboard siding with white accents, both weathered by the years, and a tiny Arctic entryway for visitors to get out of the weather and shed their coats and shoes before going inside. I knew Uncle Vance kept his outer door unlocked at all times. I stepped inside and tried the inner door, to find it unlocked as well.

Uncle Vance was right, it looked like the troopers had been through his house. I knew him to be a particular man, even fastidious when it came to his personal belongings. He would not have left magazines strewn across the couch or all his kitchen cupboard doors hanging open. When I went into his tiny bedroom to find the contents of his closet dumped onto his bed, I started to wonder if it was the troopers or an intruder who had gone through his belongings. Should I report a potential burglary to the troopers? That would put them in their place!

I didn't have time to clean up the mess or to thoroughly search the house for my missing ledger. I checked the obvious places, like Uncle Vance's aged roll-top desk which was bursting with papers and correspondence from years gone by, and the linen closet which I knew concealed a keepsake box containing his Vietnam War medal, Boy Scout sash, and a signed baseball card of Ken Griffey Jr. The carved wooden box was still there, and a quick peek inside revealed that Uncle Vance's treasures were undisturbed. The bookshop's ledger was nowhere to be found.

I rummaged through the kitchen drawers and checked any likely hooks on the wall, but I couldn't find a house key anywhere. It was possible that Nels had it in custody, and it was equally possible that Uncle Vance had no idea where his key was if he even possessed one in the first place. We took pride in trusting one another in Ptarmigan Port—a locked door was an outward sign of paranoia or an admission that one had something to hide. I had to leave the house the way I found it, unlocked and in a mess.

I scurried back to the Shipshape Bookshop, only ten minutes late to open. A few tourists stood grumbling on the sidewalk. "We've been waiting in the rain for five minutes, young lady. Are you in business, or aren't you?"

I gave the elderly man a warm, inviting smile. "Welcome to Ptarmigan Port! You're from…Michigan, right?" I bustled inside, turning on lights and waving to Marcy who peeped through the beaded curtain. "You're late, again," she mouthed, as she moved her "Do Not Enter" sign out of the way. I didn't care. What's the point of being your own boss if you have to be on time every day?

The man from Michigan had stopped in the doorway, staring at me while his wife began to browse through the bookshelves. "What makes you say Michigan?"

I circled back to him with another big smile as if to say I had all the time in the world to attend to him. "I'm pretty good at accents. Most Americans think they don't speak with an accent unless they're from South Carolina or Texas, but there are lots of differences from region to region. I get to chat with people from all over, and I enjoy listening to them speak." I cocked my head to one side, regarding him. "There's something about the vowels that marks a person from Michigan, almost like a Canadian, but more subtle. Am I right—are you from Michigan?"

"As a matter of fact, we are." He was smiling now, his earlier grumpiness forgotten.

I tended my shop for the next couple of hours. Everything was back in its place: the bright shelves with new, up-to-date books, the crowded shelves of used paperbacks, and the well-organized shelves of battered hardbacks in library bindings with Dewey Decimal numbers on the spines. The Shipshape Bookshop was a new/used bookstore coupled with a lending library and, of course, the floating bookmobile. I loved every bit of it.

Patrick came in at 11:00 a.m., right on schedule. The bookshop was hopping so I didn't get a chance to say more than hello to him. I noticed him studiously avoiding entering the back room, and when I thought back, I remembered that he had done the same yesterday while cleaning up. Patrick looked like he was enjoying the bustle of tourists and locals pressing him for details of the crime, so I didn't worry overmuch about his sensibilities.

Throughout the morning, I searched again for the missing ledger but came up with nothing. If I were a curmudgeonly old man, where would I hide my financial accounts? More importantly, why would I feel the need to hide them? I had no answer to that question.

I left the shop in Patrick's capable hands for an early lunch at the Last Chance Café before a quick trip home to tend to Cosmo. Marcy brought me my favorite, a ham sandwich on rye with fresh tomatoes and Swiss cheese melted over all. She sat down for a brief chat before the lunch rush began.

"Nels sent Uncle Vance to Juneau, and he left without telling me where my missing ledger is. What's up with that? He doesn't seem very interested in helping me to prove his innocence."

Marcy smoothed her apron in her lap, stroking her swelling belly in a touchingly protective manner. "Maybe he's not innocent, Junetta."

I chomped a big bite of sandwich and mumbled around the edges, "I'm going with 'innocent until proven guilty.' I just wish he would act a little more innocent and a little less guilty."

"All right, Sherlock. If Vance didn't do it, who's your likely suspect?"

I sat back and thought a minute. Clearly, someone in our midst was a murderer. What an unsettling thought! "What about Angus Montgomery? There's more to his story than meets the eye."

Marcy scoffed. "That puppy dog? Just because he's from New York, you think he's a killer?"

"You know how in mystery novels the heroine looks for something that's out of place, and that's a clue? Angus Montgomery is out of place. I think he's part of what's going on here."

"Oh, that's right, you're the heroine in a mystery novel now." Marcy's teasing held a strong note of affection.

I sat up straight. "That's right. Call me Agent Beale. Here's the scene: we've got a dead body in my back room." I couldn't help shuddering. "Uncle Vance's knife is the murder weapon, the Pastor's Confession Map is stolen, and the current ledger for the Shipshape Bookshop is missing. Let's say these are all connected. What's the common link?"

"The bookshop." Marcy's answer was swift and unequivocal. "You were out of the picture at the time. Uncle Vance was here. You can't blame Nels for arresting him."

"Angus Montgomery was also here. I want to find out more about him. When did he come to town? Was yesterday morning your first sight of him?"

Marcy smiled. "You can figure out when he came to town."

I closed my eyes and took a deep breath. I wished the man were here himself to witness my sleuthing prowess. "He arrived at 10:30 am on the Saturday ferry from Juneau. He's staying at Clarissa's Bed and Breakfast, unless he has friends in town, which I haven't observed."

Marcy grinned at me. "It's easy to be a sleuth in a town with very little options."

"I'm just getting started!" I settled more comfortably in my chair. "He doesn't need to come here for breakfast because he gets it from Clarissa, yet he was here at opening yesterday to be on hand when the murder was discovered. Why? You know how killers always return to the scene of the crime?"

"In books they do."

"Well, in this case he can't leave town early without drawing real attention to himself, so he has to stay and play it cool. Where else in town would he hang out if he were innocent other than the Last Chance Café? He has to come here to act like he's innocent."

"Or maybe he comes here because he is innocent."

I shook her off with a comical "Nah!" I felt like I was treating this like a game. It was the only way I knew how to deal with the overwhelming sense of violation I was feeling at the trashing of my place of business and the discovery of a dead body in my back room. I paused to reflect that I had never particularly liked Blake Rivers. At least I wasn't also grappling with grief. Small mercies, I guess.

"No, Angus Montgomery is an outlier here, and I'm going to keep an eye on him. Did he come in here before yesterday morning? He would have been in town for the afternoon."

"I never saw him before yesterday morning." She mimicked my detective-like tone, "He probably still had jet lag from flying from back east, even if he arrived in Juneau the day before, which he would have had to do in order to get the ferry. He could have scurried straight off to the Historical Society to do his research. He seems like a conscientious person."

I shot her a sharp look. "You like this guy!"

"I am a happily married woman," she retorted, with another protective stroke of her belly. "You, on the other hand…" She gave me a wink filled with mischief. "Go follow Angus Montgomery around if you like. He's planning to take the Saltwater Tours sightseeing cruise this afternoon. I hope you find out that he's not a murderer." She lumbered to her feet.

I laid a hand on her arm. "Who would be top on your list of suspects, Agent George?"

She avoided my eyes. "Vance Peterman."

Chapter Ten

I'd never taken Blake's glass-bottom boat tour before. I was out on the water on a biweekly basis in the summertime, so I didn't need an overpriced tourist attraction to satisfy my deep desire for connecting with nature in this way. But it would be fun to see into the depths through the glass bottom of the boat.

The wooden dock was uncrowded. With only a few cruise ship tourists standing in line, it looked like there was plenty of room for me to join the tour as a walk-on. I saw Angus mingling with the tourists. He had shed his brand-new slicker from yesterday and wore a trendy forest green fleece jacket. I walked up beside him through the drizzly rain and remarked casually, "You're going to be cold in that cloth coat."

He turned with a ready smile and popped open his bright yellow umbrella. "I'll keep warm and dry."

I pulled the hood up on my waterproof jacket. "That umbrella might keep you dry in New York City, but it's worthless on the water. The wind will blow it inside out in no time. Welcome to Alaska!" I slipped past him to talk to the dock agent about a walk-on ticket.

As I boarded the *Gold as Glass*, I looked around for Connor Fisk. With Blake gone, I wondered if he automatically advanced to captain, and if he inherited the boat and the business, like Reba said.

I spied him in the doorway to the cabin, adjusting his captain's hat on his head. One question answered. I walked over to greet him. "Hey, Connor, I'm so sorry about your uncle. What a horrible thing to happen!"

He just grunted in response. I couldn't tell if he was expressing grief at a violent death or annoyance that I would bring it up at his place of work. An eager tourist clamoring for a photo claimed his attention, and he turned away from me. Our brief interaction was at an end.

I shrugged and made my way to the port bow rail, my favorite spot on any ship. I liked to see where I was going, not where I'd been. This trip wasn't solely about the joy of sailing in Southeast Alaska, however. I had a suspect to surveil.

Feeling exactly like a detective/spy, I stole a glance over my shoulder to check on the whereabouts of my quarry. Angus was coming out from the enclosed lounge, zipping up his inadequate coat as he came. He joined me on the rail.

"I'm a bit anxious about this glass-bottom experience," he confessed. "I have a recurring dream about masses of sea creatures teeming underwater, unseen from the surface. I don't know if I'm ready to actually see them."

I bit the inside of my cheek to keep from laughing, which seemed like an inappropriate reaction to such a personal revelation. "It is true, there are lots of sea creatures swimming underwater. I don't know if we'll see them underneath us, or if we might see a whale breaching at the surface." I blasted him with my hundred-watt smile. "There's so much to see in Southeast Alaska!"

He smiled back, looking a bit dazzled. "I'm very interested in seeing this shipwreck."

Me, not so much. While I loved history as much as the next person, I usually tried to steer clear of shipwrecks...too close to home.

The boat started up, sparing me the need to reply. Connor's voice came on the loudspeaker, explaining the safety features of the boat and the duration of the short cruise. "We'll pass directly over the wreck of the S.S. *Fortunate*, which went down in 1915, drowning an entire cargo of gold from the Klondike gold fields in the icy waters of Havoc Strait."

"Has anyone tried recovering the gold from the shipwreck?"

Angus asked me. "If we can see it from this boat, it must not be too deep under water."

"There was an attempt in 1937, but the divers weren't prepared for the bone-chilling cold of Alaska waters. Two divers died of hypothermia, and the rest gave up. Then there was an attempt in 1989 to raise the whole shipwreck. The salvage crew's helicopter crashed in the mountains before ever making it to Ptarmigan Port, and the financial backers got embroiled in lawsuits and abandoned the shipwreck. Locals have worked hard to block any further efforts to disturb the shipwreck. We consider it to be cursed."

Angus gave me a funny look, but I didn't retreat from my statement. All of us in Ptarmigan Port understood the peril of the seas. Three tragedies surrounded the S.S. *Fortunate*, including her initial sinking. We didn't want to risk yet another one.

Connor's voice cut through our conversation, "We're coming up on the S.S. *Fortunate* now. We'll cut the engine and linger for a bit."

Angus and I joined the other tourists in the enclosed lounge. Looking through the glass bottom was a bit disorienting, in the same way that the glass in an aquarium distorts the view of the fish inside. Like in an aquarium, we could see fish swimming below us, mostly salmon. I didn't know if they counted as sea creatures teeming below like in Angus's nightmares. I didn't get the chance to ask him, as the broken boards of an old ship hove into view.

Connor appeared in the lounge as his boat drifted on the gentle seas. "There she is, folks, the S.S. *Fortunate*," he said, raising his voice so the assembled crowd could hear. "She went down on February 4, 1915, in gale force winds. She sank so fast that no rescue was attempted. The ship's manifest listed seventy-three passengers and crew, and there were no survivors." He flicked a switch to shine a powerful light on the debris below us. "Look at this, folks! You can see the glint of gold even now, shining underwater one hundred years later! Three thousand pounds of gold went down with the ship. It's all there at the bottom of the channel."

"Amazing!" Angus knelt down to peer at what certainly looked like a glint of gold spilling from the broken hull of the sunken ship. He slipped his phone out of his jacket pocket for a photo.

"Some folks say you can see the skeletons of the doomed passengers," Connor went on with ghoulish relish. "I've never seen any bones myself, but they're down there, all right."

I averted my eyes from the murky wreck, having no desire to see submerged skeletons. I saw Angus's face lose all color, taking on the tinge of green that I associate with seasickness. The *Gold as Glass* was experiencing a slight roll, which could have caused motion sickness.

I offered him my water bottle. "Do you need to sit down?"

He waved it away with an unsteady hand. "I'll be all right. It's just the thought of all those people trapped on a sinking ship, with nowhere to go and no way to escape." He sat down and pulled his own water bottle out of his backpack.

I closed my mind to that thought. "Your recurring dream will probably contain skeletons as well as sea creatures from now on."

He groaned at that thought. "Yeah, for all the live sea creatures, there are hundreds of dead ones down there, right? Thanks for that uplifting image!"

"Sorry." His color seemed to be coming back. I didn't think he was in imminent danger of passing out or throwing up.

He shook himself. "No, I'm the one who should apologize. I'm spoiling your shipwreck tour. It's just…my great-grandfather was a passenger on the SS *Fortunate* in 1915. He went down with the ship."

Chapter Eleven

I stared at him, for once at a loss for words.

"I was ready to see the shipwreck," he went on, "but I never thought I might see his remains. I wasn't prepared for that."

"So, this trip of yours is kind of like visiting his grave in an historic graveyard?"

"I guess you could say that. Except that when I got to the graveyard, I found that somebody had dug up the graves and tossed the skeletons about, metaphorically speaking. I don't want to look."

I knew exactly how he felt, though in my case the interval was closer to a decade than a century. That wasn't a conversation I was ready to have with an outsider, charming though he may be.

"I think I'll get some fresh air." Angus walked out of the observation lounge and approached the rail, popping open his umbrella against the light rain. I followed him closely, sticking to my quarry. Good thing for him! A speedboat roared past on our starboard side with a wake that rocked the *Gold as Glass* like a tree in a gale. I grabbed the side rail with one hand and caught Angus with the other as he reeled across the deck. His bright yellow umbrella flew out of his grip and sailed overboard. I clasped him to my chest, guiding his now free hand to the railing. "I guess you really will get wet now." I pointed to the umbrella, bobbing merrily on the brisk waves.

He gripped the rail with both hands as the second wave of the wake rocked the boat. "Note to self—umbrellas truly are useless on the water." He gave me a quivery smile.

With a start, I realized that my arms still encircled him. I quickly let go and slid along the rail to a respectable distance. I pulled on the pair of waterproof gloves I always carried in my pocket, to guard against the chill of the wet railing.

"I'm lucky that wasn't me bobbing about in the waves," Angus went on. "Thanks for keeping me safe onboard."

I blasted my hundred-watt smile again. "What's a trip to Alaska if you don't have at least one near-death experience?"

"I wouldn't go that far." He pointed to the shore, a few hundred yards off. "I'm a good swimmer. I'm sure I could have made it to shore if I had actually washed overboard."

I shook my head. "The water is barely 40 degrees. Your muscles would go numb in a matter of minutes. Hard to swim if you can't feel your limbs. Even if you managed to make it to shore, you would risk succumbing to hypothermia before rescuers could get to you." I smiled sweetly. "Let's face it, I just saved your life."

He pushed wet curls out of his face and gave me a comical bow. "Then I am in your debt."

I couldn't help laughing. So much for my detective/spy persona! It was hard to focus on Angus as a murder suspect in the face of his undeniable charm.

"Sorry about that excitement, folks," Connor's voice came over the loudspeaker. "We'll be leaving the SS *Fortunate* now. I hope we'll be 'fortunate' enough to scare up a pod of orcas or even a humpback whale."

I groaned inwardly. Surely Connor knew the laws about viewing whales without disturbing them. I put his words down to patter and turned my face into the wind as the boat gained speed. The steady wind blew the light rain across my cheeks, stripping the hood from my head and sending my long, red hair streaming out behind me. I laughed out loud at the power of nature. Beside me, Angus turned up his coat collar and shoved his hands into his pockets.

I peeled off one of my gloves and held it out to him. "Never walk on an icy sidewalk or sail in a boat with your hands in your pockets. You won't be able to catch yourself when you fall."

"I'm counting on you to catch me." He accepted the glove, nonetheless. Before he could continue, I laid an arresting hand on his arm.

"Look, close in to shore at 2:00. See that puff? That's a humpback."

He whipped out a tiny pair of binoculars and peered through them.

"There's another," I said, pointing. "Smaller puff means a baby, most likely."

"Thar she blows!" Connor's voice boomed. "Whales off the starboard bow." He changed course in hot pursuit.

An excited rush of tourists crowded along the starboard bow, cameras clicking. I backed off to give them pole position, shifting to the port side of the boat. Angus stayed put, binoculars at the ready.

"Look, there's the tail," someone shouted.

I never got tired of watching whales. I preferred to do it quietly, in hopes of hearing the whale's song, or the resonant sound of their blowing. I smiled at the chatter of the tourists, happy to share my little bit of paradise with them. I didn't need to shoulder through the crush to get a glimpse of the whales.

The relative calm on the port side gave me a serene view of the water around us, despite the persistent rain. I leaned against the rail to watch the raindrops pocking the water's surface, leaving intersecting ripples behind them like an impressionist painting. I breathed in the salty air in deep contentment. Suddenly, the pattern of shimmering ripples vanished as the water began boiling below us. Large bubbles emerged from the depths, sketching a wide circle perilously close to the boat's hull.

"Bubble-net feeding!" I called out. I ran along the deck to the bridge, waving my arms to catch Connor's attention. "They're right on the port side."

Several tourists turned to gawk at me, ignorant of the danger. Luckily, Connor had his wits about him. A quick glance showed him I was right, and he threw the wheel hard over. The boat swung sharply to starboard, throwing several tourists against the rail. The sea exploded on the port side, with half a dozen humpbacks emerging from the depths headfirst, mouths open. Herring popcorned through the air, propelled skyward by the force of the whales' lunge. Trapped by the net of bubbles, they had nowhere to go except to fall back into the gaping mouths of the hunting humpbacks.

Tourists screamed and scrambled for the rails as the *Gold as Glass* rocked in the roiling seas. If not for my warning and Connor's quick action, the boat would have been right in the center of the bubble net. It's questionable who would have come off worse: the humpbacks who would have dashed their skulls against the hull of the boat, or the tourists who could have ended up in the drink if the boat had capsized on impact.

The whales sank below the surface as quickly as they had emerged, leaving a shimmer of ripples on the water's surface as the only trace of the frenzy we had just witnessed. I found myself gripping the port rail with both hands, clinging to the wet metal despite the chill. I slipped my one ungloved hand into my coat pocket for warmth and looked for Angus among the crowd of shell-shocked tourists. "What an absolute treat," I called out to him. "Locals can go years without ever seeing humpbacks in the act of bubble-net feeding."

"Is that what you call it?" He shuffled across the deck and planted both hands on the rail. "Good thing my subconscious didn't know about this phenomenon. The teeming sea creatures in my recurring dreams always stayed under water where they belonged. Real life is so much worse—it's like they've broken the fourth wall or something."

I grinned at him, happy to see that he wasn't about to freak out. "Lunch time on the high seas!"

The rest of the cruise was uneventful, thank goodness. I didn't catch Angus Montgomery doing one single suspicious thing the entire cruise. That didn't get him off the hook in my book. I'd just have to keep following him around, waiting for him to slip up and reveal himself. Maybe that would happen over dinner...

I made sure to be beside him as we disembarked. "Good to be on dry land again?"

He tapped a foot on the wet boards of the dock. "Not exactly dry or land, but yes, it's good to be back on shore."

I glanced at my watch—nearly 6:00 p.m. "Hungry? How about

dinner at the Glacial Grill? My treat." I crooked a hand in his elbow and steered him down the dock. "You can tell me about your great-grandfather's voyage on the SS *Fortunate*."

Angus gave me a pleased smile. "I'd love to. Should I go back and dress for dinner?"

I shook my head. "Nothing fancy about the Glacial Grill. It's just a short walk along the docks. Hang on a sec." I sent a quick text to Marcy, telling her I was taking Angus to dinner and could she please, please check in on Cosmo on her way home. She texted back a thumbs up emoji, which was good enough for me.

I led the way to the end of the dock and then followed a path of crushed mussel shells to the wooden building perched on a rock promontory. More of a shack than a proper building, the Glacial Grill faced the water. Loops of fishing nets festooned the front door, and the smoky scent of grilled seafood drew us in.

The indoor heat was almost oppressive after the freshness of being on the water. We stripped off our wet coats to hang on a repurposed ship's steering wheel and sat down on well-worn metal stools flanking a table made from a cable reel—an oversized wooden spool originally used to coil cables on a fishing vessel. Brenda dropped off a couple menus at our table and turned away without a word.

I passed a menu to Angus. "Their specialty is grilled halibut tacos. With a splash of special hot sauce, they're to die for."

"I'll skip the dying part, but halibut tacos sound great."

I threw him a bright smile, distracted by watching Brenda rustling around by the takeout counter. I regarded her thoughtfully. A large woman with wiry gray hair and skin roughened by years of crewing on a purse seiner, Brenda Tarkington seldom made small talk while waiting tables at the Glacial Grill. Today, her silence held a special quality—was it elation, or mourning? Hard to figure out.

I wasn't afraid to give it a try.

When she returned to take our order, I quickly piped up, "Two orders of halibut tacos, please, Brenda. Hey, I'm sorry about Blake. What a terrible thing!"

She merely grunted. "Blake's the first person to get himself murdered in Ptarmigan Port in thirty years. The chump would have gotten a kick out of his fifteen minutes of fame."

Angus watched this conversation intently. When Brenda headed to the kitchen with our orders, he leaned across the table and whispered, "Who is that?"

I whispered back, "Blake Rivers's ex-wife. They divorced five or six years ago, with no love lost on either side."

He blew out a breath. "Okay. As you say, it's a small town."

"Small world, really. Tell me about your great-grandfather and how he met his demise in the cold waters of my small town."

He folded his hands on the table as if about to launch into a lecture. "My great-grandfather, Alexander Montgomery, was a passenger on the SS *Fortunate*. He left Seattle for the gold fields of the Klondike in the fall of 1914, leaving behind a young wife who was pregnant with his first child, unbeknownst to Alexander. He was twenty-five years old." He paused in his academic delivery to add in a more conversational tone, "Lucky for me, he left her pregnant, or else he would have died without any issue, and I would not be here."

I chuckled, savoring his whimsical smile. "Good job, Alexander."

"As you know," Angus went on, resuming the professorial tone, "the ship went down in heavy seas on February 4, 1915, and there were no survivors. Alexander Montgomery was one of the casualties—his name is listed on the ship's manifest filed in Skagway before she set sail."

Angus paused to allow Brenda to set down our plates. You could almost see the tantalizing aroma of perfectly grilled halibut rising from the loaded tacos. I closed my eyes and inhaled a deep, heavenly breath, then slathered hot sauce onto the tangy coleslaw and took a huge bite of taco. Wiping a dribble of sauce off my chin, I mumbled, "Go on."

Angus sprinkled his sauce on with a sparing hand, and then crunched into his taco. "Delicious!" He was quiet for a few minutes, obviously enjoying the hearty Alaska fish.

I felt my usual flush of happiness at the chance to share my personal paradise with others. But I did want to know what came next in the tale of Alexander and the sinking ship. I didn't have to wait long.

"You probably know that the SS *Fortunate* moored in Havoc Strait the night of February 3 to repair a gash in her hull from a recent encounter with an uncharted rock in Lynn Canal. Scholars have argued that the captain should have sent all the crew and passengers ashore until repairs were complete. Although hindsight is a wonderful lens for viewing history, with no reason to believe a storm was brewing, it's hard to fault the captain for the tragedy. I know that one passenger went ashore, namely Alexander Montgomery." He took a hearty bite of taco and beamed at me around the edges.

As a lecturer, Angus was good. I'd never heard that anyone had left the ship, and I wanted to know the whole story now. I leaned forward. "Where did he go? How do you know he left the ship? I thought you said he went down with the others."

"That's the great thing about being an historian. You get to study primary documents. In this case, it's a letter that Alexander mailed to his wife, Estelle, back in Seattle. It's postmarked from Ptarmigan Port on February 4, 1915, the day the *Fortunate* went down. Alexander went ashore on the third, dropped the letter into a mailbox, and returned to the ship to meet his fate."

"Or, he could have abandoned the ship, stayed in Ptarmigan Port to mail the letter on the fourth, and then…" My voice trailed off with the realization that Angus took his research very seriously. Now was not the time to make light of his theories. "So, you've read Alexander's letter, then?"

"I have. It's very interesting." His eyes twinkled with suppressed excitement. "Alexander's letter has been passed down in my family for three generations. Estelle added a note explaining why she never acted on it and asking for the eldest male Montgomery to receive the letter on his eighteenth birthday. When I turned eighteen, it came down to me. No one in my family has tried to follow up on the letter until me. That's why I'm here."

I sat back to stare at him; my taco forgotten. "What was in the letter that Estelle didn't act on?"

He shot me a grin full of glee. "Alexander sent Estelle a treasure map leading to a hidden cache of gold."

Chapter Twelve

"Wow!" It was all I could say. I returned to my neglected taco. Questions were jostling against one another in my brain. The first to come out wasn't necessarily the most important. "Why didn't your dad or grandfather want to look for the gold?"

"As in, who wouldn't?"

"Exactly! You've heard of the Pastor's Confession Map here in Ptarmigan Port. Everyone in town studied it, and all the kids spent every summer trying to find the gold."

Angus gave me a curious glance, but his answer made total sense. "You were here in town. My family left Seattle for the east coast during the Depression. Do you know how long it takes to get from New York to Southeast Alaska? Multiple days."

I shrugged. "How much gold are we talking about? Maybe it would be worth a few days' travel to gather it in."

"Well, Alexander didn't specify the amount of gold he'd hidden." Angus picked at his taco shell for a moment, an excuse to avoid eye contact. "Fact is, the gold didn't exactly belong to him. It seems he lifted a certain amount of the SS *Fortunate's* valuable cargo and slipped ashore to stash it safely for pick-up at a later date. I guess he had to return to the ship to avoid suspicion if the theft was discovered. He mailed the letter to his wife just in case he didn't make it, so she could find the gold for herself. She had her hands full with a new baby and never made it up to Alaska."

"So, your great-grandfather was a thief."

He gave an embarrassed shrug. "Actually, it gets worse. He may have been involved in a murder."

"A murder! No one's ever said anything about a murder related to the sinking of the SS *Fortunate*. What did Alexander say in that letter of his?"

"It's not in the letter, exactly. There's some writing on the back of the treasure map. It's really only half of a map, so you can't get the whole story from the writing. I can't discern if there really was a murder, or who was killed."

I could feel my face frozen into a mask of shock and disbelief, as my thoughts raced. I fought to keep my voice neutral, "I'd love to see this map and letter of Alexander's. Did you bring it with you?"

"I don't have it on me—it's in my lodgings." He shot me another funny look, almost shy this time. "Want to stop by after dinner and I can show you?"

I was about to respond when my phone rang, shocking me back to the twenty-first century. I snagged it from my pocket—Patrick. "Excuse me, Angus, I should take this."

I stepped outside into the persistent drizzle and answered.

"Junetta, I was just about to close when Nels showed up. He's asking a bunch of questions and I don't know what to say to him."

I could hear the near panic in Patrick's voice. Any hope of seeing Alexander Montgomery's letter today vanished. "No worries, Patrick. I'm finishing up dinner at the Glacial Grill. Tell Nels I'll be there in a minute. Tell him you've been instructed to say nothing without a lawyer or your boss present, so he'll just have to wait."

"I can't tell him that," Patrick squeaked.

"Hand him the phone and I'll tell him."

"I'll just tell him you're on your way. Thanks, Junetta."

I hustled back inside and intercepted Brenda for the check. I plumped down on my stool and shoveled the last few bites of halibut into my mouth. "Sorry, Angus, I gotta get back to the bookshop. I would love to see your letter some other time."

"Could we say tomorrow, lunchtime?"

"Perfect. Just stop by the bookshop and we'll take it from there." I wiped my mouth and quickly settled the bill with Brenda.

"Sorry to eat and run." I scooted out the door with a cheery backward wave.

Angus watched me all the way out the door.

I forgot about him in my dash to rescue Patrick. By the time I reached the bookshop, I had worked up a good head of steam to unleash on my brother. Who did he think he was coming into my place of business and intimidating my employee? I slammed through the front door and charged to the front counter where Nels lounged, leaning against the counter as if he had all the time in the world. He was fully outfitted in his trooper uniform, bullet-proof vest fastened across his chest and hardware dangling from his heavy belt. He even wore his hat, the ultimate in official for him.

I swallowed the whole speech that had been playing in my head since leaving the Glacial Grill, deciding instead to meet his nonchalance with indifference. "Patrick, thanks for calling me in. What's up, Nels?"

He cocked an eyebrow at me. "I have a few questions about the bookshop's financials. Patrick didn't think he was the right person to ask."

"And he was exactly right about that." I gave Patrick my most reassuring smile. "You can head on out if you want, Patrick, or you can stay and take part in this conversation if you'd rather."

Patrick opted to take off. In fact, he skedaddled as if he couldn't get out the door fast enough.

I turned back to Nels. "What about the bookshop's financials?"

"I talked to Uncle Vance, who wouldn't say one word about the financial state of your business. Sorry, I find this suspicious. I'd like to find out for myself. Can I have a look at your books?"

"Do you have a search warrant?"

Nels glared at me. "No, I don't have a search warrant, but I can get one if you're going to be difficult." His frown dared me to oppose him.

I could never resist a tussle with my little brother. "If you can satisfy me as to your reason for reviewing the bookshop's financials, I can probably waive the warrant."

Nels slammed his hand down on the counter. "You think this is a game! Junetta, a dead body showed up in your back room yesterday. Your own uncle, the 'owner emeritus' of this bookshop, is in jail in Juneau for murder. He's not cooperating one bit, but I thought you might want to help me figure out what happened. Now, I can come back with lights and siren blaring and barge in here to ransack your shop with a search warrant which I can certainly get, or I can ask you nicely to show me your books and see if they will answer my questions."

Okay, he got me there. It wasn't a game, and I did want to figure out what happened to Blake. If Uncle Vance was innocent, I wanted him home as soon as possible. I refused to consider what would happen if he was guilty.

"Okay, you can look at the books. What questions do you have that they could answer?" I led him to Uncle Vance's desk in the back room as we talked. The smell of antiseptic was very strong. I made a mental note to open all the windows tomorrow, even if it was raining.

"I told you, the fact that Uncle Vance wouldn't answer my questions made me suspicious. I want to check on the financial status of the bookshop, to see if there might have been a money motive for killing Blake." He shot me a sidelong glance. "You might know that Blake has been accused of extortion once or twice, with no convictions resulting. I want to know if he had anything over Uncle Vance that might have led to a confrontation."

I thought about the rumors Reba had shared with me about Blake's blackmailing ways. I hadn't realized that he'd been formally accused. I pulled down the ledgers and dropped them on the desk, praying that they wouldn't reveal any hint of Blake blackmailing Uncle Vance. "Here's the thing. The most recent ledger is missing. I've searched all through the bookshop and checked at Uncle Vance's house as well."

Nels folded his arms and scowled at me. "You should have reported this to the troopers at once."

I mimicked his stance and scowled right back. "You may recall that I asked you about the ledger this morning, but you were too busy getting Uncle Vance on the plane to Juneau. You couldn't spare a moment to listen to me."

"You didn't report it as missing."

"Come on, Nels. I asked you to ask him about it. Any trooper worth his salt would figure out that such a request meant that the item was missing."

Nels closed his eyes and took a deep, deep breath. "I'd like you to file a report stating that the ledger is missing. I can get a warrant to search through Uncle Vance's house."

"Didn't you already do that?" In the face of his blank stare, I went on, "I went to his house this morning and it looked like it had been ransacked. I assumed it was the troopers. If not, it might have been the thief/murderer."

Nels looked past me, thinking aloud. "It must have happened between yesterday morning after Uncle Vance left for work and this morning when you went to his house. Was the intruder looking for the ledger, or was there something else that would cause them to go through Uncle Vance's things?" His eyes snapped back to my face.

"There is something else." I pointed to the empty hook over the desk. "I gave Uncle Vance a god's eye when I was in second grade, and it has hung there ever since. Now it's gone."

"You mean that little yarn thing? What could that have to do with anything?"

I compressed my lips, not wanting to show the emotion that welled up in me again at the senselessness of this loss. "No idea. I'm just telling you, so you won't yell at me later on for not reporting it missing."

He took off his hat and twirled it in his hands, avoiding my eyes. "Sorry for yelling at you. I was mostly frustrated with Uncle Vance. He won't say a word about his whereabouts the other night, which leaves him looking guilty as sin. He's invoking his Miranda rights, just to mess with me. I shouldn't have taken my frustrations out on you." He clapped the hat back on his head—the moment was over. "Okay, you've searched the bookshop and Uncle Vance's house for the ledger. He surely didn't have it on him when I arrested him. Where could he have hidden it if he was the one who removed it?"

"I didn't check his car. I can't think of any other place."

Nels made a quick note. "I'll take care of that. Don't go poking around Uncle Vance's car, all right?" He stashed his notebook back in his pocket. "Is there any other way to gauge the bookshop's financial status, if we never do find that ledger? You don't have any electronic record, bank statements, anything like that? Come on, Junetta, this is the twenty-first century."

I groaned. "Yeah, my bad. I put a dinosaur in charge of my books. I'll search out all that stuff and see what I can find. If there's anything weird, I'll let you know. I promise."

"Okay." He made a move toward the door handle. I laid a hand on his arm.

"You have to admit that Uncle Vance might be innocent, Nels. I think there's reasonable doubt there."

He gently brushed off my hand. "If that's true, then there's a murderer on the loose here in Ptarmigan Port. Keep an eye out, Junetta."

I saluted like an ROTC recruit. He rolled his eyes and took off, and I dutifully locked the door behind him and headed to the alley behind the shop.

It was barely 9:00 p.m. and the sun was still high in the sky. The rain had finally paused, and tendrils of mist rose from the hillsides like breath on a frosty morning. I threw out my arms and breathed in the damp freshness, letting the soothing power of nature wash over me. On impulse, I locked up my car for the night and headed home on foot.

The hike through the woods was always a treat. The trail from downtown to the Hill neighborhood wove upward through the rainforest filled with towering cedar, spruce, and hemlock trees. The understory consisted of blueberry bushes with berries starting to ripen, ferns of all descriptions, and moss covering everything. Devil's club grew in profusion, with its wide flat leaves with prickles on the underside and the spiny stem that was the bane of hikers. Tonight, water dripped softly from the treetops after a day of gentle rain. Although it was bright as day downtown along the shore, the woodsy trail was enveloped in a mossy green twilight. I heard an eagle's twittering call, followed by the steady beat of its wings. I thrilled to the sight of it flying through the trees below the canopy, sharing the magical space with me for a moment. The goofy smile was still on my lips when I turned to respond to the call from behind me, "Hey, Junetta!"

It was Brenda Tarkington.

She was huffing a little, as if the upward climb was a bit of a challenge for her. She didn't waste any words. "What do you know about Blake's death?"

The last thing I wanted to talk about was murder. "Terrible, isn't it?"

She came up to me, a little too close. "He died in your bookshop. Did you find his body? What did he look like?"

"It wasn't me. I came back from the villages to find Trooper Nels already there." I shuddered at the memory. "I've never seen a dead body before." Patently untrue, but my experience was limited to tidy corpses in coffins, not the aftermath of sudden death. They wouldn't let me look that one time.

"Did your uncle kill him, like they say?"

"I don't think so, Brenda. Uncle Vance is a curmudgeon, not a killer."

She was silent a moment, considering my words. "What about that fancy man you were having dinner with? What's his part in all this?"

I couldn't resist a smile at that characterization. "He's doing family history research. I don't think he has any connection with Blake. I'm keeping an eye on him all the same."

She gave me a sour glance. "Looked like you had both eyes on him if you ask me. Watch out for handsome strangers, Junetta, they're likely to lead you astray."

I just laughed. "I'm twenty-nine years old, Brenda. I'm a little old for a lecture on stranger danger." I swatted at a cloud of mosquitos that had discovered me once I stopped walking. "Are you coming up? Time to get moving before we get eaten alive."

She shook her head and turned to make the descent. She flung a comment over her shoulder, "The truth will out, Junetta. I'm not a fool, you know."

"Of course not," I stammered, but she was gone.

I puzzled over her words for the rest of my hike, which completely spoiled the serenity of the twilit trail. I couldn't make sense of her accusatory tone. She must be experiencing a storm of emotions after the death of her despised ex-husband. I wondered if she stood to inherit anything in his will. Not a fool, that Brenda. But could she be a murderer?

I gasped out loud. If I believed in Uncle Vance's innocence, which I most certainly did, then a murderer was still at large in our town. It could be anyone. They could be anywhere. I threw a glance over my shoulder and picked up my pace. All of a sudden, the serene trail that I loved to hike morphed into a sinister place. Soft rustlings in the bushes caused me to jump in alarm. The hammer of a woodpecker echoed the pounding of my heart. I hurried even faster, until I was running up the trail as if my life depended on it.

I burst out of the twilit woods, clutching a stitch in my side. Not a threat in sight. I stumbled through the peaceful clearing to snatch open my door and duck inside. Time for a cup of herbal tea and a comedy on TV.

But I had forgotten about Cosmo. He swarmed me as soon as I got inside, not content until I had clipped on his leash and headed back out into the approaching twilight. This time I didn't freak out. Cosmo would protect me. He frisked down the road, snapping at a dragonfly and sneezing at the mosquitos that couldn't penetrate his shaggy coat. Nothing like an energetic little dog to take your mind off your troubles!

By the time Cosmo slowed down, I was well-bitten by mosquitos and ready to call it a day. I fixed myself that cup of tea and settled down in front of the TV. Binge-watching sitcoms often soothed my nerves—or at least deadened them for the moment. For the second night in a row, I fell asleep on the couch. I dreamed of a handsome young man with unruly curly hair and a bright yellow umbrella who held a treasure map in his hand and beckoned me to follow him into the mossy woods.

Chapter Thirteen

I stopped by the Last Chance Café for a cup of coffee the next morning. I didn't intend to tell Marcy that I'd dreamt of Angus Montgomery last night, but somehow his name came up in our conversation. In fact, she started it.

"Did you learn anything from following Angus Montgomery around yesterday?" She deposited a brimming cup of café au lait and a cinnamon sweet roll on the table and sat down across from me. "Either about him or about yourself?"

I deliberately picked up a spoon and stirred the coffee. "Only that his great-grandfather went down with the SS *Fortunate*, after stealing some gold and mailing a treasure map to his wife down south." I took a slow, savoring sip. "Sorry, it was only half of a treasure map."

Marcy stared at me, for once rendered speechless.

"I'm going to have lunch with him today, so he can show it to me." I chomped a huge bite of sweet roll.

"You don't think...?" Marcy whispered.

"I kinda do. I'll let you know when I see it. It'll be obvious one way or another."

Marcy ran her hand through her straight black hair. "He must have something to do with the theft at the bookshop. This can't be a coincidence."

I washed down the sweet treat with a swig of coffee. "You look let down. I knew you were taking his side."

"Oh, and you're not? A harbor cruise wasn't enough time to surveil him, so you had to have dinner together as well?" She laughed at my surprised look. "Oh, yes, I have my sources. What's the verdict, Agent Beale? Cold-blooded murderer or irresistible heartthrob?"

It was my turn to laugh. "Neither. He is a nice guy, though. And kind of cute the way his hair curls at the ends. Also, a good storyteller. I can't wait to hear the rest of his family history. But a murderer? I hope not."

She poked me playfully. "Just as I suspected. You're smitten. Have you asked him the most important question? Is he a hockey fan?"

I choked on my coffee. "I'm not getting engaged to him, for goodness' sake! We just had dinner together. He's one of our suspects, after all."

She gave me a knowing smile. She did have a good point.

Hockey was the cause of my broken engagement last year. It sounds crazy when I put it like that, but it's true. When I met Liam, I was living in Florida, working for an independent publisher, and basking in the sun far from the Southeast Alaska rainforests. He bowled me over with his charm. Things had gotten serious very quickly, before I learned that he was a rabid Tampa Bay Lightning fan. When hockey season started, Liam went AWOL. He had season tickets and never missed a game, for any reason. If the Lightning were playing out of town, he watched on TV. He lived, slept, and breathed hockey. He tried to fit me in around the edges, but I could tell that his heart was with hockey. When he gave me an engagement ring in the shape of the Stanley Cup, I knew I had to call a halt. It broke my heart, because I really did love him, but I didn't want to be a hockey widow for the rest of my life. I gave him back the ring, packed up, and moved back to Alaska, which is about as far away from Florida as you can get. I hadn't regretted it for a moment.

I took another drink of coffee, focusing on today. Was I smitten with Angus? Well, what if I was?

• • •

I spent the next few hours at the computer before opening the bookshop at 10:00 a.m. as usual. I had very little luck. I had completely trusted Uncle Vance to keep the books for the shop.

I didn't have any passwords for our online bank accounts, if he even had set up any online accounts. Without the missing ledger, I couldn't tell if our bills were paid. If they were up to date, with Uncle Vance in jail, I would have to make sure the upcoming payments were made. What about Patrick's paycheck? I didn't even know that. I spent the whole time kicking myself for not taking more interest in the financial side of my business.

By the time I turned on the lights and flipped the sign to "Open," I was in a sour mood. Not only did I have very little grasp of my own business, but I would have to confess that fact to my little brother in his official capacity as murder investigator.

It was a busy morning at the Shipshape Bookshop. After our drizzly day yesterday, the sun came out and brightened up the whole world. One big cruise ship was tied up at the dock while two others were moored in the harbor, with tenders plying back and forth from ship to dock like water beetles in a never-ending cycle. Shedding their matching raincoats emblazoned with the name of their ships, the tourists sported polo shirts and sunglasses instead. Their chatter lifted my spirits, like it always did. I met a newlywed couple from Pennsylvania who were on a ten-day cruise. They prowled around my shop for over an hour, peering out the window so many times that they started to make me nervous. Were they hiding out from the law, guilty of some crime? Could they be the ones who had killed Blake?

I mentally shook myself, before I went down the heebie-jeebies rabbit hole. The murderer couldn't have been a random tourist. The cruise ships pulled out around 8:00 p.m. or 9:00 p.m. every evening, leaving our town to breathe overnight and prepare for the next busy day. Blake was killed in the night, so the only suspects were Ptarmigan Port residents—people I had known my whole life. Talk about heebie-jeebies!

I banished that thought and approached the couple with a big smile. "Are you looking for bears out there? You can sometimes see them in town, although they usually stay away from people."

The young woman gave a guilty start. "Oh, no, we're actually hiding out from my parents. We're on our honeymoon, and they're cruising with us to celebrate their thirtieth wedding anniversary. Every conversation is about their wedding day and their honeymoon to Niagara Falls. Chris and I just want a few minutes to ourselves to enjoy our own honeymoon."

"Say no more." I pulled out a handy booklet of local attractions and flipped through the pages until I came to the section on the Tongass Glacier. "You're going to want to see the glacier, but you don't have to go with the tour bus full of visitors like your parents. The Ridge Trail is a lovely out-of-the-way option where you can hike in peace and have magnificent views of the glacier. Heather can run you out to the trailhead in her cab." Heather Forten was a local schoolteacher who drove tourists around on her summer vacation. She could never resist the opportunity to school her fares, both about local history and culture and about national politics. This young couple would get their money's worth.

They happily bought the booklet, accepted Heather's card, and went on their way.

That little interaction bolstered my confidence in my ability to solve problems. Pushing aside the financial state of the bookshop, which required much more time and effort, I focused on my upcoming lunch with Angus Montgomery.

He showed up at the stroke of noon. I'd propped the door open to take advantage of the sunshine, and he slipped inside without a word. I was ringing up a harassed mother with a whiny child who obviously needed some lunch. Angus leaned on the counter with a wide smile and said, "I just saw a bear outside, wandering down the street like he owned the place." He leaned down to face the child. "If you're very quiet, you might be able to get a glimpse of him out this side window." He strolled over to the window, followed by the now calm child, and pointed. The child gasped in excitement; all his whininess forgotten. The mother and I both gaped at this little interaction. It's hard to say who was more pleased by it.

Mother and child left with many cautious glances down the sidewalk, and I watched them go. "You're a child whisperer, Angus."

"This is the first bear I've ever seen in the wild. Not a big deal to you, but I figured that kid had probably not seen one before either. It's fun to share something special like that." He pushed back his tousled curls and beamed at me. "You live in paradise, you know."

I returned his smile. "I do know."

I called out to Patrick that I was off to lunch and led Angus out the door. "Let's get some food from Larry's food truck, and then you can show me your documents."

We made our way along the dock, sidestepping the hundreds of tourists seeking their best Alaska adventure. They had one day in Ptarmigan Port to make their memories, and today was as good a day as they could hope for. The sun beat down at a whopping 70 degrees, sending local kids crying inside because it hurt their eyes. The pale blue of the sky was mirrored in the deep blue waters washing softly against the rocky shoreline under the dock. The salty smell of the sea mingled with the savory scent of fry bread coming from Larry John's food truck. We joined the line, feeling thankful that most of the tourists would eat onboard their cruise ships, leaving something for the rest of us.

Angus gazed around him with an expression of contentment. "Everything is so beautiful. I want to savor every minute. I've only got one more week here in Alaska."

I tore my eyes from the sight of a lone eagle sitting on a piling, surrounded by the tourist paparazzi. "One week is all? Does that give you time to finish your research?" Or give me time to conclude my sleuthing? Maybe Nels would detain Angus if his murder inquiries weren't finished.

"I will have to knuckle down and focus on the documents at the Historical Society. Hard to do on such a beautiful day, though."

"Yeah, there's a tradition here in town where shop owners shut down and go out hiking or fishing on a lovely day. I have a sign, "Closed for Sunshine," at the bookshop. Last time I hung it out was in May when I wanted a whole day out at the beach."

"Isn't that bad for business?"

I chuckled ruefully, thinking of how poor my business sense really was. "What's the use of money if you can't enjoy the best things in life?" I waved an arm at the sparkling water, where two harbor seals popped their heads up and down to the delight of a crowd of visitors. "I can't see this from the front counter of the Shipshape Bookshop."

"You don't spend all your time in the bookshop, right? I understand you sail off to remote villages with your floating bookmobile." His voice held the faintest note of query, as if to ask how such an activity could possibly be profitable.

I nodded with pride. "I've got a culture grant to fund the bookmobile. It's a huge rush to see the kids come running to the beach to get their hands on their next literary adventure." I smiled at the thought. "My boat is the *Northern Dream*, the very boat that my ancestor, Rev. Denton, used to minister to the villages in the early twentieth century. You remember Rev. Raymond Denton, the pastor who took the confession of a supplicant who left him with the Pastor's Confession Map, which is now missing from my bookshop."

I watched Angus closely as I said this, looking for any kind of reaction. Either he was an actor as well as an historian, or he didn't fully grasp the importance of my comment. "I see that you're a family historian, just like me," was his only response.

We finally reached the front of the line and ordered our fry bread topped with smoked salmon, a delicious treat. We settled on a bench looking out at the water, with the warm sun on our backs and the gentle wash of waves under our feet.

"Did you bring the map and letter?" I asked.

He patted the backpack sitting next to him on the bench. "I'd rather not take it out outside. It's kind of fragile. Let's take it to the Historical Society, and I can show it to you there. Ms. Cornell wants to see it as well. I described it to her, but I haven't had a chance to show her yet."

"Okay. Probably best not to risk it getting blown away or something awful like that."

Angus took a bite of fry bread, and said with a shy smile, "Have you lived in Ptarmigan Port your whole life?"

"I was born and raised here, except for a few summers when we would go to my mom's remote lodge. She's still running it: the

Sourdough Lady Lodge. If you think Ptarmigan Port is quaint and countrified, you should check out the lodge. It's completely off-grid, perched on the unspoiled hillside and surrounded by forest, beach, and ocean for as far as you can see. Fantastic place to spend summers as a teenager." I glossed over the loneliness I'd felt, having only my little brother for a playmate while all my friends in town hiked and fished and camped together in the long Alaska summer days.

"How about your dad?"

I busied myself with my fry bread. "My dad commercial fished. His boat went down when I was fourteen." I raised my eyes to his face. "There's more than one shipwreck in Havoc Strait."

He reached out and took my hand. "I'm so sorry. Under all this beauty, Alaska really is a harsh land, isn't it?"

I nodded, swallowing a lump in my throat that had as much to do with the pressure of Angus's hand as the pain of losing my dad. "It was a long time ago, but I still miss him. I went away to college and then spent time in Florida working in publishing. I thought I'd never want to come back, but there's no place I'd rather be than here." I didn't elaborate on the part Liam had played in my desire to return to Alaska.

I gently eased my hand out of Angus's grasp. "What about you? You told me you're a student at Columbia. Did you grow up in New York City?"

"No, I'm a fairly recent transplant. I grew up in Pittsburgh, a couple blocks from the zoo. On a quiet night I could sometimes hear the lions roaring. That's the closest I've come to bears and moose wandering through the streets in broad daylight."

I laughed, grateful for the change in mood. "The moose don't usually come into town. They like the marshy area around Seven Mile Creek where it flows out of the glacier. I've never heard a lion roaring in real life. It's not an experience I would normally associate with a city like Pittsburgh."

"It's a place that's full of surprises." He gathered up his trash from lunch. "Shall we go take a look at Alexander's last messages to his wife?"

Chapter Fourteen

We walked in companionable silence down the dock and past the bookshop to the Ptarmigan Port Historical Society, marked by a small brass doorplate on the deep green door.

Angus knocked and then pushed the door open. "Anybody home?"

A cluttered desk stood to the right of the door, and the rest of the entry was filled with deep cabinets with narrow drawers to hold maps and other flat documents. A dark hallway lined with floor-to-ceiling bookcases opened into a reading room. A couple of tables with straight-backed chairs stood in the middle of the room, and low bookshelves ranged along walls hung with black and white prints from the early days of our town's existence. A faint whiff of mustiness permeated the space, and the overall impression was that of an old lady's personal abode.

The lady in question bustled out from the inner recesses of the building. "Ah, Mr. Montgomery. Have you brought me those documents from your ancestor?" Belatedly, she registered my presence. "Hello, Junetta. Are you here for the grand unveiling as well?"

I blasted Reba with my hundred-watt smile. "Angus was telling me his great-grandfather's story. I can't wait to see the letter and the map."

Reba shuffled through a pile on the desk and pulled out an ornate guest book. She held it out to us. "Please sign in, with the date and where you're from."

I chuckled as I wrote "Ptarmigan Port, AK." Of course, Reba knew where I was from. If she was keeping this guest book as an historical record, I supposed that information might be handy.

Reba retrieved the book when we were finished. She dropped it back on the desk and moved to the closest table. She pushed aside a pile of books to make room. "Lay it out here, so we can all see." She held out her hand for the letter, while somehow blocking my view of the table, in spite of her words.

Angus hefted his backpack onto the table and pulled out a large waterproof document holder. He placed it on the table and then donned a pair of white cotton gloves before extricating a yellowed paper envelope. Bypassing Reba's eager outstretched hand, he eased out a brittle packet of papers and spread them gently on the table. Both Reba and I leaned in to look.

The top page was a very short note from Alexander to his wife, Estelle. It had faded over time and the old-fashioned handwriting was hard to make out. I read aloud, haltingly,

My dearest Estelle,

This map points the way to a cache of gold from the ship. I shouldn't have taken it, but the temptation was too great. I got absolution from a pastor in Ptarmigan Port, Alaska. I've left him the other half of the map. If I don't return, go collect it from him, put the two halves together, and you will be rich beyond your wildest dreams.

In haste, yours ever,
Sandy

I straightened up and exchanged glances with Reba. Her jaw was clenched, and her eyes glittered with excitement. "Let's see the map," she said.

Angus gazed fondly at the letter. "Sandy. Short for Alexander, you know. He clearly felt remorse for the theft. He didn't mention the extent of his crime to his wife. He must have loved her very much."

Reba reached out a hand to brush the letter aside. "Show us the map."

Angus forestalled her. He carefully lifted the letter to reveal what lay beneath. It was a pencil-drawn map showing natural features like the glacier, a wooded knoll, and a "well-worn path." It had a ripped edge along the entire right side of the paper. The X to mark the spot was missing—it was on the other half of the map, the one we called the Pastor's Confession Map. The one that was now missing.

There was no mistaking it. The size, the jagged tear along one side, the pencil lines—it was clearly the other half of our historic map. Angus had the left side, and we had the right side—or we did, until recently.

I wasn't surprised. I had suspected this after hearing Angus's tale about his great-grandfather. But I was shocked. Somehow, the long arm of history had reached down through the ages to touch us in this moment. And for some reason that I couldn't fathom, that intrusion of history had led to the death of Blake Rivers.

Reba gasped aloud at the sight of the map. She sought my eyes again. "But this is…You have no idea…" She staggered backwards to fall into one of the wooden chairs.

Angus glanced from her to me and back again. "Are you all right? Do you need some water?"

She waved him away with an unsteady hand. "You have no idea what this is. And you call yourself an historian!"

Before he could respond, I rushed to his defense. "You've never seen it because it was stolen right when you came to town. This is the other half of the Pastor's Confession Map. There's no doubt about it."

"I knew it!" Angus's triumphant cry cut across my words. "As soon as I heard your story in the bookshop the other day, I was sure the Pastor's Confession Map was the same one as my great-grandfather's. I just wanted you to see it for confirmation."

Reba's color flooded back. "Are you telling me that this entire unveiling was just to gauge my reaction? That you're using me to prove your historical theories?"

"Oh, no, not at all. Sorry, I didn't mean to give you that impression. It's just super exciting to find that my great-grandfather's story is alive and well here in Alaska."

"Do you mean to tell me that you never heard of the Pastor's Confession Map until it was stolen? You've never even seen pictures of it online?" Reba glared incredulously at Angus, as if he were responsible for the theft of our town's history.

He shook his head. "I came here to follow up on Alexander's story, maybe find some mention of him in local histories of the shipwreck. Imagine how fantastic it is to find the missing half of our family heirloom!"

I was scrolling through my phone while he talked, looking to see if there were any images of our map online. "Look, here's a picture, but it's too blurry to make anything of it." I held out my phone for them to see. The image was totally blurry, and the caption simply read, "Confession Map, Alaska." When I searched Ptarmigan Port, nothing about the map came up. "There's no way Angus could have known in New York City that the missing half of his family's map was on display at the Shipshape Bookshop."

Reba turned her stern gaze to me. "It should never have been there in the first place," she snapped. "I've told you and your uncle before you that the proper place for such an important piece of history is the Historical Society." She appealed to Angus, "The reason you can't access the other half of this important document has everything to do with the stubbornness of the Peterman clan who passed down their willful disregard for historical preservation to the Beales."

I turned and walked away, not willing to engage with Reba on this old, bitter argument. The fact that she may in fact have been right didn't make me feel any better. Although my back was turned, I could hear her admonishing Angus, "You should keep this under wraps, you know. Don't go around showing people your map, or they might think that you stole the one from the bookshop."

"Good point," Angus said. Keeping a gloved hand on the paper he looked over his shoulder and called out to me. "Want to see the back?"

Of course, I wanted to see the back.

I hustled back to the table and leaned over his shoulder, ignoring Reba who did the same on the other side. Together, we bent over the document to see what was written on the back.

In the same pencil and the same handwriting as the letter to Estelle was written:

> gold. We went to Cousin
> us where to bury the
> Bob was drunk and pulled
> too. He killed him and we
> back and moved the gold and
> can't trust anyone.

"That's why I say he might have been involved in a murder," Angus said with an apologetic glance.

I couldn't take my eyes off the severed note. Questions surged through my mind. The first thing that came out of my mouth was not very helpful. "I never knew there was anything on the back."

Angus looked at me in disbelief. "You never turned it over?"

"It was in a frame, for my entire life. The map was discovered by Rev. Denton's daughter Betty when she was clearing out his things after he died in the 1950's. She's the one who framed it. She might have looked at the back, but I guess she didn't think it was important to preserve that story."

"Well, I'm very interested in finding out the rest of this story," he said. "It sounds like there were at least three people there that night: Alexander, Bob, and Cousin."

"Cousin could be Cousin Bob." Reba's cheeks were flushed. She was obviously enthralled with this historical mystery.

"True. There were at least three people, though, because 'he killed him.' Alexander didn't do the killing, and we know he wasn't killed, so there was a killer and a victim present as well as Alexander." He turned to Reba. "Are there any historical records of a homicide victim on the night of February 3, 1915, or thereabouts?"

"I've never heard of a death on land associated with the shipwreck. It's something to research…"

"You say, 'on land,'" I chimed in. "Could Alexander and his buddy have killed the guy and then taken him back to the ship to go down with the rest, and that's why he was never discovered?"

Angus cocked his head to the side, considering. "I doubt it. It was a stormy night, but no one knew the ship would sink. It would be far easier to hide a body in the woods than in a crowded ship."

"Okay, I'll give you that. It sounds like Cousin was related to Alexander. What do you know about your great-grandfather's relations? Did he have a cousin who lived in Ptarmigan Port?"

Angus shook his head sorrowfully. "That's where the historical record breaks down. I've searched through census records for Montgomerys in the area without finding any. Alexander's grandfather came to America from Scotland in the mid-1800s as a result of the Highland clearances, and the family dribbled westward for the next few generations. Families tended to be large, with ten children being quite common. I've tried to put together a complete family tree, but there are multiple gaps." He turned to Reba. "I guess you're right, I'm not acquitting myself well as an historian. That's what I was hoping you could help me with."

She straightened up until you could almost see her preening, like a seagull after a storm. "Let me see what I can find about that time period." She bustled off toward a particular bookshelf.

Angus called after her, "I remember you mentioned that the map was found in the pastor's things in an envelope along with a letter marked Mr. A. Mont. No doubt that was Alexander Montgomery. Could I possibly have a look at that letter and envelope?"

I glanced at my watch. "I gotta get going, Angus, to give Patrick a chance for a break. Thanks for sharing this fantastic historical discovery with me."

"I'll see you again, won't I? Maybe at the Founders' Day picnic?"

"Of course. Your great-grandfather confessed to my great-great-grandfather. We're practically related."

"Oh, I hope not!" He smiled warmly and waved me out the door.

Chapter Fifteen

I savored his smile all the way down the sidewalk to the Shipshape Bookshop. Maybe he would pop in before closing--or I could check in on his progress at the Historical Society...

I zipped home to give Cosmo a quick outing before heading back to the shop to spell Patrick. The cheery bell rang as I entered the bookshop. Patrick hustled up to me, anxiety written all over his face. "I was just about to call you, Junetta. I know you say you don't allow anyone in the back room, but she wouldn't listen to me. She barged right past me as if I wasn't even there."

I pushed down the apprehension that his words ignited and assumed my most reassuring tone. "No worries, Patrick. You can't always control what other people do. Is she still there? Who is it, anyway?"

"It's Brenda. I don't remember her last name. She works at the Glacier Grill? She just burst in and said she wanted to see where it happened and off she went."

"Brenda Tarkington. She's Blake Rivers's ex-wife, you know. I guess she has a right to see the place where he died." I laid a soothing hand on Patrick's arm. "Go ahead and take your break, Patrick. I'll see if I can sort things out with Brenda."

I watched him head out, his shoulders relaxing in relief. I'd have to settle down and be more present in the bookshop, to take the pressure off Patrick now that Uncle Vance wasn't around. I closed my eyes, took a deep breath, and walked into the back room. "Brenda. What's up?"

Brenda Tarkington stood in the middle of the back room with her eyes closed, her arms spread wide, palms down. She almost

98

looked like a diviner, feeling for the spirits in the room to reveal themselves. Her eyes snapped open at the sound of my voice.

"Hello, Junetta. I'm here to see the spot where Blake was killed. Is there any video camera footage?"

"No, we don't have any security cameras. It never occurred to me in a million years that we would need to have video evidence of a murder in my bookshop."

Brenda grunted and turned away from me to scan the room. "Is this where his body was found?"

I pointed to the floor, which was mercifully free from any kind of bloodstains. "That's where he was." I clamped my mouth shut before I accidentally went into detail about how he was killed. Just the facts, ma'am.

And Brenda wanted all the facts. "I heard Vance Peterman's knife was stuck in Blake's gut. No wonder Vance has been hauled off to jail."

"No wonder," I echoed.

She turned to Uncle Vance's desk, her eyes taking in every detail. "Any clues here as to what happened?"

"You know the troopers have been all over this room, Brenda. If you're wondering about the progress of the investigation, you should talk to Nels."

She grunted again. "Your brother isn't handing out any bulletins that I've seen." She ran her finger along the row of ledgers on the shelf behind the desk. "Looks like one's missing here."

I shrugged, trying to appear unconcerned. What did she care if one of my bookshop's ledgers was missing? I was starting to feel paranoid about the whole question of the bookshop's finances. I decided to go on the offensive. "Speaking of money, I was curious how Blake's estate will be settled? Do you know if Connor Fisk will inherit his business, for example?"

She swung around to face me. "I don't see how that's any business of yours."

I shrugged again. "Just curious. I took the Saltwater Tours shipwreck cruise for the first time yesterday. It was really cool. We saw whales bubble-net feeding and saw the shipwreck through the glass bottom of the boat."

Brenda ignored this conversational gambit and continued her scrutiny of my back room. She put out a hand to open a desk drawer, but I had had enough. I gently covered the drawer pull with my hand and said, "Brenda, I need to get back to tending my bookshop now. If you'll just…"

"Oh, don't mind me! I just want to feel the space a bit more and then I'll be off. I can't really do it with you here, you know."

"But I can't really leave you alone in my storeroom with all my personnel files and financial details. Sorry, Brenda, you need to leave." I said it with a bright smile, but my outstretched arm indicating the exit hinted that I wasn't kidding. Luckily for me, she took the hint.

"Fine. I'll be back if I can't get my questions answered somewhere else." She marched out of the back room and straight out the front door, leaving the bell jangling furiously behind her.

I heaved a sigh of relief. I didn't know why Brenda was taking such a close interest in the investigation into Blake's death. I didn't even know what questions she wanted to answer. I would be much happier if she took her interest and her questions down to the public safety building and pestered Nels with them instead of me.

I spent the better part of the afternoon combing through the computer, searching out any financial data I could recover from its innards. Once again, I silently cursed my poor judgment in trusting Uncle Vance to take care of the accounting without supervision. I resolved to change my ways, until a customer came into the shop. Then I eagerly dropped my search to do what I did best: engaging with the people and the books.

Marcy stopped by for a bit of a chat in the middle of the afternoon. She leaned both elbows on the front counter and looked up into my face. "Well?"

"Well…?"

"The map. Is it?"

"It is." I felt like we were passing quick notes like we did in middle school. "Angus's great-grandfather's map is obviously the other half of the Pastor's Confession Map. Alexander confessed to Rev. Denton, tore the map in half, left one piece here and mailed the other home to his wife. Get this, Marcy. There's writing on the back of the map."

I let that sink in for a minute before continuing, "It's only half of a note, that references Cousin and Bob and says somebody was killed. It's like an historical murder mystery."

"Well, I prefer the historical kind to the one in your back room. Have you found out anything else about Blake's death?"

"Nothing. Brenda Tarkington keeps showing up. I just chased her out of my back room, where she was exploring the place where Blake died and asking about my missing ledger. Marcy, I'm starting to freak out about that ledger. Is there something really wrong about the bookshop's financial status? Does Brenda know or have something to do with it?"

"Have you asked Vance?"

I scoffed. "He must think he's a noble hero in a mystery story, clamming up and refusing to speak so he can protect someone."

"Yeah, I could see him doing that." She leaned in close. "Who is he protecting, Junetta?"

Her intense words almost took my breath away. "I don't know. I guess it's time to start finding out."

She patted my hand. "Off you go, Agent Beale. I'll stop by tomorrow for an updated report."

"You could come with me. I could use your astute mind and mad sleuthing skills to figure this out."

She laughed. "Tempting, but no. Rob gets home tonight for the next two weeks. I expect to be practicing my mad wifely skills instead."

Marcy's husband, Rob, worked on the North Slope on a two-weeks on, two-weeks off schedule. They were used to the separations, but I knew it would be hard once she had a newborn to care for. Luckily, she had plenty of family in town, and as a loyal friend, I foresaw some sleepovers and babysitting in my immediate future.

Marcy wiped a sappy smile off her face. "This is all so weird. We lost one half of the treasure map and miraculously found the other half in the very same week. I don't think this could be a coincidence."

"I thought you had Uncle Vance pegged as the culprit. You just said he's protecting someone. He's got nothing to do with Angus's map."

"I'm starting to rethink my theory." She let that statement hang in the air for a moment. "The first step is to figure out who Cousin and Bob are. I've never heard of them. Could there be any notes or diary entries from old Rev. Denton?"

"That's a great idea. Well done, Agent George! We do have some boxes of family papers and such—which we've never entrusted to the Historical Society, by the way. I think Uncle Vance has most of them. I'll stop by his place and have a look."

"You're starting to sound like Angus Montgomery and his research." She shot a glance over her shoulder as the bell jangled and Angus entered on cue, as if Marcy had conjured him up. He gave a cheery wave. Marcy lowered her voice, "Be careful when you're with him, Junetta. We really don't know enough about him to judge if he could be a thief or murderer."

I nodded and waved back at Angus. I could feel a big smile spreading across my face at the very sight of him. Marcy evidently saw it because she shook her head and mouthed at me, "Be careful." She melted away as Angus came up to the counter.

"How was your research this afternoon? Did you find out who Cousin and Bob are?"

He shook his head ruefully. "There's no lack of primary sources, but Reba hasn't created any kind of cataloguing system for them. She might know where something is because she saw it the other day. Otherwise, it's a question of searching through documents willy-nilly. I spent the entire afternoon browsing through the stacks and sifting through some fascinating stuff, while making very little forward progress on my project." He leaned one elbow on the counter. "I did find one delicious tidbit today. In the early 1920s, the volunteer fire department here consisted of the mayor and a miner named Will Redwing. Several small houses in the center of town caught fire on a dark winter night, and it was suspected that Redwing set the blaze out of boredom and a desire to be hailed as a hero. There was a general outcry in the town, 568 occupants at that time. They didn't care about the fire per se—they were afraid that Redwing was a Communist sympathizer who was going to set fire to their way of life. A group of citizens launched a very successful smear campaign against him. They had irrefutable evidence of his Marxist sympathies. His name started with Red, you see."

I started to laugh. "You're making this up."

He pulled out his phone to show me a picture of a newspaper article. "I had to snap this photo on the sly so Reba wouldn't see me. She's very protective of the good name of Ptarmigan Port and all its citizenry throughout the ages."

Sure enough, the article from the *Ptarmigan Times* identified Will Redwing as a danger to society, not because he was an arsonist, but because he was undoubtedly a Communist loose in their midst. It clearly stated that his name was an indication of his politics. "What happened to him in the end?"

"I never did find out." He cocked his head to one side, lost in thought for a moment. "It would be interesting to wander through the local graveyard, to see if there was a headstone for him, to find out his date of death. Church records are another place for that kind of data. But Will Redwing is not the object of my research— just a tantalizing distraction."

"Speaking of distractions…" I excused myself from Angus to greet the silver-haired couple who placed a large pile of Alaska picture books on the counter for checkout. Normally I would chat with them about their grandchildren, but my mind was occupied as I watched Angus browsing through the shelves in the history section. I was supposed to be focusing on figuring out who besides my Uncle Vance could have killed Blake Rivers in the back room of my bookshop. For me, Angus was nothing more than a tantalizing distraction. Such a charming one, too…

It couldn't hurt to be distracted for one more evening.

• • •

I waved a cheery goodbye to the grandparents and locked up behind them. "What's your next move, Angus?"

He turned with a ready smile. "Reba asked me to join her for dinner at the Orca Inn."

"Ooh, she must be impressed with you. The Orca Inn is the toniest place in town. The food is probably even up to New York City standards, and the view is to die for."

"She wanted to drive me out to the glacier afterwards, but she's got a planning meeting with the city assembly to go to. She gave me quite the lecture because I haven't visited the glacier yet."

"And well she should. The Tongass Glacier is one of the Seven Wonders of the World, or at least one of the seven places to visit in Ptarmigan Port if you've only got one day in town. You've got more than one, so you have no excuse." I glanced out the window. Some light clouds were gathering to the north, but it looked like our sunny day was not over yet. "How about this—call me after dinner and I'll meet you at Clarissa's. You can change your shoes— you did bring hiking shoes, didn't you? — and we can hike the trails around the glacier. It's much better than just driving up for a photo op."

"How did you know I'm staying at Clarissa's Bed and Breakfast?"

I laughed. "It's a small town, Angus. Ten people could have told me where you were staying if I had asked. I didn't need to, because I know there's only one place for independent travelers to rent a room in town. Clarissa's." I gave him my phone number and headed home for my own dinner.

When Angus called, I loaded Cosmo in my car and drove down the hill to Clarissa's B & B. Perched on the uphill side of the road overlooking the water, Clarissa's Bed and Breakfast commanded the best view in town. Built in the mid 1950s, it combined rugged Alaska style with what could only be described as flowery fluff. A massive front porch held up by varnished tree trunks sported bentwood rocking chairs overflowing with ruffled patchwork pillows and wooly hand-crocheted blankets for a chilly evening. The painted sign above the front door depicted a moose head with a daisy chain draped over his majestic rack. A visitor might put that down as whimsy, until they entered the foyer to see a stuffed moose head mounted above the stone fireplace, a wreath of fresh flowers encircling its antlers. I happened to know that Clarissa changed the flowers several times a week in the summertime, only falling back on fake flowers when the rains of autumn settled in for the duration.

I rang the doorbell and then walked right in. The front desk was unmanned. I called out, "Hey, Clarissa, it's Junetta."

Clarissa emerged from her office. She embodied the same mix of rugged Alaska and cozy comfort as her business. Dressed in a long, flowery cotton dress with a crocheted shawl around her shoulders, her brown rubber boots would seem out of place to anyone but a local. Her graying hair was twisted up in an elaborate bun, and moose nugget earrings dangled from her ears. "Evening, Junetta. Lovely day, isn't it?"

"It sure is. I'm looking for Angus Montgomery."

"Nice young man." She pointed me down the hall.

I rapped on the door and waltzed in when he opened it. "How was dinner at the Orca Inn?"

Angus sat on a chair, lacing up his brand-new looking hiking boots. "Very nice. I had king crab legs, which were delicious. Not quite as good as the halibut at the Glacial Grill yesterday, though. Or maybe it was the company." His smile held a hint of shyness.

I could feel a blush rising on my cheeks. I played it off by pirouetting around the room, taking in the thick afghan on the bed and the fresh flowers in a salmon-themed mug by the bedside. Suddenly, I stopped, shocked into stillness by the last thing I expected to see.

From a small hook in the wall above the dresser dangled a small yarn decoration—a god's eye. I approached it as if in a trance. The purple, blue, and white yarn blended perfectly with the ocean tones of the room's décor. I picked it up off the wall and turned it over in my hands. "Where did this come from?" My voice sounded strange to my ears.

He looked up with a shrug. "It came with the room?"

I stroked it gently. "It's very sweet. It looks like a child made it." That child was me, of course, back in second grade Sunday school to give to my Uncle Vance for Christmas. I didn't think I would ever see it again. How it came to be hanging on Angus Montgomery's bed and breakfast wall was a mystery.

Or maybe it wasn't so mysterious after all. The god's eye was stolen from the back room of my bookshop as part of a burglary, theft, and murder. Our working assumption was that the thief was the same person as the murderer. Angus Montgomery—a murderer!

My hands started shaking so much that I could barely hold on to the god's eye. I wanted to keep it, but I decided to leave it where it was, for evidence. I managed to hang it back up on the wall while Angus finished lacing his boots. He wouldn't need them after all. I pulled out my phone and fumbled with my screen. "Oh, no, I've got a text here from Nels. He says he wants to talk to me about Uncle Vance. We'll have to postpone our hike, Angus." I shoved the phone in my pocket and fled from his room without giving him a chance to respond.

I jumped in the car, eased Cosmo over to the passenger seat, and took off. I had intended to drive straight to the public safety building and file a report for Nels to follow up on. Instead, my car took me speeding out the road to fetch up at a scenic overlook at the end of our thirty miles of pavement. I stopped the car and turned off the engine, and let my head sink down to rest on the steering wheel. "He can't be a killer," I whispered, over and over, as if the repetitions would make it be true. Cosmo yipped by my side. I reached over and scooped him onto my lap and buried my head in his dense fur. His warm, wriggling body helped to calm my mind. I pulled out my phone to call Marcy, to find that I didn't have any cell service out the road. It didn't matter anyway. Rob was coming home tonight, so Marcy wouldn't have any time for me. I thought of driving back to town to call Nels, but that felt like too much effort. Time enough to call him in the morning.

I sat for hours in the car, watching the sun slide to setting behind the mountains across the water. Finally, I clipped on Cosmo's leash and walked him up and down the roadside, up and down until we were both exhausted. Then I loaded him back up and drove home.

Chapter Sixteen

I didn't feel any better the next morning. But I knew I had a civic duty to report the god's eye to Nels. I hoped he would take it seriously.

It's hard to do your civic duty when the authorities don't pick up the phone. I called the station a couple times, and I called Nels's personal phone as well. I didn't want to call 911 because it really wasn't an emergency. Finally, I spent twenty minutes crafting a text to send to Nels, only to delete it in frustration. It sounded ridiculous to say that I thought Angus was a murderer because I found a craft I'd made as a child in his room. I had to talk to Nels in person about it.

I grabbed a quick breakfast and packed food and water for hiking. Yeah, I was going to play hooky today. I loaded Cosmo in the car and headed down the hill to the public safety building.

Nels wasn't there. Stella held a phone to her ear, raising a finger to ask me to wait. She scribbled on a yellow notepad on her desk. "Right. I'll get right on it." She hung up and greeted me, "Good morning, Junetta."

"Hi, Stella. Is Nels in?"

"Honey, he's out in the field. We got a report that the opening to the Lucky Mine adit has been vandalized. It could be a good place for a killer to hide." The phone rang again, and she picked it up and covered the receiver with one hand. "I've got no idea when he'll be back. When it rains, it pours, so they say. I'll ask him to call you when he gets in, Junetta."

I mouthed my thanks, and she waved and turned her attention to the caller.

I said a quick prayer for Nels's safety as I walked back to my car. The Lucky Mine was a pit mine that had yielded almost two million troy ounces of gold before it petered out in the 1970s. There were plans in the '90s to dynamite the tunnels. The town council couldn't come up with enough money, so the mine adit had been boarded up and marked with danger signs and that was the end of it. Stella was right, it would make a good hiding place for a murderer.

"Well, I tried," I said to Cosmo as I hopped into my car. He gave a bright yip and scampered all over the back seat.

I called Patrick to say I wasn't coming in today, and he could either open the bookshop or take the day off as well. "Don't worry, I'll pay you either way. I just need to get out of town today." I cut across his anxious remonstrations, "No worries. The business will survive."

I texted Marcy the same message. I knew I couldn't hang up on her so easily, and I just wasn't ready to hash over the whole story with her. I needed to get out into nature to get my head straight. I texted that I was taking Cosmo to Sunny Cove. I wanted someone to know where I was if I didn't return at the end of the day. That precaution had nothing to do with the thought of a murderer loose in town, and everything to do with routine safety practices when heading out into the vast Alaska wilderness.

It was a beautiful day for a beach outing. The sky was overcast, but no rain was falling as I drove down along the highway that ran parallel to the shore. Like much of Southeast Alaska, Ptarmigan Port was made up of houses and businesses that clung to the narrow shoreline at the base of the mountains. The highway that linked our town with the one remaining working gold mine curved along the shoreline, with rocky beach on the one side and looming mountain on the other. It wasn't a route for distracted driving.

Too bad Cosmo didn't know that. He bounced around in the back seat, slobbered on the windows that I had to keep rolled up so he wouldn't jump out, and barked nonstop throughout the entire ride. He finally quieted down when I blasted the radio at top volume. He was snoozing peacefully by the time I pulled into the dirt parking lot at Sunny Cove.

When the motion of the car stopped, he leapt up, fully charged. "Come on, Cosmo, let's go run on the beach."

I kept him on his leash until we'd walked down the short path to the rocky beach, and then I let him go. He let out a single, joyful yip, and zoomed off down the beach to the rolling surf.

I followed more slowly, drawing in deep breaths. The tide was out, and the smell of the sea filled the air with hints of seaweed and slick wet sand. There were a few patches of sand and even quicksand, but the majority of the beach was made up of jagged rocks crusted with barnacles and sharp mussel shells. Good thing I wore my rain boots. I didn't need to worry about getting wet, scratched, or slimed. As long as Cosmo and I avoided the patch of quicksand to the west, we would be okay. Some stakes and a rope fluttering with triangular flags marked the risky spot. If I saw Cosmo encroaching on it, I could head him off.

I lingered at the tide pools left by the receding tide. They weren't more than a foot in diameter and a few inches deep, and they were teeming with life. I loved to hunt out the sea creatures in them. In a garden, I always stopped to smell the flowers, and at the beach, I couldn't resist peering into tide pools and turning over rocks to reveal the clinging limpets or scuttling hermit crabs underneath. My favorite was when I could find living barnacles, still green and supple rather than dead and bleached by the sun. The tiny creatures inside would swivel around and pop in and out of the outer shell as if they were sticking out their tongues. Today, I found a whole rock face alive with them, busily poking themselves in and out and sounding like a bag of popcorn in the microwave.

I was so intent on this subtle symphony that I almost missed the whoosh of a passing whale. It was on its second breath before the sound registered in my mind. I whirled around to face the sea, scanning for the puff of steam that signaled the mighty creature's presence.

Two steam puffs drifted in the air, indicating that there were two whales offshore. I stood still, looking and listening with my whole being. My vigilance was rewarded when a humpback whale surfaced with a resonant whoosh, followed immediately by a smaller whale with a higher pitched whoosh—her baby, no doubt. They both went underwater without displaying their tails, which meant that they weren't diving yet. With any luck, I would see them again. I called to Cosmo to accompany me as I meandered along the beach in the direction the whales were swimming. He ran up to me, barking lustily, ever willing to come along.

The beach ran along the sheltered cove to a promontory and then bent around to a more exposed stretch of sand and rock. I followed the whales around the point, enjoying the freshening of the wind and the strengthening of the surf as it rolled along the shore. I scanned the waves for the return of the two whales, while Cosmo raced down the beach to bark at a lone figure bending over at the edge of the water. As I got closer, I recognized her—Annalisa Martin, Marcy's grandmother.

I had come out to the beach for solitude, but Annalisa wouldn't disturb that. I called out a cheery hello. The whales surfaced and blew in sync with my calls.

Annalisa straightened up and turned to greet me, a smile lighting up her seamed face. "Have you come out to collect seaweed with me?" She indicated a woven basket brimming with slimy wet seaweed.

"No, I just came out to find the peace that the beach always gives me." I wanted to share with Annalisa the heaviness on my heart. "Can I sit and talk with you for a while?"

I sat on a flat rock while the whales surfaced and dove with a flip of their tails. I told Annalisa all about Angus's half of the map, the writing on the back, and the missing god's eye that had reappeared in his bed and breakfast room. "How can I think anything else except that Angus is the thief and murderer?"

She picked up a long strand of brown seaweed covered with inflated sacs to keep the weed afloat. "This popweed is very tasty when it's fresh." She swirled it in the water, plucked off a popper and handed it to me. "Pop it in your mouth."

I wasn't a big fan of seaweed, but I closed my eyes, popped it in, and bit down. The sac burst in my mouth, releasing a slightly sweet taste overridden by the briny taste of the ocean. I washed it down with a quick drink of water from my water bottle.

Annalisa laughed and munched on her own handful of poppers.

I wiped my mouth with the back of my hand and looked her in the eye. "I don't want him to be the killer, Annalisa."

She returned my gaze, her eyes filled with sympathy. "Marcy says you like this guy?"

I shifted on the hard rock. "Yes. He's very sweet and charming. I can't possibly imagine him as a murderer."

She swirled another long strand of seaweed in the water. "At this point you are just imagining, not knowing?"

I looked up from the pattern I was forming in the sand with my boot. "There's the evidence of the god's eye in his room. I didn't imagine that."

"Because of the missing god's eye that you found, you know he is the murderer?" She handed me another popper.

I turned it over and over in my hands, reluctant to meet her eyes. "I think I know."

She dropped the long strand of seaweed into her basket and dusted her hands on her pants. "There's two ways of knowing, Junetta: in your head, and in your heart. Your head tells you he is guilty, and your heart says he can't be. Either one could be the right way of knowing."

She fell silent, cutting and rinsing strands of seaweed while I sat quietly and watched. I pulled my sandwich out of my backpack and munched. A couple seagulls swooped and called above us. I could see Cosmo frisking down by the waterline, barking at a seal that popped his head up offshore. The scent of the sea air was like a tonic.

I still felt lost.

"How do I know which way is the right way in this case, Annalisa?"

"How do you know the sun will rise in the morning? How do you know the bear will run away from you in the woods? How do you know this old woman won't make you sick by feeding you popweed?" She grinned mischievously. "You know."

I waved my water bottle at her and took another big drink. "Okay. I know."

She nodded, turning her gaze to the ocean. She shaded her eyes and pointed, "Look, there's a pod of orcas out there, in the lee of that island."

I could just make out the slash of their dramatic dorsal fins. There were five or six of them frolicking in the ocean, their white and black sides flashing in the light. They skimmed the water like living speedboats. I longed to cling to their backs, racing through the waves with not a care in the world.

Annalisa and I watched the orcas until they rounded the island and were gone. Then she bent over to resume her gathering.

I reached down to help her collect the slimy seaweed. "I didn't get to talk to Nels this morning. Do you think I should tell him about the god's eye?"

"Oh, yes. He would think you were hiding something if you didn't."

"What if he arrests Angus and he's not really a murderer after all?"

She eased the seaweed out of my hands. "You're choosing all the old, tough ones. Let Nels do his job and let me do mine."

I laughed and dried my hands on my pants. "I don't much like seaweed, so I never learned how to harvest it correctly. Give me nagoonberries any day."

She waggled a finger at me. "You need the sour and the sweet in your life, Junetta. I will ask Marcy to cook you the best seaweed you've ever tasted in your life."

I gave her an impulsive hug. "Thanks for talking, Annalisa. I should get back to the real world now."

She patted my arm. "This is the real world, Junetta."

I threw out my arms to encircle the ocean, sand and rocks, mountains, and sky. "Yes, it is!" I gave her another big hug, then whistled for Cosmo. That didn't work in the slightest. It took me a good twenty minutes to round him up. Mercifully, he had not strayed into any quicksand while Annalisa and I were talking. His white fur was covered in wet sand, and he smelled like a romp in skunk cabbage was in his very recent past. I clipped on his leash to walk back to the car, where I set him up with water and dog food in the back seat. As I drove back along the winding shoreline under the darkening clouds, back to the anxieties of a murder investigation, I felt better equipped to face whatever it was that I needed to know.

Chapter Seventeen

All the way back to town, I debated with myself—should I go straight to Nels, or should I stop by Uncle Vance's house first to roust out the family documents from Rev. Denton's time? Did I even want to explore the history behind Angus's map if he was hauled away for murder? In the end, I headed for the public safety building, hoping to find Nels at home this time. I had spent hours at the beach, and it was going on 5:00 p.m., but Nels didn't work a nine-to-five job.

I caught him on his way out. He was in a hurry, like always. I planted myself in his path.

"Nels. I have some new evidence in the theft and murder case."

"So do I." He brushed past me and made for his cruiser.

I ran after him and jumped in on the passenger side. "You first."

He scowled but didn't kick me out. "It has to do with an altercation between Blake Rivers and Uncle Vance the night before the murder." He peeled out from the parking lot as the clouds let loose with a fine rain.

"I know all about that," I said brightly. "Kirk Dunbar said they argued over darts."

"Oh, he did? Did he tell you that Davey Harper took part in the argument?" He sped down the road, fast enough to draw a ticket if he was a regular citizen, but not quite fast enough to turn on his siren.

I thought back to our conversation. It was always hard for me to focus on what Kirk was saying, for fear that he was about to go down on one knee or pull out a ring box. "I think he said Davey tried to distract Uncle Vance from continuing the fight. When it comes to Uncle Vance, Davey's always on hand."

"Okay. Where's Davey now?" He pulled to a screeching stop in front of Davey's house on the far edge of town. Without waiting for an answer, he charged out of the car and up to the door, dodging the quickening raindrops.

Davey Harper lived in a bona fide log cabin, one of the few remaining ones in town. He lived by himself, and his property reflected the lifestyle of an aging solitary male. The yard hadn't been mowed in the past decade. Pine trees and Sitka spruce stretched their branches over the cabin. Several saplings had sprouted on the moss-covered roof, giving the impression that nature was well on her way to reclaiming this particular corner of Alaska.

Nels pounded on the door, then tried the doorknob. Unsurprisingly, the door opened.

I crowded in behind him, only because he hadn't told me not to. "Davey's not home, Nels. I saw him on Sunday at Green's Grocery. He was buying propane to go camping."

He whirled around to look at me for the first time since I'd jumped into his car. "Why didn't you tell me this?"

I blew out an exasperated sigh. "You didn't ask?" When his brows lowered, I went on. "Nels, I didn't know Davey was a suspect. You'd already arrested Uncle Vance by the time I talked to Davey. Also, you're not the easiest person to get ahold of. I tried to call you this morning, and I even stopped by the public safety building, but you were off on a case." I stopped in mid-stream. "What did you find out at the Lucky Mine adit? Has somebody been hiding there?"

Nels frowned at me. "What do you know about the Lucky Mine adit?"

"Nothing. Stella said you were looking into vandalism at the opening of the adit, which might be a good place for a murderer to hide. Has someone been there?"

He shook his head. "Stella shouldn't have said anything. But no, nobody's hanging around the mine adit, as far as I can tell.

Some of the boards covering the opening have been ripped off and strewn about on the ground. Probably kids." He glared at me. "Don't try to change the subject. Tell me about Davey."

"He said he was going down to Seven Mile Creek, but not to hunt. Just camping."

"Just camping … or skipping town?" Nels turned back to scan the cabin. The inside matched the outside, exuding a general air of benign neglect. The ceramic sink was full of dirty dishes, with the remains of Davey's latest meal sitting on the table. The unmade bed in the corner was strewn with a couple days' worth of dirty clothes. A squat TV sat on a chest of drawers, turned so it could be viewed from the bed. I swung open the door to the bathroom— also grungy and in need of a good scouring. I took a peep into the fridge. Davey wasn't going to pass a healthy diet test any time soon. Eggs, hunks of cheese, and cans of beer made up the bulk of his provisions.

"Junetta, do you mind?"

I closed the door with a snap. I was amazed that Nels let me remain in the room with him, so I didn't want to call undue attention to myself. Invisibility was not my strong suit, however. "Why are you focusing on Davey now, Nels?"

"You said it yourself. Wherever Uncle Vance is, Davey's there too. I want to know if he was involved in Blake's murder. The fact that he's left town bumps him up on my list of people of interest." He threw me a sidelong glance on his way out the door to the lean-to shed. Rain drummed on its metal roof. "Uncle Vance has been in contact with Davey since Blake's body was discovered. I found several calls on his phone between the time I was called in and when I arrested Uncle Vance."

I couldn't help wondering if Nels had obtained a warrant to search Uncle Vance's phone, but I kept that thought to myself. Instead, I popped open the door of the battered chest freezer next to the back door. It was chock full of packages wrapped in wax paper, each labeled with a date. There was venison, salmon, halibut, and even a bit of bear meat dated 2010. I wasn't confident that it was still good five years later, but that wasn't my problem at the moment. I hastily shut the lid before Nels noticed me snooping again. "What does Uncle Vance say about those calls?"

Nels almost burst out laughing. "What do you think, Junetta?"

I couldn't suppress a rueful grin. "He folded his arms, stared you down, and said he wasn't going to be badgered about his personal phone conversations, thank you very much."

"Precisely. So, I thought I'd ask Davey about his side of the story, but he's skipped town." Nels led me back through the cabin and out the door. "Nothing useful here."

We got back into his cruiser. He cranked the engine, and then turned to look me in the eye as rain streamed down his windshield. "Okay, your turn. What evidence do you have to give me?"

I heaved a sigh. "I'm worried about Angus Montgomery being involved." I waited for Nels to prompt me. He stayed silent, simply watching me. "I saw something in his room at Clarissa's B & B yesterday."

His gaze sharpened. "What were you doing in his room, Junetta? I didn't know you knew him that well."

"Not that it's any of your business, little brother, but I stopped by to pick him up for a hike out at the glacier. He was tying up his boots." I tossed my head and turned to look out my window, playing off the flush on my cheeks that Nels certainly noticed.

"Okay, I can see that you're not interested in listening to me when I say to be careful. What did you see in his room?"

I turned back to face him. "Remember I told you that the god's eye that I gave Uncle Vance had gone missing?" I barely registered his nod. "Well, it was hanging on the wall in Angus's room. There's no mistaking it. I asked him and he said it came with the room. That makes no sense. All I can think is that Angus stole it from my back room, which means that he was probably the thief and the murderer." I clenched my jaw in a vain attempt to hide the tremor in my voice. I wiped away a stray tear and took a deep breath. "I tried to find you this morning, even though I don't want you to look into it because you might find that it's true and that would be horrible." I turned my face away to hide my tears.

Nels sat in complete silence, most likely shocked by my tears and unsure how to handle them. It was the thought of his predicament more than anything else that helped me to regain control.

I was just about ready to return to polite conversation when he patted my shoulder awkwardly and said, "Sounds like you like this guy."

Everybody kept telling me that. "Yes. But I love Uncle Vance, and if he's innocent I want him out of jail. And if Angus is guilty, then he's the one who should be in jail." I sniffled. "I just hope that he's not, that's all. I think you should check out his room and question him about the god's eye. Just don't tell him I sicced you on him. Please?"

Nels put the car in gear and eased out of Davey's muddy driveway. "Fair enough. I can find him at the Historical Society, right?"

I nodded. I'd fulfilled my civic duty. So, why didn't I feel virtuous?

• • •

Nels dropped me off at the public safety building to pick up my car. He didn't bother asking if I wanted to go along when he questioned Angus.

Cosmo was waiting for me when I got to the car. There was nothing patient about his waiting. He zoomed around inside the car like he was being chased by a swarm of bees. I took him out for a quick walk along the water runway behind the public safety building in the soaking rain before loading him back up again to head out to Uncle Vance's house.

My stomach growled as I drove along the shore to Uncle Vance's house. If I was smart, I would go home and fix a proper dinner. I knew that if I went home, I wouldn't set out again this evening. Better to grab a bite to eat at Uncle Vance's house and take my time going through the family papers.

I sifted through my family tree in my mind. My mother, Penny Beale, was Uncle Vance's sister. Her maiden name was Peterman. Their father, John Peterman, my grandfather, was the only son of Michael and Elizabeth Peterman. Elizabeth Denton Peterman, known to her friends as Betty, was the daughter of the Reverend Raymond Denton of the Pastor's Confession Map fame. She was eight years old in 1915 when the SS *Fortunate* went down and the events in question took place.

I always liked hearing stories about Betty Denton, mostly because her birthday was on October fifth, same as mine. We were birthday buddies. She died the year before I was born, so I never got to meet her. Mom and Uncle Vance liked to tell stories about their grandmother. She was the original owner of the Shipshape Bookshop, which passed to Uncle Vance upon her death. She was an avid quilter—her handiwork adorned the walls of Mom's Sourdough Lady Lodge. In her young adult years, Betty was a teacher, traveling with her father, the pastor, to the remote villages to teach the children how to read and write. Mom said Betty secretly longed to be a famous author. She wrote plays for the children to perform and published poetry in the *Ptarmigan Times*, but she never achieved the level of fame she dreamed of. She did leave behind a trove of her own writings, as well as carefully organized files of her father's work that I hoped might shed some light on the Reverend's encounter with Alexander Montgomery on February 3, 1915.

But first, food.

The house was in the same state of disarray that I'd seen before. It didn't worry Cosmo. He sniffed around the entire house, checking out each room in obvious joy at being home. "I hope you'll get to move back in very soon, little guy," I said. I rinsed out his water bowl and dumped out the stale dog food in favor of a fresh batch. "Bon appétit."

I rummaged through Uncle Vance's fridge, pulling out bread and cheese for a grilled cheese sandwich made in the toaster oven. I found a fresh carton of milk and poured myself a glass. I couldn't find any fruit to finish off the meal. Like his buddy Davey, Uncle Vance's solitary eating habits could be improved.

After eating, I resisted the impulse to wash dishes and tidy up the place. I was here on a mission, to seek out family documents and try to discern who Cousin and Bob might be. Ordinary housekeeping tasks would have to wait. I set my phone to silent so I wouldn't be disturbed and got to work.

I'd only seen the family documents once when my mom pulled them out in a moment of nostalgia. I didn't know where Uncle Vance kept the file box I remembered. I began a thorough search of his house. I told myself that if my searching turned up a bookshop ledger gone AWOL, then that would be a bonus.

Half an hour and no ledger later, I found two cardboard file boxes tucked away in the top of Uncle Vance's bedroom closet. I hauled them down and dusted them off before lifting the lid of the first one. Reverend Denton's papers were neatly filed in dozens of file folders organized first by category: sermons, correspondence, taxes, and photographs. Within each category the files were then organized by date.

I started with the photographs. There were only a handful of old photos showing scenes like the log cabin church where Rev. Denton was pastor, the pastor and his wife holding Betty as a baby, and various shots of local places. There was a magnificent black and white picture of the Tongass Glacier which filled the valley and extended probably a mile further than it did today. Rev. Denton was pictured on a horse in the foreground—an early tourist to Ptarmigan Port's natural wonder.

I had seen all these photographs once before. They still brought a smile to my lips. I savored the photo of the reverend's young wife, who died in childbirth in 1909 along with her second baby. She looked exactly like my mom, only dressed in turn of the century clothing. I used to tease Mom that she was the reincarnation of her great-grandmother.

I didn't expect to learn anything new from these photographs, although I did check the back of each one for stories or maps or anything like that. There was nothing unexpected.

Next, I turned to the sermons. I leafed through the folders and pulled out the one for 1905-1915. If Rev. Denton took the confession of a murderer when he received the map, he might have been moved by the experience to include it in his preaching.

I remembered from my Local Lore class in school that February 4, 1915, the day the SS *Fortunate* went down, was a Thursday. If Rev. Denton took confession on a Wednesday, he might have slipped something into his Sunday sermon on February 7, 1915. I searched for his notes from that date.

It was a nice idea, but apparently Rev. Denton did not write out his sermons, choosing to preach from a very spare outline. His notes from that Sunday included two texts: Psalm 116 and John 8: 2-11, and his theme was "repentance." A quick internet search revealed that the psalm talked of calling out to the Lord for help and then praising him for deliverance. The passage in John was the story of the Pharisees bringing a woman to be stoned for adultery, and Jesus telling them, "Let him who is without sin among you be the first to throw a stone at her." I guessed that Rev. Denton was moved by the sins of theft and murder that were confessed to him just days earlier. I was heartened by the thought that Rev. Denton focused on the mercy of both God and Jesus. His faith in God's grace, however, didn't help me uncover details about the events of that wild Wednesday night.

I slipped the sermon notes back into the folder and moved on to "Correspondence." This series of folders was brimming with letters that Rev. Denton received, paired with carbon copies of his side of the correspondence. If Angus wanted to do a research paper on the history of the Presbyterian Church in the early 1900s in Southeast Alaska, I had a treasure trove of primary sources for him. Assuming that he wasn't locked up for murder, that is. I pushed all thoughts of Angus into the recesses of my mind.

I got lost in a fascinating exchange between Rev. Denton and a parishioner who wanted to obtain marital counseling because her husband was often seen in the saloon downtown. As I made my way through the thick stack, it became clear to me that Rev. Denton was getting increasingly concerned that the woman was looking for more than pastoral comfort from him. I reflected that he was probably the most eligible widower in town. I was deep in the woman's fifth plea to meet with the reverend at her house while her husband was off hunting, when the sound of Cosmo's barking snapped me back to the present.

Cosmo lunged at the back door, barking lustily. Once my concentration was broken, I realized that he had been barking for some time before I even noticed.

I shushed him as best I could, then opened the back door a crack to peek out. The rain still came down steadily, and twilight was settling in. I must have been lost in history for hours. I could hear shuffling, as if someone was hanging out behind the corner of the house. It sounded like a large being—people sized, or maybe a bear. I called out, "Anybody there?" Silence. The rustling stopped, and no one called back in response.

This silence spooked me. If it was a wild animal, my voice and Cosmo's barking would probably have scared it off, in which case I would have heard it take off. If it was a friend of Uncle Vance's, they would have called back, and we could have had a conversation. Or it was a person who wished to remain hidden— that thought creeped me out.

I shut the back door with a snap, but there was no lock on it. Short of dragging the furniture across the room, I had no way of keeping anyone out. For most of my life I wouldn't have given this a second thought. Tonight, it made me uneasy. Close proximity to murder changes a person—what an unwelcome thought!

I blew out a gusty sigh to settle my nerves and packed the folders back into the cardboard file boxes. There was no reason why I couldn't go through them at my house. I did have locks on my own doors. Even if I couldn't always find my keys, I could lock the doors from the inside.

Cosmo zoomed around the side of the house when I opened the door to load the boxes into my car. I didn't hear any growling, so I was confident that it wasn't a bear that lurked there. Lucky for Cosmo—I was sure that he was just impetuous enough to try to take on a bear, even though he was technically eagle bait himself. I'd never witnessed it personally, but Uncle Vance liked to tell the story of a hapless little dog who was snatched up in an eagle's talons back in 1993. The story had a happy ending—the dog was too heavy for the eagle to get any altitude, so it was dropped off over the water and managed to swim ashore unharmed.

I called for Cosmo, to no avail. I resolved to tell Uncle Vance to try harder to train his dog and followed Cosmo around the corner of the house. Between the woods beyond, the rain, and the deepening twilight, I had a hard time telling if someone stood in the shadows or not. I didn't really want to charge over to find out. I called Cosmo again. To my relief, a white blur zoomed past my ankles, barking all the while. I grabbed him by the collar and clipped on his leash. "Time to go home, buddy. My home."

By the time I got home and washed a very muddy little dog, I was tired out. I stashed the cardboard boxes in the back of my closet, checked all my doors, and turned in for the night. I checked my phone—I'd missed a call from Nels, two calls from Angus, and a pile of texts from Marcy. I powered the phone off and turned out the light—time enough to deal with everybody in the morning.

Chapter Eighteen

I overslept the next morning and had to scramble to get Cosmo settled before heading down the hill through a patter of raindrops to open the bookshop on time. Even in my mad rush, I took time to breathe in the fresh wet air and enjoy the rainbow that arched over the water, illuminated by a shaft of sunlight breaking through the one tiny bit of blue sky visible. We called those "sucker holes"—breaks in the clouds that let the sky peep through and tricked people into believing that the weather was clearing up, only to have the clouds close in again. I brushed the rain out of my face and laughed up at the sky, "You can't fool me!" As always, the wonder of nature cheered me like nothing else could.

Flush with the joy of the rainbow, I burst through the front door of the bookshop and threw my arms wide. "Today is a new day!"

Marcy waved at me from the café. She glanced over the few customers sitting at tables and then ducked through the beaded curtain to talk to me. "You made it! I thought I was going to have to start selling books along with my lemon scones."

"Lemon scones? Yes, please."

She folded her arms over her belly and faked a scowl. "Not yet. First, I want you to account for your actions last night. You totally ghosted me the entire evening."

I threw out my hands in supplication. "I didn't want to intrude. Rob came home yesterday, right? That's why you're glowing even as we speak."

She laughed. "Yeah, there is that. I wanted to see how you were doing, after Nels…" A quick glance at my face told her everything she needed to know. "You ghosted Nels last night, too? Junetta! Have you even looked at your messages?"

Her voice trailed off as I pulled out my phone and called up the voice messages. The first one was from Angus: "Hi, Junetta. I'm sorry you had to rush out. Maybe we could try again for the hike out at the glacier?"

The second was from Nels: "Hey, Sis, I want to talk to you before you read about it in the news. Call me."

"News?" I mouthed to Marcy, my good mood evaporating with the sucker hole. She grimaced in sympathy.

Marcy's texts escalated from, "How's it going?" to "U OK?" to "Where U at?"

What was going on? I closed my eyes, steeling myself to listen to the final message from Angus.

Marcy eased the phone out of my hand. "I'll listen to Angus's second message and tell you what he says."

She paced to the end of the counter before hitting the play button. The frown on her face deepened as she listened. "He says he never stole your map. He says he doesn't know how it got there and maybe he's being framed. He says he hopes you know it wasn't him."

She handed back my phone. I held it to my ear.

Angus sounded bewildered, more than anything else. "Junetta, I swear, I never stole your map. I don't know how it got into my room. Maybe somebody's trying to frame me? I hope you know it wasn't me that took it. I promise." I could hear someone in the background, and he hung up abruptly.

At that moment, a pair of hikers wearing waterproof gaiters and backpacks that looked heavier than they were came up to the counter with a pile of travel guides. I rang them up as quickly as I could, with no pleasant chatting about their destination, readiness for backcountry camping, or tips on how to stay safe in bear country. I simply bagged up their books and said goodbye.

I hung up my "Closed" sign and turned out the lights in the bookshop. I found a seat in the café and waited for Marcy to join me. She dropped two lemon scones on the table, poured me a cup of coffee, fixed herself some herbal tea, and sat down next to me.

"Tell me everything you know," I said.

"Rob wanted to go to the Grizzly Bar last night, so we both went for a bit. Kirk had all the news." She paused, refraining from her habitual teasing over Kirk's infatuation with me.

"What's the news?"

"Nels found the Pastor's Confession Map—it was in Angus Montgomery's room at Clarissa's B & B."

"In his room?"

She nodded. "I heard Nels went to Angus's room with a warrant, looking for a little trinket that might be significant."

"Yeah, my god's eye that I made for Uncle Vance when I was a kid. It disappeared from his desk the night of the break-in."

"Okay, Kirk didn't know that part. Cool, I know something Kirk doesn't."

I gave her a bleak stare, and she wiped the pleased smile off her face. "When Nels was there, he went through the whole room and found the map in a drawer, still in its frame. That's the big news."

I looked through the beaded curtain to the pale spot on the wall where the map had hung for decades. "Where is it now?"

"That I don't know. Probably at the public safety building for evidence. Nobody at the Grizzly Bar had seen it."

"And what about Angus? Did Nels arrest him?"

I knew what her answer would be before she said a word. "Yeah, he did."

"Did he arrest him for murder or just theft?"

"Yeah, I don't know that either. Nels wants to talk to you, so you can ask him." She pulled my empty plate away from me. I didn't even remember eating the scone. "Go talk to him now, Junetta. Find out what's what." She lumbered to her feet. "And next time? Don't turn off your phone all day when momentous stuff is happening."

I stood up and gave her a hug. "Thanks for being a buffer for me, Marcy."

"Do you want me to come with you to talk to Nels?" She scanned the café doubtfully. "I can probably get away if you want moral support."

I hugged her again. "No, I'll be okay. I'll text you if I need anything." I waved my phone at her. "I'll keep it on, I promise."

She bagged up a few extra scones and handed them to me. "Off you go, then. I'll fill Patrick in when he arrives."

I groaned. "Poor Patrick. I'll have to give him a bonus when this is all over." I waved on my way out the door.

I chose to drive to the public safety building, so I wouldn't have any chance to think before tackling Nels. Sometimes, forethought just serves to make you crazy. This was one of those times.

Lucky for me, Nels was in when I arrived. I burst through the front door, causing both him and Stella to jump in surprise.

"Honey, you should know better than to crash into a police station like that. It never pays to startle a person with a gun." Stella winked at me, "Especially if it's your own brother."

Nels reholstered his gun, proving Stella's point. "Come talk to me. Let's walk and talk." He led me back outside without another word.

The soft rain had petered out, replaced by snatches of sunlight that set the wet ground steaming. Maybe the sucker hole was the real deal after all.

"So, you went to Angus's room and found the Pastor's Confession Map. That was unexpected."

He stopped in his tracks. "You've heard the news. I would have preferred to tell you myself, but you didn't answer your phone. I guess I'm not the only Beale who's hard to get ahold of."

I couldn't suppress a rueful smile. "Okay, you got me there. Marcy gave me the same lecture about ghosting. Sorry. Tell me how it went down."

"I caught up with Angus at the Historical Society and asked to take a look at his room." He gave me a sidelong glance. "After your stubbornness the other day, I was ready with a search warrant, although he never asked me to produce one. I found the god's eye straight away, hanging on the wall just as you said. For form's sake, I asked Clarissa if she had hung it up. She said she'd never seen it before and had no idea how it came to be in her best room. Angus had no explanation for its presence, and unless he's a really good actor, he had no idea of its significance."

"That's what I thought when I asked him about it." I thought back to that conversation. I had been so shaken by the sight of the missing item that I wasn't thinking straight. I wasn't sure I was thinking straight now either.

"I went ahead and searched the rest of the room, to be thorough. That's when I found the map tucked away in a dresser drawer. Again, Angus seemed astonished to find it there." He blew out a gusty breath. "I brought him in, since not one but two stolen items showed up in his bed and breakfast room. I don't know how long he plans to stay in town. I can't have him taking off before I get everything sorted out."

I averted my eyes. "Are you sending him to Juneau or holding onto him here?"

"I have no evidence to link him to Blake Rivers's murder. I'm just detaining him here until I can process the map and your god's eye." He paused to watch a couple bald eagles riding a thermal above our heads. They soared in ever-widening circles, calling out in their high-pitched tones. With his eyes on the skies, Nels said, "You can go talk to him if you want to."

I would have given him a hug, but my brother and I didn't have that kind of relationship. Instead, I found myself struggling to contain the emotion that welled up in me at his unexpected compassion. I took refuge in watching the eagles as well. We must have made quite a sight; two adult siblings staring at the sky so they wouldn't have to look each other in the eye and admit to their vulnerabilities. I might have laughed if I wasn't the one feeling vulnerable. "Not right now," was the best I could manage.

Three more eagles jumped onto the thermal, making it quite the community event for them. Vultures are noted for circling over the carcasses they scavenge. I liked to think that eagles ride the thermals for the sheer joy of soaring. The sight of them enjoying themselves in such a majestic fashion made me smile, as always.

I tore my attention from the sky to face my brother. "Where are the god's eye and map right now?"

He started walking back toward the station. "They're here, set to be processed for fingerprints. I'd like to get your prints done, Junetta. Stella can set you up."

I followed Nels back into the station. "Can I see them?"

"The map and craft? Ok, if you can look without touching."

I rolled my eyes at him. He led me to his office and pointed to his credenza. The blue, white, and purple god's eye sat on a piece of computer paper labeled, "Found hanging on wall at Clarissa's B & B, 06/10/2015." The framed Pastor's Confession Map lay next to it, with a nearby sticky note that read, "Found in dresser drawer at Clarissa's B & B, 06/10/2015."

I clasped my hands behind my back and bent over the framed map. There was the familiar "tall tree" that we spent summers trying to pinpoint in the woods, and the X to mark the spot where the treasure was hidden. It was like seeing the face of an old friend after an extended absence. I snatched my right hand back before it could make contact. I longed to stroke the glass, caress the frame, and then pop the map out of its housing to see what was written on the back. I wondered when Angus had put the two halves together to read the entire message. Did he know the whole story when he took me to the Historical Society to first view his map? Was he acting all along?

"Come on, honey, let's get your prints taken." Stella waved the inkpad as if it were a palette of makeup for a five-year-old's birthday party.

I submitted to having my fingerprints taken. I called out to Nels in his office, "Okay, now my fingerprints are in your system. Handle them with care."

He lined up the papers on his desk and typed into his computer. "As long as you don't break the law, you've got nothing to worry about." He stood up and gathered up his jacket. "Stella, I'm off. If Junetta wants to talk to the prisoner, that's okay. Bye, Sis." And he was gone.

I stood in the middle of the public safety building, looking at the door swinging closed behind him. "How long will it take to process the map and god's eye for prints?"

"Come back tomorrow, honey, and we'll see if it's done by then." I had to be content with that.

I didn't feel up to talking with Angus at the moment. I just walked out of the public safety building and headed back to the bookshop. Time to act like a responsible business owner and sell some books.

When I got back to the Shipshape Bookshop, I steeled myself to meet Patrick's anxiety, guessing that he was probably frantic with worry. I was not wrong.

"Junetta, you're back! Marcy said you'd gone to the police. Five customers were lined up at the door when I got here. They were not happy."

I pasted on a reassuring smile. "Thank you, Patrick, for holding down the fort. I'm not worried about a few unhappy customers."

"But they'll leave bad reviews online, and our reputation will suffer." He twisted his hands together at the thought.

I shrugged. "A couple bad reviews aren't going to break us. It's a tradition in Southeast Alaska to close down for sunshine. People are used to that dynamic." I forestalled his next comment, "Sure, the sun has only just come out, so they might reasonably expect us to be open, and normally we would be. Murder in the back room changes things, at least temporarily." I bustled to my favorite spot behind the counter. "If you want to take a break, go ahead. You've earned it."

He shook his head and leaned in close to whisper, "Did you hear the news, about the map?"

"Yes. Nels recovered the Pastor's Confession Map from Angus Montgomery's room at the bed and breakfast. I saw the map just now, down at the public safety building. Once the troopers are finished with it, we'll get it hung back up where it belongs."

• • •

A steady trickle of tourists flowed through the bookshop throughout the afternoon, helping to keep my mind grounded rather than circling through the events of the last few days like those bald eagles riding that thermal. Every time I thought of Angus or pictured his eyes lighting up when he smiled, I doubled down on my efforts to help my customers find the books they were looking for.

Minutes before closing, I was surprised to see Connor Fisk come into the bookshop.

In a small town, everyone knows everyone else who lives there. I knew all my regular customers quite well and could often anticipate their tastes in books before they even asked. I couldn't recall ever seeing Connor in the bookshop. He would come into the café for coffee or a sweet treat from time to time, but he'd never shown any interest in books before. Yet here he was, hovering over a shelf full of humor collections, five minutes before closing time.

Patrick had already gone home for the day and Marcy had closed the café after the lunch hour, and I knew the cruise ship in town had a 6:00 p.m. sailing time. I was alone with Connor in the building.

"How can I help you, Connor?"

He approached the counter and loomed over me. At such close proximity, I could smell the alcohol on his breath. "I heard your brother found the missing map." He waved a hand at the bare spot on the wall. "Where are you hiding it now?"

I relaxed, though I'm not sure why. "Oh, Nels has it down at the public safety building. I don't know when they'll be done processing it. You could go down and ask them about it if you want." I held my breath and leaned in close, crowding him just a little bit. "What's your interest in the map, Connor?"

As I had hoped, he backed off. "I wanted a good look at it, after all this time. That's all. I haven't seen it since a field trip in fourth grade if you can believe it." He forced a chuckle and turned away. "I'll see if Nels will show it to me."

I breathed a sigh of relief as he ambled out the door. He was like a bear one encountered in the woods. If you kept your wits about you and treated the bear with respect, chances are it would turn and walk away. But if it was a sow with cubs, the story could end up very differently. Unpredictable—that was Connor Fisk in a nutshell.

I hustled to the door and turned the sign to "Closed." It had been a long day.

• • •

At home, I curled up with Cosmo for popcorn and a movie. We had gone for a long run through the woods followed by a quick doggy shampoo, leaving him calm and willing to snuggle in my lap instead of zooming around the house. Unfortunately, every movie I could find fit into the rom-com category, where the girl finds her true love only to discover that he isn't good for her after all before they finally get together in the end, often years later. Those storylines hit a little too close to home to be mindless entertainment for me.

I hoisted Cosmo off my lap and pulled Betty Denton's boxes out of my closet. I opened up the second box this time, which contained Betty's personal papers. This box was as neatly organized as the other one, with sections marked: plays, story ideas, poetry, diaries. I caught my breath and reached for the packet of diaries. Betty had used small date books as diaries. Each daily entry was no more than a few sentences. The diaries dated back as far as 1914, when Betty was only seven years old. She wrote of having potatoes for dinner and wishing she could play with her friend Emma on the weekend.

I took a moment to savor the diaries before beginning my historical quest. I found the one dated 1962 and opened to the fifteenth of August. Sure enough, "John and Alma had a baby girl, Penny Louise, 7 lbs, 10 oz. Mother and baby doing well." The one from 1954 was a bit more expressive, "Baby Vance Michael born at 2:47 am. I'm a grandma!" I smiled at the joy that babies bring. My own birth wasn't recorded in these diaries, since Betty died the year before I was born. But I wasn't here to read about the beginning of life so much as the ending of it.

I went back to find the diary from 1915 and opened to the month of February. Betty was eight years old when her father had a late-night visitor. Had she been a witness to their conversation?

On February 4 she wrote, "Daddy talked to a man at night about a dead man. The man's cusin Cray stabbed him. He had a tresure map for gold. I know where it is."

The entry for the next day said, "The gold ship sank in Havik Strate. Daddy said evrybody died, even the man that came to our house at night. Daddy was sad."

Betty returned on the next day to her usual notations of games with her friends and struggles with her schoolwork. I couldn't find any other mention of the late-night visitor or the enticing map. What did she mean when she said, "I know where it is?" Surely, if she had found the hidden gold, she would have written about that in her diary. I spent several hours paging through the next ten years. I found no mention of any treasure discovery.

I wondered who Cray was. Maybe Reba would have census records at the Historical Society that gave names of the citizens of Ptarmigan Port in 1915. I realized I had an ulterior motive here. If I asked for Reba's help, she might feel kindlier towards me when I declined to give her the Pastor's Confession Map like she wanted. I could also get a feel for Angus's research, to see if I could figure out if he really was the thief and murderer.

Chapter Nineteen

It was a quiet morning at the Shipshape Bookshop the next day. If I were Betty writing in a tiny diary, I would have noted, "Sunny day—tourists all out in nature." Who would want to browse in a bookstore when they could be out whale watching or viewing a glacier?

I took an early lunch to spend some time in the Historical Society before Reba took her own lunch break. Unsurprisingly, I was the only one there. I called out to Reba, who emerged from a back room.

"Hi, Reba. Beautiful day, isn't it? I've got a few historical questions to ask you."

Reba was dressed in a tweed skirt and matching blazer, as if she'd never heard of a rare day of sunshine and warmth. She could have passed for British royalty out for an afternoon grouse hunt. "Good morning, Junetta. Please sign in." She handed me the guest book, and then excused herself to take a phone call.

I signed my name and then scanned the entries in the guest book from the past few days. There was my signature along with Angus's when he showed me and Reba his half of the treasure map. The first time Angus had signed in was on Saturday, June 6, when I was enjoying the children in Mallory. I stared at the page, my heartbeat quickening. On the line above Angus's signature, on the same day, was written, "Blake Rivers."

I quickly shut the book and placed it on Reba's desk, laying the pen carefully on top. What could Blake Rivers have been doing at the Historical Society the afternoon before he died? I picked the guest book up again and held it open, waiting for Reba to return. Might as well ask.

Reba bustled back into the room and took the guest book from my hands. "What can I help you with?"

I waved a careless hand at the guest book. "I noticed that Blake Rivers was in here on Saturday, the afternoon before he died. Was he doing some kind of local research?"

Reba cradled the book to her chest. "Junetta. Surely you of all people know that a person's research or choice of books is confidential. I couldn't possibly comment on that to you." She replaced the book on her desk and then turned back to me with an insincere smile. "How can I help you today?"

I smiled back, big and wide, to let her know that she wasn't fooling me one bit. I pulled Betty's little diary out of my purse. Maybe I should have kept it under wraps, but I found myself wanting to one-up her in the field of historical documentation. I had something she'd never seen.

"I was looking through my great-grandmother's papers, and I found this diary from 1915." I held it out to her. "I'm curious about her entry from February 4."

She eased the little book from my fingers. "How extraordinary." She turned it over gently, almost reverently. "Where did you find this?"

"We've got a couple boxes of Betty Denton's papers, and her father's sermons and correspondence. What I'm wondering…"

"You must let me see these documents! They might illuminate the history of Ptarmigan Port like nothing else has done. Can you bring them in this afternoon?" Face flushed, she leaned forward eagerly, clutching Betty's diary in both hands.

"Not today. I'll find some time to bring them in." I reached out for the diary. I literally had to take her hands and pull back her fingers to retrieve it from her grasp. I opened the little book to the date of February 4 and held it out for her to see the childish handwriting.

"Betty was eight years old when her father, Rev. Denton, spoke with Alexander Montgomery and received the Pastor's Confession Map the night the SS *Fortunate* went down. Evidently, she witnessed her father's conversation with Montgomery, and learned the name of the man who killed someone: Cousin Cray. That fits in with the words on the back of Angus's half of the map. I'd love to find out who Cray was."

Reba stared at me as if I had said I'd caught a moose munching on her rhubarb. "Did Angus Montgomery send you here to continue with his research? You know he's in jail for stealing the map, right?"

"Yes, I did know that, and no, he did not send me here. I'm curious about the story now, and I'd love to find out as much as I can about it." I tucked the diary into my purse for safekeeping. "What better place to find out about history than the Historical Society? I told Marcy that the only person who could help me find the answers to my questions is Reba Cornell."

I expected Reba to puff up with pride and hasten to assist me, but she fooled me this time. Her face got even redder, and she said, "Did you show this diary entry to Marcy? Who else has seen it besides you two?"

She'd caught me in a lie. I hadn't mentioned the diary to Marcy or anyone else. I was simply trying to butter her up so she would give me the information I wanted. I've always found when lying that finding the path closest to the truth was the safest way to go. "I didn't share the diary with Marcy, I just mentioned that I have historical questions and I knew you could help me find the answers. I was hoping you could show me census records or other documents that would list the names of the residents of Ptarmigan Port in 1915."

"I see." The flush receded from her cheeks. "It will take me some time to roust out those kinds of documents. Perhaps you would like to leave the diary with me and come back, say, tomorrow afternoon?"

I laid a protective hand on my purse. "Tomorrow afternoon would be fine. I'd rather not let the diary out of my possession. I'm sure you understand."

Her face darkened again. "You think I'm going to keep it, like you kept the Pastor's Confession Map instead of turning it over to the Historical Society where it belongs."

I flashed my big smile again. "We wouldn't want that to happen, would we?"

Reba sputtered.

I glanced at my watch. "Yeah, I gotta get back to the shop. I'll stop by tomorrow afternoon if that works for you?"

She tossed her head. "I'm sorry, I forgot that I am otherwise occupied tomorrow. I could fit you in next Thursday at 4:30 p.m. I will look for census records to have them ready for you." She turned on her heel and marched out of the room, leaving me to wallow in my defeat.

It was definitely a defeat. I didn't get to see any census records, I wasn't any closer to knowing who Cray was, and Reba had clearly indicated that battle lines were drawn over the permanent home of the Pastor's Confession Map. She didn't know that I had a secret weapon—the law. The map belonged to my family, not the town, and my brother was the agent of the law here. Even though we had our disagreements, I felt sure that Nels would turn the map over to me and not to Reba. Pretty sure, anyway...

• • •

Afternoon sales picked up at the bookshop, as a direct result of the weather. Clouds rolled in, the light changed from bright and clear to heavy and green, and a misty rain began to fall. It was a tricky rain, seemingly light, but leaving one soaked in a matter of minutes. Tourists came inside to seek shelter and stayed to read or buy books.

I was in the middle of ringing up a sweet couple from Albuquerque who were buying books on the Alaska Railroad in advance of their upcoming train trip into the Interior. They had taken train journeys in every state except Alaska and Hawaii, so they were close to their lifetime goal. I was taking a photo of them to post on the bookshop's social media pages when Nels walked into the shop. He wore his full uniform and held a flat parcel under his arm. I hoped I knew what that contained.

"Look, an Alaska State Trooper, just like on TV!" The couple snapped a quick photo as Nels approached the counter. He tried to suppress a grimace, and even unbent enough to allow me to take a picture of him with the couple for their memories. Then he placed the parcel on the counter without a word.

I said goodbye to the sweet couple and turned my full attention to Nels. "Is it the map?"

He gave an exasperated chuckle. "What do you think?"

"Can I touch it now?" Without waiting for an answer, I ripped off the packaging and ran both hands over the frame. "What did you find out? Were there any fingerprints?"

"It was wiped completely clean on all sides. Very thorough thief."

Just what you might expect from an academic. I gently turned the map over and began to pry back the tabs holding the frame together.

Nels put out a hand to stop me. "What are you doing?"

I pushed his hand away. "I want to see the writing on the back." I paused at his quizzical glance. "Didn't I tell you that Angus's half of the map has writing on it, that references a death on the night in question? We've never looked at the back of our map, so I don't know what it says." I pried up the final tab and lifted off the back of the frame: nothing.

I carefully extracted the map from the frame, to see if there was an extra piece of paper for backing: nothing.

The back of the Pastor's Confession Map was blank.

I looked Nels in the eye. "I don't understand. Angus's map is clearly the other half of ours. His has half of a narrative written on the back. It's the same handwriting as the letter that came with it, passed down through his family since 1915." I threw out my hands. "What happened to the writing on the back of this map?"

Nels bent down to examine the back of the map. He ran a finger over the paper, looking for evidence of erasure. Without raising his head, he said, "How can we be sure that Alexander Montgomery wrote the letter and the half of the map? Maybe it was Angus Montgomery who did that."

I shook my head, bewildered. "Why would he do that? He's never seen the Pastor's Confession Map. What could his long game be?"

I pulled out my phone and took several photos of the front and back of the map, and then replaced it in its frame. Then on an impulse I pulled it out again and reached for an eraser.

"Stop," Nels cried.

Too late. I swiped the eraser over a very small portion of the image. Nothing happened. I scrubbed a little harder, but the writing did not disappear.

"It's a photocopy." Nels slammed his hand down on the counter, startling a couple of kids who were browsing through the chapter books. They dropped their books and scurried out of the shop.

"Shush. You're bad for business." I held the map up to the light. "Couldn't you have figured this out when you were processing the map?"

"We were dusting for fingerprints. We're investigating a theft and murder here, not art fraud. We never took it out of the frame." He stared glumly at the map. "So, where is the real map?"

Chapter Twenty

I leaned on the counter and studied the frame. "I'm sure this is the real frame. See here, where there's a chip out of the side. I remember doing that when I was moving in the glass-fronted bookcase last year. I felt guilty for three days, until I realized that nobody even noticed. I'm sure if somebody tried to switch the frame, they wouldn't notice the ding."

Nels peered at the chip, and then straightened up abruptly as the doorbell jangled. In a flash, he settled the map back into the frame and pushed down the tabs to secure it. "Don't tell anyone about the switch, Junetta. Not even Patrick or Marcy. Everyone in town should think that we're overjoyed to have the map back unharmed." He flipped the frame over to admire the map.

I barely had time to acknowledge his words with a nod before Reba Cornell bustled up to the counter. "Thank goodness, it's back!" She ran her hands over the frame just as I had done. "I thought we would never see this again." She turned to speak to Nels, her back turned firmly to me. "I'm sure you will agree that the only safe place to house such an important piece of our town's history is the Ptarmigan Port Historical Society. Please make arrangements for the Pastor's Confession Map to make its way to its proper home without delay."

Behind Reba, I made slashing motions across my throat with my hand in the universal sign of "not on your life." I shook my head vigorously from side to side, just in case Nels missed the message.

He got it.

He took the framed map with both hands and lifted it up to hang on its usual hook, where it had hung since the 1950s. "This is the map's home, Reba. It belongs to Junetta's family—to my family. Junetta has every intention of improving her security at the bookshop. I'm sure it will be safe here."

Behind Reba's back, I rolled my eyes at Nels. Looked like he was going to get his way when it came to increased security measures. Still, I would much rather lose to Nels than to Reba Cornell. "It's only a matter of time before all the new security measures are in place, Reba. The map will be safe at my bookshop. I promise."

She scowled at me, turned on her heel, and marched out of the bookshop.

"If the map goes missing again, you'll know who to arrest," I said. "Seriously, Nels, thanks for sticking up for me. Reba's been after that map for years now. It's an old, annoying conversation. Maybe it will finally be put to rest."

He leaned his elbow on the counter and regarded the map. "I'm trying to figure out a timeline here. We have two distinct crimes: the theft of your god's eye and the map, and the murder of Blake Rivers. Then there's a missing person case—Davey Harper is still unaccounted for." He didn't pause, despite my exclamation of dismay at this news. "I've got Uncle Vance in jail in Juneau for murder, and Angus Montgomery in custody here in town for the two thefts. But the map we found in Angus's room which led to his arrest was a fake. The question is, did Angus switch the maps, or did a person unknown plant the fake map in Angus's room so he would be arrested for the theft?"

I bit my lip and stared at the map. "And the god's eye?"

"Same question. I'm starting to wonder if Angus is being framed."

The two of us stood and stared at the map, as if a hundred-year-old document could answer our questions. Nels broke the silence first.

"Who else knows about the writing on the back of our map besides Angus? The map was already missing when he told you about the back."

I pictured the scrawled signature in the Historical Society's guest book. "Somebody else did know about the writing on the back. I saw Blake Rivers's name in the guest book at the Historical Society the day Angus told Reba about his half of the map."

Nels stared at me. "Blake Rivers is dead."

"He was killed that night. Suppose he went back to his ship and told his nephew, Connor Fisk, about the map. You know how he was always trying one get-rich scheme or another. If he got his hands on the two sides of the treasure map, he could have found the gold. What a great story for his glass-bottom boat shipwreck tour."

"Junetta, Blake is dead. Are you suggesting that he saw the back of Angus's map on Saturday afternoon, then came back and stole the map and the god's eye that evening? He switched the maps, planted the fake on Angus Montgomery, and then got himself killed in the bookshop? It doesn't make sense."

A chill ran down my back. "Connor came into the bookshop yesterday afternoon at closing. He was asking about the map and wanting to see it. To my knowledge he has never set foot in the bookshop before." Nels didn't stop me, so I kept going. "Maybe Blake came with Connor to steal the map, and somehow, he died in the back room. He could have fallen or had a heart attack or something. Connor panicked and stabbed him with Uncle Vance's knife to make it look like a murder and took the map to finish the job the two of them had started. He photocopied the map and planted the fake on Angus to further confuse the issue…" My voice trailed off. Nels was staring at me as if I had sprouted wings. "What?"

"What you just said: that Connor stabbed Blake with Uncle Vance's knife to make it look like murder. That could be exactly what happened. I shouldn't tell you this, but Blake didn't die from being stabbed. He had significant trauma on the back of the head consistent with a sharp blow to the head. That's what killed him. The knife was an afterthought."

It was my turn to stare, open mouthed. "Does that mean that Uncle Vance is innocent?"

"It doesn't mean anything. Not yet. And this information can't get out, okay? I never should have told you."

"Your secret is safe with me." I held out my hand, pinky extended for the most solemn of vows, the pinky promise.

He reached out to hook pinkies with me. For a moment we were twelve and eight, conspiring to keep our parents in the dark about the deer we were secretly feeding in the woods. Mom fussed about her perennials getting munched all summer long, but neither Nels nor I broke our pinky promise.

Nels squared his shoulders and plucked his hat up off the counter. "That's settled." The moment was over. "I need to check on the search efforts for Davey. We've identified his campsite, but it's been abandoned. Then I'll look in on Connor and see what he's up to." He pointed a stern finger at me. "You stay away from him, Junetta. Connor Fisk is a real piece of work. I wouldn't put much past him."

I gave my annoying salute, just to let him know that I didn't like him telling me what to do. I didn't take it any farther than that. I was grateful to be included in this brainstorming session, and I owed him one for the way he shut Reba Cornell down. "Thanks, Officer, for everything."

He pulled a small parcel out of his pocket and handed it to me without a word, then sauntered out of the bookshop.

I pulled back the tissue paper, and my god's eye fell into my hand. I took it to Uncle Vance's desk and hung it up with reverence. Now the only thing missing was the man himself. I wondered when Nels was going to let him out of jail.

Toward the end of the afternoon, Marcy ducked through the beaded curtain to talk to me. She had already taken her apron off for the day, preparatory to heading out. "Hey, Junetta, come with me to the Grizzly Bar after you close. Rob's gone hunting for the weekend and I'm not ready to go home to an empty house right now."

I leaned on the counter and regarded my friend. "Are you sure that's where you want to go? We could take a hike or go home and watch a movie or something."

She rubbed the small of her back with both hands. "Yeah, I'm not doing a whole lot of hiking just now."

I laughed. "Are you on your final countdown? How many more days?"

She closed her eyes. "Two and a half weeks. Don't remind me." Her eyes popped open, wide with apprehension. "Baby Rain has to come out somehow, but darned if I know how. I'm petrified."

I reached out and took her hand. "Surely you have some idea. Haven't you done those birthing classes at the clinic?"

"Oh, sure. It's one thing to read about something or watch videos. It's another thing to actually do it. Grandma tells me that our people have been giving birth since time began. That doesn't make me feel any better. This will be my first time."

"Would it make you feel better to have the baby at the hospital in Juneau, with a doctor instead of a midwife? I'm sure Gary could get you there safely."

She squeezed my hand. "That's not the problem I'm looking to solve tonight. I'm just feeling lonely with Rob out hunting when he's supposed to be hanging out with me, so I want to hang out with my best friend. I like the Grizzly Bar. We can play pool, and I'll beat you like I do every time."

I moved to close up the shop. "You'll never beat me this time. You won't even be able to reach the table with that baby in your way."

"Game on, girl!" She pitched in to help me put things away for the night. We checked the locks and lights and then walked down the street through the misty rain to the bar.

Chapter Twenty-one

Kirk was holding a boisterous happy hour at the Grizzly Bar. Several fishermen wearing waterproof raingear bellied up to the bar, enjoying a round of pretzels with their beers. A group of younger men surrounded the pool table, alternately hitting the balls and hitting on the few women in the bar. I saw Stella there, sipping a beer and addressing everyone as "honey." No better way to squelch unwanted attention from a young man than calling him "honey" in a motherly tone. It worked for Stella, even though she was no older than thirty-five at the most.

Marcy cast a look of disappointment at the pool table.

"Let's try to get on the waiting list," I said, leading her to a small table in the corner. "Want something wholesome to drink?"

She gave me an affectionate smile. "You can get me...never mind, here's Kirk."

Kirk materialized at our table, his smile advertising his delight at seeing me. "Junetta, Marcy, how great to see you in here!"

He leaned an elbow on the table and beamed at me. "I've been thinking about you, babe. You're at the center of a real mystery. I wouldn't be surprised if Scotland Yard showed up in Ptarmigan Port any day now."

I couldn't help laughing. "Oh, Kirk, Scotland Yard doesn't operate in America. Last I checked, Alaska is part of the United States."

He winked at me. "I tell tourists that a dozen times a day. Three out of ten don't believe me." He waved a hand at a couple of slates hanging on the wall behind the bar, covered with chalk tick marks. "Davey convinced me to start keeping track. He's pledged drinks for everyone if I go a full day with every single person convinced that we're not part of the US. We haven't gotten there yet. One day it was up to eight out of ten thinking they were in a foreign country."

Marcy poked me, her eyes full of fun, "You should keep track at the bookshop as well, Junetta."

"Only if Davey pledges a free book to everyone." The laughter faded from my voice. "Kirk, what do you know about Davey? Nels said he's still missing."

Kirk pulled up a chair and sat down next to me. "Well, I heard he was going camping. He's an experienced outdoorsman. I wouldn't worry too much." He patted my arm. "I also heard that Nels has asked Gary to scout around the area by air, and he's got a couple Mountain Rescue folks from Juneau coming in tomorrow to launch a larger search. They'll find him, and when they do, he'll be lounging by his campfire wondering what all the fuss is about." He jumped up and said, "What can I get you two?"

"I'll have a virgin pina colada." Marcy turned to me. "Get whatever you want, Junetta. I'll be your designated driver."

"You'll be no such thing. How can I beat you at pool if I'm buzzed?" I turned to Kirk. "Make it two. Hey, any chance of us getting a turn at the pool table?"

"You just say when, babe, and I'll make room for you." He winked again and ambled off to get our drinks.

Marcy leaned in close and said, "You know, Junetta, you could do worse…"

I rolled my eyes, refusing to give an inch on this silly topic.

True to his word, Kirk shooed the men away from the pool table when we said we were ready to play. They didn't go far, however. They crowded around the edges, commenting on our every move. It was such a distraction that I completely messed up my game. I lost to Marcy in ten minutes flat. It couldn't have been more embarrassing. Then when we retired to our corner, the men flocked to our table, offering to buy us drinks and give us tips to make us better pool players. I was pretty sure Stella's technique wouldn't work for me, but I tried a few "honeys" anyway, to test it out. They just thought I was flirting.

Finally, Marcy stood up, rubbed her very pregnant belly, twirled the wedding ring on her finger, and proclaimed, "I think it's about to rain."

I stared at her quizzically. Before I could ask her about her weather prognosticating, Kirk materialized at our table. He shooed the annoying men away from us, saying, "Less talk, more action, fellows. Show us how to win at pool." He dispensed pool cues and steered the men to the pool table we had abandoned.

Marcy sat back down and took a long swig of her virgin pina colada, a satisfied smile on her face.

I looked from her to the men now engrossed in pool, and back again. "What just happened?"

She leaned over and patted me on my left hand. "Kirk set me up with a safe phrase. He really is a sweetie, Junetta. I like to come here and play pool, but the crowd can get rough, and Rob's out of town half the time. Kirk makes sure I'm okay."

I regarded the man with new eyes. Okay, I still saw a guy who was deluded enough to think he was going to marry me one day, but I had to admit that he was, as Marcy said, a sweetie.

He caught me looking and flashed me a huge smile. I mouthed "thank you," and turned away before he could read anything more into my glance. As I swung my head around, I caught a glimpse of Connor Fisk, sitting at the end of the bar, guzzling a foaming glass of beer.

I had been surprised to see Connor at my bookshop yesterday. I was not surprised to see him at the bar tonight. I wondered if Nels had already investigated him, and if so, what had he found? Maybe I could find out something on my own, in spite of Nels's warnings.

"Hey, Marcy, I gotta get going. Thanks for a fun time at the Grizzly Bar tonight."

She sputtered into her drink. "Are you taking off on me?"

"I just have a few things I want to look into." I chugged down my drink and began to gather my things.

She laid a hand on my arm. "Are you taking off to go sleuthing? I wanna come."

I paused in the act of putting on my jacket. I leaned in close and said quietly, "Connor Fisk is here drinking, which means he's not on his boat. I want to go check out the *Gold as Glass* and see if there's anything suspicious going on."

She accepted this statement at face value, for once. "I can be your lookout on the dock. I won't be doing any running away, but I can warn you if he's coming back."

"Okay. Just to let you know, Nels says I should steer clear of Connor."

"And Nels is exactly right about that. That's why you need a lookout. Let's go."

We donned our jackets, paid our bill, and said a warm goodbye to Kirk.

"Come back any time, babe. Marcy knows, I've got your back."

I grinned back at him. "Thank you for tonight, all of it." I waved behind me on the way out, checking over my shoulder to see if Connor had noticed our departure. He was completely focused on his beer.

The *Gold as Glass* was tied up at the cruise ship dock. In the quiet evening light, it didn't look as exotic as it had when I took the shipwreck tour. Tonight, all I could see was an ordinary wooden hull above the water line, concealing the signature glass bottom beneath. It looked like the wood could use the ministrations of Captain Evan. The bright blue painted trim was flaking around the edges and the varnished boards had lost their sheen. Although it wasn't quite bad enough to frighten off the tourists, the worn appearance of the boat told me that Saltwater Tours was not making a fortune with their shipwreck excursions.

Marcy stationed herself on a bench. She assured me she would sing out, "Ninety-nine bottles of beer on the wall" if she saw Connor coming. I could tell she was thoroughly enjoying her new role as Agent George.

No one was aboard the boat. I made sure by calling out and scanning the area before I boarded her. She barely rocked under my weight.

I prowled through the vessel, beginning with the main lounge where Angus and I had peered through the glass bottom at the bones of the sunken SS *Fortunate*. He had shared his recurring dream about sea creatures teeming below the surface. I shook myself. I was here to investigate, not get sentimental about a nice guy who may or may not have killed the owner of this boat.

I wanted to find any evidence that might link Blake, or by extension Connor, to the break-in at my bookshop. What that evidence might be, I had no idea. I tried to ignore the glass bottom, and methodically checked all the nooks and crannies in the lounge: nothing.

I moved on to the engine room with its gleaming control panel. I searched for a ship's log or some other documentation of Blake and Connor's sailings. I came up with nothing. All I saw were nautical charts of the surrounding waters. "I don't know what I'm looking for here," I said aloud in frustration.

Then I remembered that Connor, and Blake before his death, had living quarters on the boat, well forward of the glass bottom lounge. I followed a narrow hallway that led to two cabins, one on either side of the boat. The head was wedged between them, in the bow.

I chose the cabin on the port side. It was unlocked.

I slipped in and closed the door behind me. It looked like this cabin was Blake's. The narrow bunk was neatly made with clothes piled on it, sorted by category. A photograph of a younger Blake striking a heroic pose on the deck of the *Gold as Glass* hung on the wall. I rifled through the latched cabinets without finding anything interesting.

I crept out of his cabin and crossed to the starboard side to Connor's cabin. It was the mirror of Blake's, with a narrow bunk and built-in cupboards--but Connor's cabin looked well-lived in. His clothes were jumbled into an upright hamper at the end of the bunk. Several hats lay about the cabin, captain's hats emblazoned with the words, "Gold as Glass." Clearly, Connor was enjoying the role of captain. Was that a role he would have killed to achieve?

Like in Blake's cabin, I unlatched one cupboard after another, just to see what I might find.

When I found it, I almost didn't recognize its importance. All I saw was a grungy little notebook with a spiral spring at the top. The pages flipped over like a movie detective's interrogation pad. I pictured Connor flipping those pages.

Mimicking what I imagined his motions to be, I flipped open the notebook to the last page. The first thing I saw was a scrawl that looked like, "Second half of the treasure map. He says gold was stolen from the ship. Can't let that story out."

Curious, I flipped to the front of the notebook. Printed on the inside cover was the phrase, "Property of _____." The blank was filled in with the name "Blake Rivers." I gave an audible gasp. This was Blake's notebook, not Connor's. But it was in Connor's cabin, so he must have known of its contents.

That's when I noticed the singing.

I heard Marcy belting out at the top of her voice. She was already on eighty-five bottles of beer. Connor must be almost upon me.

The boat rocked to a heavy weight. I shoved the notebook into my jacket pocket and zipped it up. I looked around for a place to hide. The last thing I wanted was for Connor to find me in his personal cabin.

There was no way I could get off the boat without him seeing me.

I slipped out of the cabin and into the head at the bow. Once inside, I clattered around, flushed the john two or three times, and then lurched out and headed down the hallway. I met Connor at the door to the lounge.

He leaned heavily on the doorjamb, peering at me through a drunken haze. He was big, drunk, and furious. "What the hell are you doing on my boat?"

I held my breath, almost gagging on the pungent smell of beer and whiskey emanating from him. He was clearly as dangerous as Nels had warned me.

"Oh, Connor, honey," I drawled in a loud, high voice. "Thank God your boat was here. I was out with Marcy at the Grizzly Bar, and I really had to pee. I'm so sorry for barging in—I just couldn't wait." I continued down the hallway, hoping he would move out of my way of his own volition. "Did you see us at the pool table, Connor? Marcy wiped the floor with me. She's waiting for me up on the dock." I leaned past him and called out, "Yoo-hoo, Marcy! I'll be right there."

She must be frantic by now.

Connor blocked my way. "This isn't a public toilet," he slurred. "But maybe you're looking for something else?"

Blake's little notebook burned in my pocket, until I realized that Connor was referring to something else altogether. No thank you!

He reached for me.

I pulled my phone out of my other pocket and illuminated the screen as if I was on a call. I held it to my ear, "Oh, hi, Nels. Yeah, I'm here on Connor Fisk's boat, the *Gold as Glass* at the cruise ship dock. I just had to use the head, but now he's blocking my way. Uh huh…yeah, that would be great." I clicked off the phone. "Trooper Nels is on his way. He gets very protective, with me being his sister and all." I smiled sweetly at Connor.

He moved aside and let me pass.

"You tell your brother to back off," he hollered at me as I scurried through the lounge and out onto the deck. I gauged the distance from the deck to the dock and leapt from the side. Marcy stood on the dock, white-faced, looking like she wasn't sure if she should climb on board or call the cops. She pulled me into a fierce hug.

I pushed her off. "Let's get out of here before Connor realizes that Nels isn't coming after all."

We hustled down the dock as fast as Marcy could manage. I kept checking over my shoulder every few minutes to reassure myself that Connor wasn't after me. I should have listened to Nels. I remembered a few newspaper articles about Connor's brushes with the law. Nels had arrested him twice for public drunkenness and at least once for fighting. Most fights never made it to the level of trooper intervention, which made Connor's record all the more impressive. Could he have fought with Blake, ending up by clobbering him over the head and then planting a knife in his chest? It wasn't hard to picture at all.

Chapter Twenty-two

Marcy and I finally found ourselves back at the Last Chance Café. We tumbled in, locked the door behind us, and burst into near-hysterical laughter. Eventually, we settled down, had a bit of herbal tea, and brought our heart rates back down to normal. I looked at Marcy's flushed face and damp hair and silently vowed not to involve her in my snooping ever again, no matter how much she wanted to be Agent George. We had Baby Rain to think of. But the least I could do was show her my find.

I pulled the little notebook out of my pocket. "I found this in Connor's cabin. It was Blake's notebook."

She leaned in close, and we flipped through the pages together. "This looks like a record of all his get-rich-quick schemes," she said. "Remember when he wanted to build an ice hotel on top of the glacier?"

"Here's his idea to pressure the school board to require his shipwreck tour for tenth grade History classes during the off season." I had to admire the guy for coming up with innovative ideas to promote his business.

"Look at this," Marcy said.

It was a couple pages in the style of a ledger, listing names and sums of money. "Collections" was written at the top. I didn't see myself or Marcy on the list, but a number of people I knew were there, including Uncle Vance. Next to his name was the notation, "$1000 weekly." I gasped and looked at Marcy. "Is this an amount that Uncle Vance was paying to Blake?"

She was as mystified as I was.

I lingered on the Collections page for a long time, looking at the names and amounts and wondering what kind of racket Blake had been running. If he was pressuring all these people to pay him money, there were a lot of people who might have wanted him dead. Brenda Tarkington's name was on the list, as was Davey Harper. My eyes kept returning to Uncle Vance's name.

Finally, I showed Marcy the last page, where Blake had indicated that he knew of Angus's half of the map and did not want the story to get out.

"Sounds like he was absolutely a candidate for map thief," she said.

"It could have been Connor, though. The notebook was in Connor's cabin, so he must have read it all." I reached for my phone. "I have to give this to Nels. He's going to be furious with me for getting involved with Connor, but he needs to see this."

Marcy covered my screen. "Junetta, it's past 10:00 p.m. Call him tomorrow. It can wait."

I bowed to Marcy's good sense. I would be better equipped to confess to Nels in the light of day, after downing a couple cups of Marcy's good coffee. She and I headed out to our respective homes.

I settled Cosmo for the night, which involved a run up and down the switchback road of my neighborhood and a friendly tussle over a pair of slippers that would forever after be dog toys. I resolved to go back to Uncle Vance's house in the morning to pick up a few of Cosmo's chew toys.

The good thing about having to care for a vibrant little dog was the healthy feeling of tiredness at the end of the day. When I finally made it to my bed, I fell asleep almost immediately.

I wasn't able to get a good night's sleep. I was used to the sun coming up at 3:00 a.m., and my blackout curtains worked for the most part to keep my room dark. It was the noise that woke me. With Cosmo in the house, I kept my bedroom door open at night, in case he needed anything. Usually he was a good sleeper, only jumping up onto my bed three or four times during the night. Tonight, he started howling. Whenever I hear a dog howling, I look for bears nearby. There's no better warning signal. I was barely awake, but I wanted to see the bears poking around in my yard. I flung up my blackout shade and peered outside. It was 4:15 a.m., and the sun was already up as bright as day. I scanned the edge of the woods, looking for a big, furry shape. It's possible the bear had already fled into the woods at the sound of Cosmo's howling. It was only then that I realized that the howling was coming from outside. Somehow, Cosmo had gotten out of the house.

I stumbled into the living room, gaping at the sight of the open front door. That's how Cosmo had gotten out. Worse, someone had gotten in. I spun around in what felt like slow motion. There was a scattering of papers on the floor, flung off my desk in the corner. Books had been pulled out of their shelves and thrown to the floor. A stiff breeze stirred their exposed pages. It was a horrible echo of the trashing of the Shipshape Bookshop.

I staggered to the front door, calling frantically for Cosmo. No doubt he had bolted out the door along with the intruder, whoever he was. If it was a bear, and I couldn't rule out that possibility, then Cosmo's life might be in danger. A little dog like him had no business taking on a bear, of any description. "Cosmo!" I shouted to the quiet morning.

I ran through the yard in a panic, searching for any sign of Cosmo. He wasn't sniffing through the long grass, chasing the birds twittering around my birdfeeder, or rooting through the strawberries in my garden. Just as I was hurrying inside to get dressed and mount a wider search, he zoomed through the door, barking triumphantly.

I slammed the door shut and shot the deadbolt. I couldn't remember if I'd done that simple action when I went to bed last night.

I knelt down and gathered Cosmo into my arms, submitting to his slobbery kisses and bestowing quite a few of my own. After this mutual lovefest was over, I clipped on Cosmo's leash and led him from one room to another in my house, looking for damage and making sure that no one was lurking in a corner waiting to jump out at me. Cosmo gave no warning barks, and everything looked undisturbed, except for the living room.

I checked the back door, which was unlocked, and secured it. My windows had no locks, so they were a weak spot in my defenses. Other than that, I felt like I was in a fortress. A fortress that had been breached in the middle of the night by someone intent on…what? I had no idea.

I started picking up the books, but then I realized that this was a case for Nels. I shouldn't touch anything until the troopers had taken a look. I sank down on the couch and pulled Cosmo into my lap. "Not again," I whispered into his damp fur.

By the time I was dressed it was almost 5:30, late enough that I felt okay calling the troopers. Unsurprisingly, I got a recorded message. I wasn't sure if this break-in counted as an emergency since I wasn't currently being threatened by anyone. I jumped up and checked all the windows, just to make sure that no one was lurking in the yard hoping for a second crack at me. Nothing. Maybe they had found what they'd come for and were long gone.

I couldn't stand the wait. I called Nels on his private phone.

He picked up on the fifth ring. "Junetta? Do you know what time it is?" he slurred.

"Yes, it's 5:45. I'm sorry to wake you. My house was broken into. Cosmo was howling at 4:00 a.m. I'm trying not to touch anything, but it's a mess."

He cut across my babbling. "Are you okay?"

"Yeah, they didn't come in my bedroom." I shuddered at the thought of my open bedroom door. Whoever had come in could have stood in the doorway watching me sleep. "Listen, I don't know if a bear wandered in and Cosmo chased him off, or if a person tried to rob me. Can you come?"

I heard a muffled groan. "I'll be right there."

To give him credit, Nels arrived in less than fifteen minutes. He was dressed in his uniform, unshaven and looking none too happy at this early morning call. But he didn't grumble, which was probably best. I couldn't guarantee a calm response if he had.

He stood just inside the front door, surveying the mess in my living room. "You're sure Cosmo didn't do this?"

"Come on, Nels! The front door was open, and Cosmo was outside howling when I woke up. He's a talented little dog, but I'm pretty sure he can't open the front door."

He ignored this outburst. "You got any coffee on?" He examined the door jamb while I fetched him a cup from the kitchen. I'd already had three cups and was feeling jittery as a result.

"I don't see any signs of forced entry."

I sighed. "I can't be sure that I locked the door last night." I braced myself for the inevitable lecture, but he was slurping down his coffee and missed his chance. Instead, he said, "Is anything missing?"

I wrapped my arms around my chest. "I don't know. I didn't want to touch anything until you came."

"Okay. I'm going to get Mark in here to take photos and dust for prints. You were right not to touch anything. Can you look around just with your eyes and see if anything is missing, or can you think of something valuable that a thief might be after?"

"I don't own anything valuable. I've got some cash in my desk drawer." I pointed to the desk.

Nels pulled out a handkerchief to ease the drawer open. "I don't see any cash."

I reached in and caught up a heart-shaped cardboard box that had once held Valentine's candy. I could smell the faint whiff of chocolate and coconut when I pried off the lid. My wad of cash was inside, undisturbed.

Nels frowned at the money. "The intruder either missed the significance of this box or wasn't looking for cash. Could he have been searching for something related to the map or the murder at the bookshop?"

I gasped and ran into my bedroom. Nels followed close behind, trying not to show his confusion.

I pulled my bedside table drawer open and lifted out the notebook I'd filched from Connor's berth. "They didn't find this." I handed it to Nels.

He turned it over, then flipped it open to reveal the front page with Blake's name written on it. "Where did you get this?"

Here comes the lecture. "I went to Blake's boat to see if I could find anything there, and this is what I found." I reached over to flip a few pages. "Look, he's got Uncle Vance's name on a list of 'Collections.' What could that be about?"

Nels snatched the notebook away from me. "I guess we'll never know, will we?" He slammed the notebook down on the bedside table. "You stole this book from Connor. I can't use it as evidence. Whatever is in there is now off limits. I shouldn't even look at it without a warrant." He glared at me. "Didn't I tell you not to mess with Connor Fisk?"

I nodded, chastised. "I'm sorry. I should have listened to you."

Startled out of his anger by my apology, Nels fingered the little notebook. "Did Connor see you take this? It could have led him to break in here to recover it."

I shuddered at the thought of Connor Fisk peering through the open door to my bedroom. "I did run into him while I was on his boat. He was drunk, and I pretended that you were on your way over to make him let me get by."

Nels struck his forehead in a classic face-palm. "You're lucky to be in one piece, Sis. Connor's a mean drunk. It could have been your murder I was investigating next."

"If you put it that way…"

He pressed on. "You told me that Connor was in your bookshop the other day, asking about the map. Now we find out that he's got access to Blake's notebook…"

"That mentions that Blake knew that Angus had the other half of the map," I cut in. I leaned over and flipped the pages to the end. "See, Blake says 'can't let that story out.' He must have gone to steal the map, and then Connor killed him."

Nels frowned down at the notebook.

"Listen, I'll sneak the notebook back onto Connor's boat, and then you can go get a warrant and make it official."

Nels shook his head. "Doesn't work that way." He held up a finger to stop my next words. "Here's what you're going to do. Nothing. Lock your doors behind you, keep Cosmo close, and leave the policing to me. Got it?"

I bowed my head in defeat. "What about the notebook?"

"I'm going to take it back to the station and see if Connor comes looking for it. If he does, I'll tell him it turned up as found property. If he mentions your trespassing, I'll tell him that I will give you a warning. I'll also warn him to leave my sister alone. Happy?"

I guess I had to be. "Thanks. I'm sorry to cause you all this trouble."

He just held out his coffee cup. "Can I have a refill?"

He sat down to drink his coffee, and I sat beside him on the couch.

I waved a hand at the mess surrounding us. "It's the same, but different."

"What do you mean?"

"Just like at the Shipshape Bookshop. Books thrown off the shelves and stuff tossed about. It's like they were looking for something here, even though I can't find anything missing. At the bookshop, the Pastor's Confession Map was stolen, but the thief didn't have to search for it, it was hanging on the wall. The mess there was just for the sake of destruction." I turned to look at my brother. "Do we think it was the same person that did both break-ins?"

He massaged his temples. "If it was, then I've got two innocent people in custody."

Chapter Twenty-three

I didn't stick around to watch Trooper Mark process the crime scene in my house. I loaded Cosmo into my car and drove down to the bookshop. I had some more questions to find answers to. It was all very well for Nels to tell me to stay safe and do nothing. That didn't mean I was going to do as he said. My inner child, the one that often got me into trouble, wanted to chant, "You're not the boss of me."

I had a mystery to figure out.

I wanted to go to the back room of the Shipshape Bookshop and set up an easel with a pad of newsprint on it to list off all my suspects, like they do on TV. I could picture a color-coded flip chart, drawn up with my scented markers. But Ptarmigan Port was a small town, and privacy was an almost nonexistent concept. There was no way I could keep such a display under wraps. Instead, I settled down at Uncle Vance's desk and opened up a document on my laptop. I typed up a list with three categories: map theft, Blake's murder, and the break-in at my house. The list looked like this:

Map Theft:

-Blake—he knew about Angus's map and didn't want the story to come out and threaten his shipwreck tours.

-Connor—he had Blake's notebook in his possession. He knew what Blake knew.

-Brenda—not sure why she would steal the map.

-Angus—he had the other half of the map. The fake map was found in his room.

-Uncle Vance—he was the 'owner emeritus' of the bookshop. Why would he steal from himself? That makes no sense.

Blake's Murder:

-Connor—he could have gone with Blake to steal the map and then killed Blake, either by accident or on purpose. Question— would he inherit the *Gold as Glass* or other assets after Blake's death?

-Uncle Vance—his knife was found in the victim. He argued with Blake at the Grizzly Bar.

-Brenda—she was Blake's ex-wife and disliked him.

-Angus—he was an outsider—no motive to kill Blake.

Break-in at my house:

-Uncle Vance—he was in jail in Juneau—INNOCENT

-Angus—he was in jail in Ptarmigan Port —INNOCENT

-Brenda—She was clearly looking for something in the back room of the bookshop. Did she continue searching at my house?

-Connor—he might have missed Blake's notebook and remembered that I had been trespassing on his boat.

I stared at the screen, then added another category:

Other Strange and Mysterious Things:

-Davey Harper is missing. He said he was going camping, but Nels thinks he skipped town.

-The current ledger for the bookshop is missing. What does this have to do with the map or murder?

-The stolen map was recovered but it was a photocopy. Where is the real map? Who would want to hide the writing on the back?

By now my head was aching, and I was having a hard time seeing how one person could be responsible for all these incidents, or why. I closed my eyes to sit in silence for a moment, hoping that a pattern might emerge. I didn't have time to meditate on the case, however. It was time for the Founders' Day picnic.

I closed my laptop and hustled out of the back room, ready to close up for the rest of the day to enjoy the picnic. The shop was empty except for Patrick helping Brenda Tarkington in the true crime section.

Although Brenda was a voracious reader, trending toward mysteries and historical romances, she rarely bought a new book at the bookshop. She was a faithful library patron and spent her tips on used books from the fifty-cent table. It wasn't Christmas and she didn't have any grandkids to buy birthday presents for. I couldn't think of any reason for her to be browsing the true crime section of the new books. She was definitely out of place.

I sauntered over to Patrick and Brenda. "Hi, Brenda, nice to see you this morning." I looked from her to Patrick and back again. "Are you finding what you're looking for?"

Patrick gave me an anxious glance and melted away. I groaned inwardly. He probably thought I was questioning his competence in waiting on a customer. When this was all over, I truly needed to find some way to recognize Patrick for his efforts.

Brenda fiddled with her purse strap, as if annoyed with being interrupted. "I was looking for a book on forensic methods, actually. I was reading an Agatha Christie novel where Poirot investigates a stabbing, but the person was dead before he was stabbed. I wanted to know if that storyline really makes sense."

I regarded her thoughtfully. Was she investigating Blake's death, using an Agatha Christie novel as cover? Did she suspect that Uncle Vance's knife had been planted on Blake's body after he was already dead? Did she merely wonder if her ex-husband's murder was not all that it seemed, or did she know for a fact because she was the one who killed him?

I poked through the books on the shelf, selecting one that purported to be a resource for mystery authors who wanted to get their details correct. "This is the best thing I can think of." I checked the table of contents and turned to a discussion on how to pinpoint the time of death and other forensic details. I held the book out to Brenda. "There's not much on the subject of faking a murder weapon. You might find this part to be helpful."

She took the book with a grunt of thanks. I watched her closely as she scanned the chapter and then settled down in one of my easy chairs to thoroughly read a few pages. Clearly, she wasn't planning to buy the book. I shrugged off a slight feeling of annoyance, focusing on my overall mission of bringing the joys of reading to the community. Other people would buy enough books to make up for it.

When she finished the couple of pages, after shamelessly taking a picture of one page spread with her phone, Brenda dropped the book on the top of the bookshelf and made a move to go. I wasn't ready for her to leave yet.

I intercepted her with a book in hand. "Hey, Brenda, I got a couple more cozy mysteries in since the last time you were here." I held out the brightly colored, well-worn paperback. "Want to take a look?"

She took the book, one of her favorite authors, and gave me a glance of thanks. I led her over to the fifty-cent table. I rooted through the piles of books and pulled out another Agatha Christie book that I thought she would like. "Have you read this one yet?" While she turned it over, I went on, "I know you like to read mysteries, and now we've got a real-life mystery in our town. How do you think Hercule Poirot would look at Blake's death?"

"He'd use his little gray cells and figure out what's going on that nobody else can see." She gazed around the shop, looking for what no one else could see, perhaps?

"I'll bet he would interview everyone in town, to find out their whereabouts on the night of the murder," I went on in a light voice, as if this discussion was nothing more than a parlor game. "I was on board the *Northern Dream*, returning from the villages. How about you, Brenda?"

"I was home in bed, like always." She shot me a sideways look, as if daring me to contradict her.

I took a breath to continue, but she cut across me. "Are you working for your brother, now, Junetta? He's no Poirot, but he did ask me this very question. I figure I owed him an answer. I don't owe you one."

I stifled a laugh. "No, he would never let me work for him. In fact, he asked me the same question. It was kind of intimidating, to be honest."

She sifted through the piles of paperbacks. "He's feeling mighty self-important if you ask me. But don't go telling him I said that."

"Not me—my lips are sealed." Out the corner of my eye I saw a group of tourists enter the bookshop. I turned my back as if I hadn't seen them, leaving Patrick to wait on them. I didn't want to sever this rare connection with Brenda until I got the answers I was looking for. "Brenda, I heard that Blake and Uncle Vance were arguing in the Grizzly Bar the evening of the murder. They say it was about money. What do you know about Blake's finances?"

I swear, the temperature dropped twenty degrees in the bookshop. "I don't answer for Blake Rivers anymore. We got divorced five years ago come December, and we settled our joint finances at that time. If you want to know about Blake's finances, go talk to the bank, or get your brother to break confidentiality to tell you everything you want to know." She scooped up three books and marched over to the cash register. "Thanks for pointing out these books."

"Please don't be offended," I said as I rang her up. "It's just that I heard that Blake was collecting money from a number of people in town, and I thought I heard you were one of them." I busied myself with bagging up the books, trying to gauge her reaction without seeming to be staring at her.

If I had to pick one word to describe that reaction, it would be "stunned." "Who told you that? What does your brother know?"

"I just got the impression, maybe from his nephew, Connor? Was Blake running some kind of racket? Uncle Vance's name was on the list, which is what worries me."

"List?" Brenda's voice rose, causing the group of tourists to glance over at us. I ducked my head and smoothed the bag once or twice.

"List," I said firmly. "There were a lot of townspeople on the list. I'm guessing Blake had a lot of enemies. Any one of them could have killed him. Even you."

She leaned in close and hissed, "Where is this list?"

I countered with a question, "Do you know who his enemies were? Who would want to kill him?"

She took the bag from my hand, dropped a dollar fifty on the counter, and turned to leave.

I called out to Patrick to lock up behind me and go enjoy the picnic, and followed Brenda out the door. "Brenda, please. I don't think my uncle killed your ex-husband. I'm trying to figure out what happened. You might be the best person to help me, especially since you know so much about murder mysteries."

She strode down the sidewalk with me in hot pursuit. "How can I trust you?" she shot over her shoulder. "Anything I say will get right back to the troopers. Don't tell me that you and your brother don't talk."

I caught up to her and we walked side by side. "Yes, we talk. The last thing he said to me was that I was to do nothing about trying to figure out this case. As if I'm going to take direction from my little brother! I'm not about to go running to him with information, because he's just going to shut me down. Brenda, if you didn't kill Blake, then maybe you want to figure out who did. We could work together." I held my breath after delivering this remarkable line. If she was a murderer, I was putting myself in danger. I tried to remember if Nels had warned me to steer clear of Brenda Tarkington.

Brenda stopped short in the middle of the sidewalk. At first, I thought she was going to hit me. Instead, she burst into laughter. I didn't think I'd ever seen her laugh. "If I didn't kill him? You're not very far along the road, are you? Why would I want to kill him? I got free of him five years ago. If I was going to kill him, that's when I would have done it. I don't know anything about a list to collect money from me, but I can guarantee you that he would have had a hard time making that happen." She regarded me searchingly. "You're not much of a sleuth, Junetta. You're making a fatal assumption about me. I don't care about Blake Rivers."

"Then why are you trying to figure out who murdered him? I could have sworn that's what you were up to."

She waved her newly purchased Agatha Christie novel at me. "Use your little gray cells, Junetta." She got into her car and slammed the door behind her, leaving me standing alone on the sidewalk, wondering.

What did I really know about Brenda Tarkington?

Chapter Twenty-four

I was lost in thought when Marcy came to the door of the café and called out to me. "Are you just going to stand there all day?"

"I'm waiting for inspiration to hit me out of the blue."

She laughed. "Well, you picked a good day for it. There's more blue sky up there than we've seen for the past week and a half." She turned her door sign to "Closed" and came out to stand beside me.

"You're closing? Are you coming to the picnic, then?"

She shook her head. "You know I'm not. We're all going down to the beach for a bonfire. Grandma's bringing herring eggs." She indicated a basket dangling from her arm. "I've got five different kinds of jam here, and my cousin Nathan is going to make fry bread on the beach. He's already dug the pit for the salmon. The kids are going to gather the skunk cabbage leaves to wrap it in."

My mouth watered at her description, but despite our close friendship, I knew I wasn't invited on this particular day. It was a sad fact of life in Ptarmigan Port that there were two separate gatherings on Founders' Day. The descendants of the European settlers considered June 13 to be the birthday of our town in commemoration of the date in 1902 when Craig Cornell discovered gold in Seven Mile Creek and started a mini gold rush and a prospecting town. The Alaska Natives, who had lived in the area for centuries, saw nothing to celebrate in the influx of white settlers who took over the land and its resources and forever changed their way of life. Really, we were approaching a moment in history when it would be best to drop the Founders' Day celebrations completely and come together for a summer solstice party instead. The old guard like Reba Cornell resisted any efforts at change. As the granddaughter of Craig Cornell himself, Reba always took center stage at the annual event.

I gave Marcy a hug. "Have fun at the bonfire. Don't feel shy about eating for two."

She hugged me back. "I'll save you a piece of fry bread. Enjoy your picnic. What are you taking, anyways?"

I ducked my head. "I'm picking up some drinks on the way over."

She punched my arm. "That's the classic bachelor picnic offering. Grab some chips and dip while you're at it."

I couldn't help laughing. "Things have been so crazy. I didn't even think to order a cake from you."

She handed me her basket and turned to unlock the café's door. "I thought you'd never ask." She led me inside to the walk-in and pointed to a stunning chocolate layer cake decorated with chocolate frosting roses and fresh raspberries. "I had a hard time sleeping last night, so I threw this together for you." She boxed it up in one of her white and red cake boxes and eased it into my hands. "I'll send you a bill next week sometime."

I set the box down gently on the counter and wiped my eyes before engulfing her in a big bear hug. "Marcy...you're the best!"

• • •

The picnic was in full swing when I arrived. I parked on the edge of the sandy lot, leaving Cosmo in the car with the promise of a run after lunch. The picnic was held at Prospectors Park on the shoreline north of town, not far from Uncle Vance's Miner's Beach neighborhood. There was a short stretch of rocky beach, a playground with the super-long swings that I loved as a girl, and a covered picnic shelter with enough tables to seat dozens of people if it was raining. Today's sunshine drew families out onto picnic blankets spread on the grass. Two long tables inside the shelter were filled with casseroles, platters of fruits and veggies, and more desserts than anyone could possibly eat. There were even seven different varieties of chips.

I found a place of honor on the dessert table for Marcy's magnificent cake and started to fill a plate with three-bean-casserole, pasta salad, and the loveliest smoked salmon. I found a seat at the end of a long picnic table and dived into my food. Everything was the same as it ever was. I'd been going to Founders' Day picnics since before I could walk. I had fond memories of playing frisbee with my dad on the beach and scolding him when he let the frisbee sail into the water and wouldn't let me swim after it. Nels and I played hide and seek at every Founders' Day picnic, even if we never played together any other time. I looked around for Mom. Sometimes she would come into town for the picnic, but I didn't see her today. She was probably fully occupied with her Boston wedding party.

Uncle Vance was also noticeably absent, as was Blake Rivers. I didn't miss Blake's loud voice and abrasive personality. I didn't see Davey Harper either. I hoped he was simply enjoying his camping trip, not skipping town for some crime. As I ate and observed the friends and neighbors around me, I realized that the ever-present topic of conversation was the murder and the theft of the Pastor's Confession Map. I heard Clarissa tell Brenda Tarkington, "I never would have guessed. He was such a nice man, too." Stella Turner said to Patrick, "Honey, you mustn't let it bother you."

I saw Kirk Dunbar roll in, a bag of nacho chips and a six-pack of soda in his hands. Classic bachelor offering, just like Marcy said. I averted my eyes before he saw me looking. Some might say that it was my fault he was still a bachelor. If it was up to me, he could stay in that state forever. You had to admire his persistence, though.

He loaded up a plate and plumped down next to me with a huge smile on his face. "Junetta, how great to see you here, babe. Things getting back to normal at the bookshop?"

"Hi, Kirk. Yeah, we've got things cleaned up. I'm just waiting to get Uncle Vance back to where he belongs."

He popped an entire deviled egg into his mouth and mumbled around the edges, "Sounds like Vance didn't steal the Pastor's Confession Map after all. I heard Nels found it in Angus

Montgomery's room. He didn't stay locked up for long, though."
He leaned forward and whispered. "Lookout behind you, babe."

I whipped around to see Angus hovering on the edge of
the covered area. Nels must have released him from custody. I
turned back around before he saw me, my mind whirling. Did
his presence here mean he was innocent, or just lucky that there
wasn't enough evidence for Nels to hold him? Whatever would I
say to him if he came up to me?

Kirk laid a hand on my arm. "If he bothers you, I'll take care
of him, babe. Just give me the safe word."

I threw him a genuine smile. It fairly dazzled him. "I don't
know the safe word, but I appreciate the thought."

"That's the great thing about it," he said, when he could
speak. "You get to make up your own safe word. It should be
something you might really say, so the offender doesn't know
what you're saying, but not something so common that you'll say
it accidentally." He looked at me expectantly. "What's your safe
word, babe?"

I chuckled, then took a deep breath. How could it hurt for
me to set up a safe word with Kirk? As long as it had no marriage
connotations, it could be very useful. "Let's say, 'Is that a mouse
I see?'"

He shook his head, laughing all the while. "Have a heart!
You'll have my patrons scrambling onto the bar to get away. Try
again, babe."

I couldn't help laughing at the image of the hard-bitten crowd
at the Grizzly Bar squealing over a mouse. "Okay, how about,
'peanut butter?' I don't love peanut butter sandwiches, so I'm not
likely to ask you for one."

"Peanut butter. That works. If I hear you say, 'peanut butter,'
I'll step in." He took my hand. "Anything for you, babe."

I gently disengaged my hand and popped a piece of watermelon
into my mouth. "Thanks, Kirk. You're a sweetheart."

I threw a quick glance over my shoulder to see if Kirk's
services would be needed right away. Angus sat alone at a table,
a full plate of food in front of him. He picked at a pile of potato

salad morosely. He glanced in my direction, and I looked away in a flash. I knew I wouldn't be able to avoid him indefinitely. Besides, that wasn't my way. If he was guilty, I wanted to expose his guilt, and if he was innocent...? I took a deep breath, smiling slightly to myself. If he was innocent, I wanted to hike out to the glacier with him and see what might happen after that. If only I could figure out which one it was.

I pulled my attention back to Kirk's story about a bear cub wandering into the bar this morning. "The tourists wanted to cuddle him like he was a teddy bear. I shooed him outside and shut the door before Mama bear could come in to teach us all a lesson for messing with her baby." He laughed at his remembrances. "One old guy was seriously bent out of shape that his wife didn't get to pet the cute little bear. I just asked him if his accidental death and dismemberment policy was up to date."

I laughed out loud, causing heads to turn. They were going to come away with the wrong idea. In any other place it wouldn't matter, but our small town had an active gossip mill that would pair my name with Kirk's and expect wedding bells to ring out. I'd successfully avoided that conclusion for the past ten years, mostly by keeping my distance from Kirk. I made a move to gather up my plate, when Reba Cornell approached the microphone set up next to the food tables.

Reba was decked out in a long woolen skirt and a cotton chemise in the style of the early 1900s. With her gray hair piled high on her head to augment the period costume, she was the spitting image of her grandmother, Lucy Cornell. I knew the dress was a replica because I'd seen the original on display in the Historical Society next to a formal portrait of Craig and Lucy Cornell hanging on the wall.

Reba launched into a speech detailing Craig's miraculous find of gold in Seven Mile Creek in 1902, and his subsequent work to establish the town of Ptarmigan Port and eventually become mayor, an office he held from 1927 to his death in 1954. "If not for Craig Cornell, Ptarmigan Port would be nothing more than a creek flowing into the sea, rather than a vibrant center of culture and commerce in Southeast Alaska."

It was the same speech she made every year for Founders' Day. We all knew it by heart. I was stuck in my seat because Reba would take it personally if I got up and walked out, but I didn't have to pay attention. I tuned out her words, turning over in my mind how to find out if Angus was a murderer or the victim of framing. Maybe Nels would tell me...

Reba finally wrapped up her speech with her iconic line, "Gold is the heart and soul of our beloved Ptarmigan Port."

I gathered up my plate and said goodbye to Kirk. He clasped my hand for a moment, a sappy smile on his face. "Till next time, babe."

Yeah, time to establish that distance again.

• • •

Angus must have slipped out at the end of Reba's speech. I decided to leave him for later. I waved to a couple friends on my way back to my car to liberate Cosmo for a ramble along the beach. He greeted me with barks of joy, and we both took off running down the beach. The tide was high, and we splashed through the shallows. My shoes got soaked. I knew better than to run barefoot on a beach in Southeast Alaska where I could step on mussels with their razor-sharp shells or barnacles clinging to the rocks. We ran at top speed to the rocky point, where I turned Cosmo around and slowed to a more leisurely walk. He abandoned his quest for speed and set out to poke his nose into every bit of seaweed or pile of rocks that we passed. I let him take his time while I tried to empty my mind of any worry about murder or theft or guilt or innocence. I breathed in the fresh, salty air and focused on my immediate surroundings.

That's the only reason I saw him.

In a patch of alder trees along the edge of the rocky beach lurked a big man. I narrowed my eyes at him. Even from the shoreline I could see his long, white Santa Claus beard. I gave Cosmo's leash a gentle tug and called out, "Hey, Davey!"

He didn't hear me, or if he did, he pretended not to. He slipped back under cover of the alders and disappeared.

Well, that was suspicious enough for me to go right after him. It never occurred to me that this might not be wise. I'd known Davey Harper all my life. There was no way he could be mixed up in theft and murder. I just wanted to know why he was hiding out when people were out there trying to rescue him.

I hustled up the beach with Cosmo frisking at my heels. By the time I reached the stand of alders, there was no sign of Davey. Cosmo and I stumbled around among the trees for a few minutes until we emerged onto the roadway running along the shoreline. A truck was rounding the bend, headed for the Miner's Beach neighborhood. We set off in hot pursuit.

It took us half an hour on foot to make it to the cramped collection of houses in the Miner's Beach neighborhood. Cosmo was panting pretty heavily by now. I postponed my pursuit of Davey to stop at Uncle Vance's house for some water. I threw open the front door and Cosmo zoomed inside, barking lustily. He ran straight to Uncle Vance's bedroom. I followed him closely, to find him leaping at Davey Harper's feet.

"Junetta! I wasn't expecting you or Cosmo here. Didn't you go to the picnic?"

Was there a furtive note in his voice?

"Yeah, I was just exercising Cosmo after the picnic. Where have you been, Davey? Nels has people out looking for you."

He ran his hands through his hair and blew out his breath like a humpback whale. "Didn't I tell you? I went out Seven Mile Creek to go camping. I never needed rescuing."

I unclipped Cosmo's leash to let him roam around the house. "So, why was your campsite abandoned? People have been worried about you, Davey."

"Well, they shouldn't be. I've lived in this town all my life. I can take care of myself out in the wilderness. People need to stop minding other people's business."

I sat down on Uncle Vance's bed and gazed at him. "What are you hiding?"

He gave a guilty start and glanced at the closet. "I'm not hiding anything. Why would you think I'm hiding something?"

I jumped up and beat him to the closet by three steps. It gave me just enough time to throw open the door and scan the interior. He had obviously stashed it minutes earlier.

I pulled out a heavy, leather-bound book—the Shipshape Bookshop's missing ledger.

I slapped the ledger down on the bed and faced Davey. "If I open this up, will I find pages torn out or altered accounting or something?"

He gazed at the ledger with his mouth hanging open. "I have no idea what that is or what you're talking about. This is Vance's house—you should take it up with him."

I shook a finger at him. "You are the worst liar I've ever met in my entire life. Did Uncle Vance put you up to this? Is that why you've been hiding out ever since Blake was killed, so nobody would find this ledger?" I kept a hand on the book, afraid to open it for fear of what I might find. What was Uncle Vance's long game here?

Davey drew himself up in a passable imitation of Reba Cornell when she saw fit to take umbrage like she often did. "A man's got a right to go out camping and not be bothered by questions and accusations."

"Okay." I scooped up the ledger and held it close to my chest. It was ice cold to the touch. "I won't ask you any questions. I'll tell you what happened. After Blake was found murdered, Uncle Vance called you and told you to hide this ledger in case he got arrested for the murder. There must be something in here that incriminates him. You took the ledger and hid it for him." Inspiration hit me. "You hid it in your chest freezer underneath your packets of game from 2010."

Davey gaped at me. "What are you, a mind-reader or something?"

"I'll take that as a 'yes.' You could have hidden it there forever and no one would have looked. Why did you bring it here today?"

Davey heaved a sigh and sat down on the bed. "I'm tired of hiding out. Vance is going to have to face the music for what he's done. I had nothing to do with it."

My hands went cold, which had nothing to do with the icy book I clutched. I sat down next to him. "What did he do? Did Uncle Vance stab Blake?"

Davey reached over to ease the ledger out of my hands. He opened it to a page towards the last third of the book and pulled out a yellow legal-sized sheet of lined paper. He handed the paper to me.

I read the handwritten words in growing horror. The message was simple enough. "Vance Peterman attests that Blake Rivers won full ownership of the Shipshape Bookshop in a game of straight poker on this date of February 22, 2015." Uncle Vance's signature at the bottom was unmistakable. Davey Harper was listed as a witness.

Chapter Twenty-five

My hands were shaking so hard that I dropped the paper. "He didn't tell me." I pointed a trembling finger at Davey. "You didn't tell me either."

He spread his hands wide, palms in the air in the age-old gesture that says, "Not my fault, not my problem."

I scrabbled through the ledger's pages, checking notations of income and outgoing funds. Even without knowing Uncle Vance's system, I could see that there were regular payments of $1000 a pop that had no explanation indicated. I waved a finger at the most recent payment. "Was Uncle Vance paying off Blake to regain ownership of the bookshop?"

Davey shook his shaggy head. "I'm pretty sure that was hush money. He didn't want you to know."

I gripped my head in my hands, trying to make sense of the depth of my uncle's betrayal. He had gambled my bookshop and lost it to Blake, and then used bookshop profits to pay to ensure Blake's silence, presumably buying himself time to figure out how to get out of this mess. I gasped out loud. Had Uncle Vance seized on murder as the best way to make this whole bad dream go away?

I stared unseeing at the yellow piece of paper. Here was evidence of the strongest motive for Blake's murder. I had to turn this in to Nels.

As if he could read my mind, Davey slid the paper out of my hands. "I'll just slip this back in the book and stash it in Vance's dresser. If your brother wants to search his uncle's house, that's his business. Nothing to do with me."

I snatched the paper out of his hand and caught up the ledger in one smooth movement. I retreated across the room and faced him. "I'm not covering this up. This shows that Uncle Vance had a motive to kill Blake."

Davey stood up and held out his hand for the ledger. "Honey, stop and think a minute. This paper is from February. We're into June now. Why would Vance have waited so long, and paid Blake so much money, if he was just going to kill him?" He came closer to take me by both shoulders. "Hey, Junetta. I've known Vance since before you were born. You couldn't find a more cantankerous old fool with a heart of pure Alaska gold. He wouldn't kill nobody. He might start a fight with Blake in front of the whole town, but he wouldn't stick a knife in him in no back room. That's not his way."

I waved the ledger at him. "Why did he tell you to hide this, then?"

"You can figure that out. He knew it looked bad. Just because something looks like evidence doesn't mean it is evidence." He laid a hand on the ledger without attempting to wrench it from my hands. "Listen. Before you take this to Nels, talk to Vance about it. Look him in the eye and ask him if he killed Blake. You'll see that he's innocent."

I groaned out loud. "Uncle Vance is in jail in Juneau. I can't talk to him. When I did talk to him before Nels sent him off, he wouldn't say anything. He refused to say what he was doing that night. He's trying his best to look guilty. What am I supposed to think?"

Davey scratched his head in silence. "I guess I can't help you there. I never did know anyone more stubborn than Vance Peterman. Whatever he was doing, I'd stake my life that he wasn't stabbing anyone in the back room of his bookshop."

I clutched the ledger like it was a life ring to save me from drowning. "It's my bookshop! At least I thought it was." I pulled out my phone. "I'm going to call Nels. I don't have to tell him that you hid the ledger, but he needs to see this paper."

Davey just nodded. "I'm going to head on home. You can tell him I showed up and I'm fine, and he had no call to be worried." He waved and slipped out the door before I could answer.

Of course, Nels didn't answer when I called. I left a message with Stella saying that I had seen Davey and I found something Nels would want to see. I left it at that. Then I collected Cosmo, tucked the ledger under my arm, and trekked back to the beach to pick up my car.

The picnic was breaking up when I got back to my car. I didn't want to go into the matter of the ledger with anyone other than Marcy, who was otherwise occupied. I loaded Cosmo into the car and slid the ledger under the front passenger seat to keep it safe.

I wasn't ready to go home and face the mess left behind from the break-in. I didn't want to disturb Marcy at her bonfire on the beach. I settled for driving up and down the shoreline. Living in a small town with no roads in and out was a disappointment when you just wanted to hit the road to get away. I could go about fifteen miles in each direction from town—it was the road trip version of pacing—so, I paced, and talked over my predicament with Cosmo.

"It looks bad, Cosmo. Uncle Vance gambled away my bookshop, and then paid Blake Rivers $1000 a week for five months to keep it from me. That's $20,000!"

Cosmo raised both ears at my near-hysterical tone. His dark eyes blinked sympathetically.

"Then, he got Davey to hide the ledger to keep this story from coming out. He must have known how it would look—like he's the killer." I leaned over to look Cosmo in the eyes. "Do you think Uncle Vance is the killer?"

Cosmo jumped up and barked once.

"Yeah, me too. I wish he would stop playing games and try not to look so guilty." I eyed Cosmo speculatively. "What about Angus? Do you think he's a killer?"

Cosmo lay back down on the front seat, seemingly losing interest in this conversation. I wasn't ready to let it go.

"I can't figure any connection between Angus and Blake. They couldn't have even known each other. Angus just wants to follow up on his family history story." I scratched Cosmo's head to get him to look at me. "The map that Nels found in his room was a fake. Why would he plant a fake map in his room? It looks like somebody is trying to frame him, to divert suspicion away from themselves. That couldn't be Uncle Vance because he's in jail. Unless…"

I reached the end of the road and turned around in the cul-de-sac to start my next lap. "If Uncle Vance stole the map and wanted to plant a fake on Angus, he could have arranged that with Davey when he contacted him about the ledger."

Cosmo's ears perked up again at the mention of Uncle Vance and Davey. "I'll bet you could sniff out their guilt or innocence. Want to be a police dog, Cosmo?"

He gave another sharp bark, and then started lunging at the window. I glanced over. Cosmo was right, something was up. I was driving past Clarissa's Bed and Breakfast. A trooper car with lights flashing idled in the front parking area. It looked like trooper Mark's car, not my brother's. "Good boy. We'll go check it out."

I clipped on Cosmo's leash and hopped out of the car. Mark was just disappearing inside the building. I didn't think twice about following him in. Marcy liked to remind me that curiosity killed the cat, to which comment I always retorted that the cat came with nine lives. Losing one or two along the way wasn't that big of a deal.

Trooper Mark stood in the hallway rapping on Angus's door. Of course, this trooper visit had to do with him.

I lingered in the foyer, wondering what I would say to Angus and how to explain my presence there.

Clarissa paved the way for me. She bustled out of her office; her graying hair twined into a long braid studded with buttercups from her front garden. "Isn't it dreadful, Junetta? Never in my thirty years of business have I had a guest's room violated like this. The poor man's things were all thrown about."

I gaped at her, with visions of other break-ins dancing in my head. "How did it happen?"

"Well, the troopers never did this, I can guarantee you that. Someone must've snuck in during the night, while the poor man was in jail. He just got back from the picnic, and this is what he found. None of us are safe in our beds, Junetta. Your brother needs to figure this out before anyone else gets killed. Come, take a look."

I shortened Cosmo's leash to keep him close to my side and crowded after Clarissa in the doorway to Angus's room. As she said, the room was a mess. Drawers were pulled out and flung onto the floor, the contents of a suitcase were scattered everywhere, and in the midst of the mess a despondent Angus sat on the bed with his head in his hands.

My heart went out to him. Even though he was on my list of suspects, I wanted to sit down next to him, take his hands in mine, and say, "Don't worry—everything's gonna be okay." The sheer force of this desire practically took my breath away.

He didn't notice me in the doorway. I heard him say to Trooper Mark, "My laptop is missing. All my research."

Cosmo gave a sharp yip, and Angus looked up. Before I could back away, he jumped off the bed and came to me. "Junetta. I didn't steal your map. It wasn't me; I promise."

I was touched that in the midst of his own trouble his first thought was to establish his innocence in my eyes.

I looked deep into his eyes, searching for truth or deception there. Some might say that I wouldn't recognize either one if I saw it, but I was satisfied. "I believe you," I said.

He closed his eyes with a deep breath of relief.

Well, that awkwardness was over. On to the crime at hand. "What about your map, Angus? Was that taken too?"

Mark shot me a quizzical look, as if to say, "Who's the trooper here?"

I didn't care. I had my eyes on Angus.

He spun around and hustled into the bathroom. I didn't know if I was supposed to follow him, but in my book, a man's bathroom was not a place to go without an explicit invitation, and maybe not even then. I heard a clanking, as if he'd set something heavy down on the toilet. Then he emerged with a smile of relief on his face, holding a soggy, plastic-wrapped packet. "I duct-taped this to the inside of the toilet tank lid. It's too precious to leave it laying around in a town where historical maps keep disappearing and reappearing." He unfastened the waterproof covering and pulled out his family's letter and map. "Whoever came in got all my research, but they didn't get the most important thing."

"All right, everybody out." Trooper Mark brandished his fingerprint duster. "This will take me a couple of hours. Come on back about 5:00 p.m. and I'll put in a report for your missing laptop."

Angus nodded and slipped the envelope back into its protective covering. He slid it into a small backpack and slung that across his shoulders. "You look like you're out to walk your dog," he said to me. "Mind if I come along?"

"If your hiking boots haven't been stolen, we could take that glacier hike we missed the other day."

He hesitated, biting his lip. Then, "Are you sure Kirk won't mind?"

I stared at him. "Kirk? What does Kirk have to do with anything?"

He colored a little. "I thought Kirk was your boyfriend. You looked so cozy together at the picnic."

I burst out laughing. "I dated Kirk in high school, a million years ago. He's a sweet guy living in a fantasy, but he's definitely not my boyfriend."

Angus's face lit up like a sunrise breaking over the calm, clear waters of Havoc Strait.

Chapter Twenty-six

I didn't care that clouds had overtaken the clear blue sky. I ignored the fact that I had planned to reopen the bookshop after the picnic. The only thing that might have enticed me to turn around was if Marcy was going into labor, but that didn't happen. Nothing else could stop me from taking Angus out to see our glacier.

The Tongass Glacier was our town's biggest attraction. A towering river of ice that flowed out of the mountains until it melted at the face to become Seven Mile Creek, the glacier provided numerous opportunities for the tourist trade. There were helicopter flightseeing tours and guided hikes, as well as a growing cadre of artists who gathered along the Fireweed Meadows to paint the glacier while tourists strolled nearby as if they were on the Left Bank in Paris. But the best way to see the glacier was to hike along its west side on the Ridge Trail to a secret spot that provided safe access to the ice.

Angus put on his brand-new hiking boots and climbed into my car for the short drive to the trailhead. Before I could say anything, he said, "Well, this is kind of awkward. I'm not quite sure how to act, now that I'm an ex-con."

I gave him a sharp glance and was reassured by his whimsical smile. Adopting a similarly light tone, I said, "Yeah, most of my brother's friends turn out to be some kind of hooligan or other. It's an occupational hazard. I'm using Cosmo as a judge—if he likes you, you're good."

Indeed, Cosmo wriggled all over Angus, slathering him with doggy kisses. Angus settled him down with a thorough scratching behind both ears.

"I'm sorry Nels arrested you. It's kind of my fault. I saw that god's eye in your room and assumed that you had taken it from the bookshop. So, I sicced Nels on you." I kept my eyes on the road. "Sorry."

"Yet something happened in the meantime, while I was cooling my heels in jail, to convince you that I wasn't a thief after all. Presumably. Otherwise, I doubt you'd let me into your car. Unless you're kidnapping me, of course. You're not kidnapping me, are you?"

I laughed and pulled into the parking area. "No, though you might think otherwise by the time we reach the glacier. You were locked up when someone broke into my house last night, and then your room was broken into as well. It had to be someone else, not you at all."

He gave me a glance of sympathy. "I'm sorry your house got broken into. You must feel like somebody's out to get you."

I tried to hide a shudder. "Yeah. But I don't want to worry about that now. Nothing like being out in nature to take all your worries away."

I settled my day pack on my shoulders and waited for Angus to don his backpack. He re-tied his right shoe and fished a water bottle out of his pack for a long drink. Finally, he was ready for our hike.

"Lead on, O fearless leader!"

I had to laugh. "Stick with me, you trusting follower. Wonders await us."

The first part of the trail ran through old-growth forest, with massive red cedar, Sitka spruce, and western hemlock trees in profusion. The green of the moss, ferns, and trees was intensified by the increasing clouds.

I kept Cosmo on his leash, mostly because I knew I wouldn't be able to corral him if he wanted to run down the trail. He had plenty of leash room to explore a fairy ring of mushrooms, or a pointed tree stump marked by the gnawing teeth of beavers, or a tiny stream that burbled over a smattering of mossy rocks.

Angus showed as much enthusiasm as Cosmo, taking pictures of every natural wonder that the little dog discovered. Between the two of them, a forty-five-minute uphill hike stretched into an hour. Finally, we reached my favorite part of the trail, where it swung around a bend and opened up to a magnificent vista of the glacier. The sight of the grand river of ice carving its way through the valley always took my breath away. At that moment, the sun broke through the clouds, kissing the tips of the nunataks on either side of the glacier. These sharp rocky peaks had once been the only things that protruded above the ice sheet. Now, they framed the Tongass Glacier in a picture-perfect vision.

Angus stopped in awe, for once forgetting his camera. "Wow," he breathed.

I could feel a goofy smile lighting up my face. I do love sharing my corner of paradise with others. "Take a picture, quick, before the light changes."

My words shocked him out of his stunned silence. He took a series of careful photos, posing me in the foreground in one, "for scale." "It's breathtaking," he said, so many times that it became a mantra.

I just kept on grinning.

Finally, he was ready to move on. "That was magical. How did you arrange for the sun to come out at that particular moment?"

"I aim to please. Let me show you something else, every bit as magical but on a small scale." I pointed to a lupine plant.

He exclaimed over the tall, dark blue spikes of flowers, reaching nearly waist high.

"Yes, the flowers are lovely. Do you see the diamonds?" I showed him the raindrops that collected in the center of each swirl of leaves, left over from last night's rain. Sparkling in the sunshine, they truly did look like diamonds.

"Who knew Alaska was the home of diamonds as well as gold?" Angus snapped a few close-up photos. "Are you taking me to your private gold mine next?"

"Better." I led the way down the steep trail that led to the beach at the face of the glacier. "I did find a gold nugget once, sitting among the rocks along the creek side. It sparked a mini gold rush among my friends at school, but no other nuggets turned up. That's the closest I've ever gotten to striking it rich. If we could put the two halves of your ancestor's map together and find the missing gold, that would be a huge triumph."

Angus puffed a little as he scrambled down the path. "No reason not to. Your map is back on the wall in the bookshop, and mine is safe in my backpack as we speak. Let's hope nothing else happens to keep the two halves apart."

I paused to look back over my shoulder at him. "Do you think that's what this is all about? Somebody trying to keep the two halves of the map from coming together?"

He paused to lean against a tree to catch his breath. "I think so. I feel like we're in a moment of intersection." His vibrant brown eyes shifted their attention from me to focus on a spot over my right shoulder. I glanced behind me, expecting to see a scavenging raven or something. Nothing was happening there. I had the distinct impression that Angus was looking past me, back through time to see some historical person or event. It was very disconcerting.

"What do you mean, 'moment of intersection?' Intersecting with what?"

Angus's attention snapped back to me. "I have a theory about history, that's all."

"Okay. What's your theory about history?" I continued down the trail, checking behind me to make sure that he was keeping up.

He slowly followed me down. "Most people live their lives in the present, unconcerned about what went before. They go places without ever wondering why that place actually exists." He paused for breath again. "Why does Ptarmigan Port exist, for example? It's pretty far off the beaten path."

I knew that one, thanks to my Local Lore class in fourth grade. "The town was founded in the early 1900s when Craig Cornell discovered gold. The Natives were here for generations before that, of course, thriving on the rich fishing. Salmon and gold—those are the reasons for Ptarmigan Port."

Angus nodded in approval. His voice took on a deeper cadence, as he lapsed into his historian persona. "I believe that the history of a place doesn't remain fixed in the past, but it informs the actions of the present, which then transform into history themselves. It's a fluid, ever-changing continuum. I look at those times as a moment of intersection, when the events of the past reach into the present and affect the course of history in the making." He paused again, breathing heavily as the slope took its toll. "I have the feeling that this is one of those times."

I slithered down the final bit of scree to land on the rocky beach at the face of the glacier where it melted to become Seven Mile Creek. Angus slid down after me, gravity and momentum combining to throw him off balance when he hit level ground. I grabbed his arm before he ended up tumbling into the creek.

He breathed a sigh of relief. "I'm counting on you to catch me."

I reached out to take his other arm and held him there for a moment with both hands, just a shade longer than necessary. Then I patted both arms and let him go. "You're back on solid ground. Want to go all the way to touch the ice?"

His breath came quickly. "Wouldn't miss it for the world."

I took his hand to lead him over the rocks and boulders left behind by the retreating glacier. His hand was warm in mine.

"Is this where you found your gold nugget that fired up your classroom?" His eyes were fixed on the ground, as much to ensure safe footing as to search for a telltale glint of gold.

"Close by, anyway. The glacier has receded quite a bit since I was ten. These rocks here were covered by ice just a decade ago. They haven't been mined for gold before. People really do find gold here from time to time, but I've only found the one nugget."

Angus selected a large boulder and sat down and pulled out his water bottle. The glacier was laid out in front of him in all its glory, the creek rushed alongside, and Cosmo frisked at his feet as the final touch of Southeast Alaska charm. We had the entire beach to ourselves.

I sat down on a sharp boulder across from him, shifting about to get more comfortable. "Tell me about your moment of intersection. Are you suggesting that something that happened in the past, in history, brought about Blake Rivers's death in the twenty-first century?"

He lifted his camera to take a picture of me on my rock with the massive river of ice in the background. "That's what I'm mulling over. I had a lot of time to think in your brother's jail cell. I think that when I showed up in town with half of the map that had hung openly on your wall for decades, I disrupted the equilibrium of this place. For some reason, getting the two halves of the map together is a threat to someone—enough of a threat to kill to prevent it from happening."

I considered this thought, while I watched a few fish jumping in the creek. "The map itself points to gold that your ancestor Alexander Montgomery stole from the SS *Fortunate*. If we put the two halves together, we might be able to find his stash. I happen to know that Blake didn't want your story to get out, presumably because it would indicate that the gold was no longer all on board the shipwreck that he has monetized. But Blake wasn't threatened enough to kill to prevent the two halves coming together—he's the one who was killed. It doesn't make sense." I shifted a few rocks with my toe, idly looking for that elusive glint of gold. Nope. "Even more interesting than the treasure map is the writing on the back. If the two halves of Alexander's message come together, they might tell a story of historical murder."

Angus waved a hand to his backpack, lying next to his rock. "Let's get the two halves together to read the full message."

I dropped my head in my hands, just for an instant. "We can't. I'm going to tell you this because I'm sure it wasn't you, but you can't let it get out. Nels will kill me if he finds out I breathed a word. Promise?"

"Cross my heart."

I heaved a quick breath. "We never knew there was writing on the back of the Pastor's Confession Map because it's always been in its frame. When it resurfaced, the first thing I did was check the back to see what it said. There was nothing there."

I paused to let that astounding statement sink in. "The map on the wall in the Shipshape Bookshop is a photocopy. The real map is still missing."

Chapter Twenty-seven

Angus stared at me, stunned. "A photocopy? Seriously?"

"It's in a frame." For some reason I felt defensive, like he was judging me for not recognizing a blatant fake like that.

"Was it always a photocopy, or did the person who stole it switch out the real map this week."

That was something I hadn't considered. But it couldn't be. "The map has been hanging on the wall since Betty Denton Peterman discovered it in 1952. She wouldn't have had access to a photocopier in those days. I suppose Uncle Vance could have taken it down at some point, copied it, and stored the original, but that would be very much out of character for him. No, I think whoever stole it last Saturday replaced it with a copy."

"Okay, that's clear proof that it's the message on the back that presents a threat to the thief and killer." Angus snapped his fingers, causing Cosmo to bark sharply. "Remember when we were in that awesome fish restaurant, and I was telling you Alexander's story? You knew the waitress, Beverly or something."

"Brenda," I cut in.

"Yes, Brenda. She was very attentive during my tale. I'm sure she heard the whole thing. Could she have something to do with it?"

"She's definitely on my list of suspects. She's been sniffing around at the bookshop like she's trying to figure out who killed Blake, her ex-husband. Now she tells me she doesn't even care about Blake, so I don't know what she's up to." I ran my hands through my hair. "The map was already missing when you told me Alexander's story, so that couldn't have been a cause-and-effect kind of thing."

"No, I guess not." Angus stashed his water bottle and stood up, abandoning our speculations. "How close can we get to the ice?"

"Ready?" I jumped up and picked my way across the rocks and boulders to the edge of the glacier itself. The retreating glacier had scraped deep striations into the rocks at its face. The terminus was gradual rather than a steep edge with calving icebergs like you would see in a tidewater glacier like those in Glacier Bay to the northwest. "We can walk onto the ice for a bit, until it gets more broken up with crevasses. I didn't bring any gear for serious ice climbing today."

Angus took a tentative step onto the ice.

The surface was friable rather than glassy, minimizing the risk of slipping. I always treat the glacier with tremendous respect, as if it were a living beast that might not want me to get too close. The ice was constantly flowing out of the ice field and melting at the face, even if that dynamic process wasn't evident to human eyes. We could hear it, though. "Hear that creaking, like trees in a stiff wind? That's the movement of the ice."

"Wow." He snapped a few pictures, and then stepped back onto solid rock. "I'd love to come back sometime with ice cleats and the whole deal to hike onto the glacier."

I followed him off the ice. "You know what they say about Alaska? Go anywhere in the world you like first but come to Alaska last. You'll never want to leave. It was John Muir who said that, though I might not have gotten the words quite right."

He nodded. "I can definitely see the attraction."

I glanced over my shoulder, to see a group of tourists emerging from the Creek Trail, which was easier than the Ridge Trail I had brought Angus on. "We only have a few minutes before the tourists overrun the face of the glacier. I want to show you one more thing."

I led Angus to the special spot I knew, on the western edge of the glacier where the ice lifted up from the rock it rested on. "We won't go in today, for lack of the proper gear, but if you lay down on your belly you can see into the ice caves."

I eased myself down on the rock and scooted forward until my head was almost underneath the glacier. Angus followed my lead. Side by side, we caught a glimpse of the magical world underneath the glacier. The hole we peered through was only a few feet high at the opening, until it spread out into a vast cave hidden under the glacier. While the ice on top was more like snow than anything else, the ice beneath was a deep shade of blue, smooth as glass, and glistening with water dripping as the glacier slowly melted away. The creaking sounds of the glacier's movement echoed throughout the otherworldly space.

"This is fantastic," Angus breathed. "Can you really go in?"

I smiled at him. His face was inches from mine, colored by the blue light of the underside of the glacier. "Technically it's not safe. The ice could crumble on top of you at any moment. But people do go in, and they come out with stunning pictures of a place that most people have never seen."

"Have you?"

I could feel the warmth of his body next to mine. "I have. I went with Marcy and her husband Rob this past winter, and we slid down into this cave and explored for an amazing and terrifying twenty minutes until we decided we'd risked enough time for one day. I'll show you my pictures sometime."

He reached out to lay his hand lightly over mine. "I'd love to see them."

A handful of ice skittered down from the cave's frozen ceiling, and I slithered back from the opening. "Best not to risk it today." I stood up and pointed to a bare spot of rock to my left. "There was an ice cave on this rock last summer, but the glacier is melting, and it collapsed on a hot July day. Luckily no one was inside at the time."

Angus scrambled to his feet. "You live in an amazing place, Junetta."

I brushed some dirt off my chest. "Yup. I wouldn't live anywhere else." I collected Cosmo, who had found a dead salmon along the creek side. "Let's take the Creek trail back. We'll have to walk along the road a bit to get back to the car, but it's a much gentler trail."

Angus put up no resistance to this suggestion. We got a head start on the group of tourists, so we had the trail to ourselves to begin with. The wide, flat trail led us alongside the rushing creek before bending into the forest. The roar of the creek couldn't penetrate the mossy depths of the forest. We walked in companionable silence.

By the time we walked along the roadside to get back to the car in the Ridge Trail parking lot it was late afternoon and a light rain had begun to fall. "I guess I have to get you back to Clarissa's to finish your police report."

"If I must." His eyes twinkled at me as he climbed into the car. "I'd much rather explore paradise with this delightful company than sit in a trashed room making out a police report."

"Well, I'm happy to have provided a temporary distraction." I grabbed a towel from the back seat and rubbed Cosmo down before settling him into the car. "I do hope your laptop resurfaces like the Pastor's Confession Map did. Such a shame to lose all your research." I pulled out of the parking area.

"Don't worry, all is not lost. I've got all my work backed up on a portable hard drive. I found that in my suitcase while I was getting ready for our hike, so the damage is minimal. It was a new laptop, though."

I dropped Angus off at Clarissa's and headed up the hill to my house to settle Cosmo and grab a quick shower before tackling the mess in my house.

Alas, no gremlins had come in and tidied up my living room while I was out. It took me over an hour to clean up the mess. At least there wasn't any broken glass this time around. Instead, I had to go through papers that had been pulled out of drawers and thrown willy-nilly about the room. I couldn't think of any documents of mine that an intruder would want, unless they were after my social security or bank account numbers. As I sifted through the papers, smoothing out wrinkles and sorting the pages into piles, I breathed deeply, trying to discern a scent of whiskey that would implicate Connor Fisk. I couldn't sense any alcohol, although I did pick up a slight floral scent that made me think of my favorite brand of lavender soap. I nipped into the bathroom to see if the bar of soap had been disturbed. It still sat in a little pile of soap sludge where I'd left it. It wasn't likely to be the source of the lavender smell in my living room.

I frowned down at the soap dish. I had assumed that it was Connor who broke in looking for Blake's notebook. But what if it was a woman?

Brenda Tarkington was the only woman on my list of suspects. She was clearly interested in figuring out who murdered Blake, although she told me she didn't care about him. What did she care about, then?

I went back to my cleaning, lost in thought. I straightened a pile of birthday cards I'd saved over the years. I thought of the boxes of family documents that I'd moved from Uncle Vance's house. Could they have been the object of the intruder's search?

I scanned the living room, but the two file boxes weren't visible. I scrambled to my feet, my heart pounding. Losing those boxes of my family's history would be as traumatic as losing the Pastor's Confession Map. I started frantically searching through the recesses of the living room, until the one sane part of my mind recalled that I had stashed the boxes in my bedroom closet. I rushed in and threw open the closet door. The boxes sat innocuously on the floor, undisturbed. If they had been the object of the intruder's search, my sleeping presence had deterred her.

I pulled out the boxes to make sure that nothing was missing from them. The files looked just the same. Abandoning my clearing-up efforts, I sat down on the bed to go through the files once more, galvanized by Angus's theory of the intersection of history and the present. I couldn't help feeling that the answer to all my questions lay in the papers of either Rev. Denton or his daughter Betty, both of whom interacted with Angus's great-grandfather, Alexander Montgomery, on the fateful night of February 3, 1915.

I shuffled through the file folders in the box of Rev. Denton's papers. I had been interrupted the other night before I finished going through the pastor's correspondence. Vowing not to get sucked into the parishioners' fascinating affairs, I sifted through the letters. Finally, I found the one I was looking for. Tucked away at the back of the folder was an envelope with the name "Mr. A. Mont." written on the front. Although I knew roughly what it said, I wanted to read the pastor's exact words.

Tonight, I had the most extraordinary experience. A young man came to the manse in the middle of the night suffering from a state of acute distress. He said he was seeking absolution. He spoke of a mortal crime in which he had played a part. He bade me not to disclose the nature of this offense according to the sanctity of the confessional. I tried to reason with him, stating that I am merely a Presbyterian minister, not a Catholic priest, and as such I am not endowed with the power to dispense God's forgiveness. He would have none of it. In the end, I agreed to hear his confession and assured him that God forgives the sinner who repents of his wrongdoing.

After revealing his sin, the young man seemed very much easier in his mind. He asked another favor—that I would keep a document safe for him until his eventual return. He pulled a map out of his pocket and tore it in two. He handed me one half, saying, "Put this in an envelope with my name on it, and keep it until I or my family comes to collect it." And so I shall.

The man's name was Alexander Montgomery. Of his crime, I cannot write. May God have mercy on his soul.

Rev. R. Denton
Dated this third day of February 1915

A "mortal crime." That surely referred to murder. All these years, our townsfolk had been so intrigued by the treasure map and the prospect of finding a cache of gold that we overlooked the clear evidence that Alexander Montgomery had been involved in a murder.

There was nothing else in the envelope—no other notes or letters to indicate who the victim was or what happened. I found myself feeling disappointed in Rev. Denton. Sure, he acted as a confessor to Alexander according to his conscience as a pastor, but he allowed somebody to get away with murder.

I dropped the envelope onto my bed. "Cusin Cray" had gotten away with murder. We needed to find out who Cray was, and how he was connected to Blake Rivers.

Chapter Twenty-eight

I lay in bed that night listening to the rain rattling on the roof while old documents whirled through my mind. On the back of Angus's map were the cryptic words making up one half of a vital message that would reveal the identity of a killer. Eight-year-old Betty Denton's diary identified the murderer as "Cusin Cray." The Pastor's Confession Map, containing the other half of the message, was still missing, and a copy hung in its place—and Blake Rivers was dead. Was he killed by my Uncle Vance, to keep the bookshop safe from his blackmailing ways? Or was his death connected to a tale of murder from a hundred years ago? Nothing made sense.

I sought out Marcy the next morning to help me sort things out. She was pulling a tray full of buttery croissants out of the oven when I popped into the café, a warm, scented haven from the light rain outside. She had her long, black hair pulled back by a colorful scarf, and beads of sweat glistened on her forehead.

"Fresh out of the oven," she called out to me. She fixed me a whopping cup of café au lait and dropped a teabag into her own cup. Two clean plates and a heaping pile of croissants appeared on the table before I had barely gotten myself settled. She eased down into the chair across from me.

I lifted my coffee cup. "To my best friend, who makes the tastiest coffee in Alaska!"

She grinned and wiped her forehead. "I'm looking forward to being able to drink it again soon."

I took a sip. "How is Baby Rain? You look a little worn out today."

She leaned back in her chair and rubbed her belly. "Yeah, I'm starting to hope the baby will come early, just to get it over with. Rob's here for another week and a half. It would be great if he could be here for the birth. But they say the baby is the one who chooses when to be born."

I leaned down and spoke directly to her belly. "Hey, Baby Rain. Help your mommy out, will you? Time to make your entrance!"

Marcy laughed, still stroking her belly. "Not today, but soon would be great." She slathered some homemade huckleberry jam onto her croissant. "What's on your mind, Junetta?"

"Murder."

Without missing a beat, she said, "Who are you planning to bump off?"

I laughed and sputtered in the middle of a big gulp of coffee. "If I tell you, then you'll be an accomplice when Nels comes to question you."

She folded her hands on her belly, the picture of innocence. "I'll just tell him that the code of friendship prohibits me from divulging any of your secrets."

"Yeah, he wouldn't fall for that any more than he did when we were in high school, and he was trying to find out what we were doing when we stayed out all night."

She gasped with laughter at the memory. "You told him we had rescued a wounded seal that turned into a fairy spirit and granted us our hearts' desires."

"Yeah, no wonder he doesn't believe me when I tell him things." My laughter died down. "He did tell me that this isn't a game. He's right about that." I took a long drink and set the cup down on the table with a thump. "I feel like there's more than one murder to solve. Blake Rivers was found dead with Uncle Vance's knife in his chest in my back room." We both shuddered. "Then one hundred years ago, Alexander Montgomery took part in a murder that got lost in history, overshadowed by the tragedy of a shipwreck that killed seventy-three people. A hundred years later, Alexander's great-grandson shows up in our town with the other half of the map left behind with the local pastor, my great-great-grandfather." I leaned forward, my coffee forgotten. "I feel like Angus and I together are linked to this murder in the past, and it's somehow connected to the murder of Blake Rivers."

Marcy stared at me, stunned into silence for a moment. But only for a moment. "Get a grip, Junetta. No one could have murdered someone in 1915 and then murdered again a hundred years later. Unless you're going with the ghost option? I'm quite sure your brother would frown on that theory."

"Yeah, I can hear him now, 'Stop wasting my time with your dumb ideas—this isn't a game.'"

Marcy laughed at my imitation of my brother's voice. "He's right, you just said so yourself."

"Yup, I sure did." I took a deep breath, trying to bring myself down from the giddiness of joking to the sober reality that someone in our town today was getting away with murder. "I wasn't thinking that the same person did the two murders. Mostly, I'm struck by the coincidence between the two halves of the map almost but not quite coming together, and the weirdness of Angus's relative and my relative encountering one another on that wild, stormy night. And then when Angus shows up in town with his story, Blake gets killed and the Pastor's Confession Map goes missing. It's all connected somehow." I placed both hands on the table and leaned forward. "Or, the map and its history have nothing to do with anything, and Uncle Vance killed Blake to cover up the fact that he lost the bookshop to Blake in a game of poker."

"Wait, what?"

Marcy stared at me in growing horror as I told her about my recovery of the bookshop's missing ledger and the damning promissory note inside. I could hear my voice starting to shake. "You see how Uncle Vance has the strongest motive for murder of anyone?"

"No." She stood up, grunting with the effort. "No, no, no. Vance wouldn't kill for money like that. I know I said he was my prime suspect, but I can't see him killing Blake just to keep you from finding out about this. That's a really cold-blooded thing to do. I've never thought of Vance as being cold-blooded. More like a hothead, if you ask me."

"Davey said the same thing. I'm not sure it makes a very good defense, to say you're impulsive and passionate, so there's no way you could be a killer."

"Yeah, Nels isn't going to buy that story, is he?" She stacked our empty plates. "And you're convinced of Angus's innocence in all this?"

I closed my eyes. In my mind I could hear Angus's voice saying, "Junetta. I didn't steal your map. It wasn't me; I promise." I believed him, without reservations. "Yes."

I opened my eyes to see her watching me closely now.

She nodded. "Okay. We presume that Uncle Vance is innocent, and you believe that Angus is as well. I'd say you should team up with Angus to help you figure out if the map is at the center of the murder. He's the historian, after all. Well, him and Reba Cornell. I'll bet you can find your answers at the Historical Society, with those two to guide you through all of Reba's musty artifacts."

"I think that's what I should do." I jumped up from the table, ready to take on the mists of history to solve today's mystery.

• • •

As it turned out, Angus wasn't available until after lunch. He apologized profusely when I called him, saying that he was struggling with a bout of intestinal distress which he hoped would pass by the afternoon.

I spent the morning in the back room of the Shipshape Bookshop brainstorming a computerized inventory system that would work for me. Sure, I could have purchased a computer program with all the bells and whistles designed for an independent bookstore, but what fun would that be? As a true Alaskan, I wanted to do it myself, using my own ingenuity to get exactly what I wanted and nothing else. In this case, however, I didn't plan be the one to do the actual programming.

"Hey, Patrick, can I turn you loose on a computer programming project?"

Patrick's head shot up from the pile of books he was shelving. "Uh, sure. Is it for accounting purposes?"

"It is." I regarded him. "What are your thoughts on our accounting issues?"

He glanced around as if fearful of being overheard. "I know Vance has us using the same system that was in place since the beginning, using paper ledgers for sales and a pile of notebooks to record inventory. There's no crossover between the two. Every book we sell has to be recorded twice." He ducked his head. "I'm not saying anything against Vance, but it does make more work for us, and if someone forgets to write something down, there's no way to track it."

I pulled him into the back room to look at my notes, which were handwritten on a stray piece of paper. "Okay, I'm as bad as Uncle Vance. Can you set up a spreadsheet or something to track our inventory and sales like this?"

He bent over the paper and then picked up my pen to make a few quick notes. I could tell straight up that they improved on my idea.

"Yeah, I can do this." He reached for my computer, and I left him to it.

I took a quick trip home to take Cosmo out for a run down the street, dodging the intermittent raindrops, then settled him at home for the afternoon. I knew he would have preferred to ramble through the woods all day, but little dogs can't always get what they want.

Chapter Twenty-nine

Angus appeared on the dot of 1:00 p.m., just like he said he would. "Ready to dive into some historical research?" he said cheerfully.

I narrowed my eyes at him. He looked quite pale, with a thin sheen of sweat on his face despite the cool, rainy weather outside.

I grabbed my jacket and called out to Patrick that I was leaving. "How are you feeling by now, Angus?"

He grimaced. "My stomach's all messed up. I must have eaten something yesterday that didn't agree with me."

I stopped in the middle of the sidewalk, heedless of the wind which was starting to blow the rain sideways. I beat back a mental picture of Angus's ransacked room. Had he been the victim of an attempted poisoning as well? "What did you eat yesterday that might be different from your usual diet?"

"I had breakfast in jail, nothing fancy there. I had lunch at the picnic—it's possible that some of the food was left out too long, I guess. Then I went to the beach and collected mussels for dinner."

"What?" It came out as more of a screech than a question.

Angus gave me a quizzical look. "Mussels. I boiled them into a stew at Clarissa's. It wasn't very good though. I only ate one bite."

My heart started thumping. Although he was an academic, Angus had acted out of abject ignorance. "Haven't you ever heard of PSP? Paralytic shellfish poisoning? The beaches are all infected around here. You have to check with Fish and Game before you go out to harvest. The old wives' tale says that it's not safe to harvest shellfish except in months that contain the letter 'r.' You don't want to mess with PSP—it can be fatal." I brushed rain out of my face and resumed our walk down the sidewalk toward the Historical

Society. "Whatever made you decide to go search for mussels on the beach for dinner?"

He shrugged. "A desire for the authentic Alaska experience? I'm a big seafood fan. I've heard a lot about scalloping around here, but I didn't come prepared for diving. I figured I could collect some tasty seafood without having to go underwater. Reba pointed out the best beach to go to."

I groaned. "Only a cheechako would go out harvesting mussels in the month of June. Reba should have known better than to encourage such foolishness."

"Cheechako?"

"I thought you were an historian! A cheechako is someone who is new to Alaska and unfamiliar with what it takes to survive in the harsh environment. The opposite of a cheechako is a sourdough—someone who has been here a long time and is well versed in Alaska ways. My Uncle Vance is the perfect example of an Alaska sourdough, and you, Angus Montgomery, are a cheechako of the most clueless kind. You're lucky to be alive right now. Repeat after me, 'Only harvest in months that contain the letter 'r.'"

He smiled ruefully and repeated my little jingle. "Luckily it wasn't fatal this time."

"Yeah, you can't count on luck forever." As we approached the Historical Society, a new and horrid thought came to me. What was Reba thinking? Had she sent Angus to the beach to try to poison him? I hadn't considered her as one of my suspects. The very idea was monstrous. You couldn't imagine a more respectable person than Reba Cornell, but the fact remained that she had been waging a years-long campaign to have the Pastor's Confession Map moved to the Historical Society. She knew about the writing on the back of Angus's map. Had she taken matters into her own hands and stolen the map? How did Blake Rivers's death fit into that theory?

I opened the door to the Historical Society, realizing that Angus was still speaking.

"I guess I'll steer clear of any further attempts to live off the land."

I instinctively lowered my voice as if we were entering a library. "Subsistence is alive and well in Ptarmigan Port, but you need someone to teach you what you can eat and what to avoid. The woods are full of red huckleberries that make the most beautiful jam. Then there are bright red baneberries that are so poisonous that as few as four can kill a small child. Most parents around here caution their young kids not to eat any red berries in the woods without checking with an adult first." I sent him a searching look. "You didn't eat any red berries last night, did you?"

He shook his head with a small smile and called out a cheery hello. There was no answer from within Reba's office.

"Reba is expecting me. I told her I would stop by today to keep going on my research. I think we can dive right in."

Shaking the rain from my jacket, I signed my name in the guest book for form's sake and followed Angus behind the counter and into the maze of bookshelves. "I'm on a mission to find out who 'Cusin Cray' was."

"Who?"

"Didn't I tell you? I found a diary from Betty Denton, the pastor's daughter, who witnessed her father talking to Alexander about a man who was stabbed by 'Cusin Cray.' Betty was eight years old..." My words trailed off in the face of Angus's starry-eyed wonder.

"Where...? Do you have the diary on you? How fantastic!"

"It's at home—I'll show you later. It's pretty cool. I feel like the answer to a lot of questions is wrapped up in the identity of 'Cusin Cray.' I'd like to find the ship's manifest or census records for Ptarmigan Port from 1915."

"Reba showed me the ship's manifest the other day." Angus rooted through the shelves until he found a slim bound book titled "SS *Fortunate's* final voyage." It was a collection of newspaper articles and historic photographs of the disaster that had been compiled by the Historical Society in 1925, well before Reba Cornell's time. The last chapter was a facsimile of the ship's manifest.

Angus pulled out a magnifying glass to better view the historic cursive writing.

I leaned over his shoulder to take a picture with my phone, only to find that the battery was dead. I pulled my charging cord out of my purse and plugged the phone in to an outlet on the wall next to our table.

Sensing that Angus's perusal of the ship's manifest might take a while, I started rooting around the cardboard file boxes shoved under the many bookshelves, hoping to stumble upon some documents from 1915. I bypassed the one marked "Peterman Family," saving it for later. Betty's husband Michael Peterman came to Alaska in the mid-1920s, so I knew that box didn't hold any answers for me. I reached for the box labeled "Cornell Family."

I flipped off the lid and started rooting through the papers documenting the history of Reba Cornell's family. As founder of Ptarmigan Port, her grandfather, Craig Cornell, was definitely present in town in 1915.

"There's no Cray on the ship manifest," Angus said, closing the little history book with a snap. "Neither first or last name, or any word that sounds like Cray."

"Word that sounds like Cray...?"

"From your description, it sounds like young Betty was eavesdropping, unnoticed by the two men. She may have been hiding. It's likely that she didn't hear the word correctly or wasn't able to write it down accurately. Her diary counts as an unreliable source in historical researching, but there are methods used to authenticate unreliable information."

I waved my hand at Angus, trying to get him to stop lecturing. "A word that sounds like Cray? Like Craig?" I hauled out a number of files from the "Cornell Family" box and shoved a few of them across the table toward Angus. "See if there's anything in here about what happened on February 3, 1915."

While Angus sifted through piles of papers, I searched the box for diaries. I'd had such luck with Betty's diaries—maybe Craig Cornell kept one of his own. All I could find was a diary from his wife, Lucy Cornell.

I paged through a few months' worth of entries. Lucy's handwriting was easy to decipher. I skimmed rapidly, picking up random phrases here and there. On July 10, 1914: "Craig was out fishing for hours and brought back nothing. We were happy to have beans for supper." On August 17, 1914: "We picked blueberries for three pies. Craig says mine are the best he's ever eaten." On September 2, 1914: "Craig's speech was magnificent. I couldn't have been prouder." On October 22, 1914: "I wore my new dress to church. Craig made eyes at me all throughout the sermon."

I smiled at the thought of this young married couple flirting during the Sunday sermon. I paged back to the beginning of the diary until I came across their wedding day, June 5, 1913. "It rained nonstop all day. Who cares? I'm the happiest bride in all of Alaska." The next few pages listed the couple's wedding gifts. I could have gotten lost in the details, but I was on a mission to find out about the events surrounding the sinking of the SS *Fortunate*.

I turned to the date of February 3, 1915. Lucy noted: "Craig left in the night after a knock on the door. Such a wild, rainy night." There were no other details. I held my breath and read the next day's entry: "He came home in the middle of last night, wild-eyed." She went on to write of the tragedy of the ship's sinking. The next day: "I won't ask him where the blood on his trousers came from. But if it was game, then where's the meat for our table?"

"Angus, you've got to see this." That's when I noticed that Angus was no longer sitting next to me. He must have gotten up to use the restroom or something. I'd been so engrossed in Lucy Cornell's diary that I hadn't even noticed him leaving.

I turned back to the diary. The next few weeks made no mention of Craig's mysterious nighttime excursion. Lucy wrote about her new friend Patsy and her efforts to cultivate a garden in the rainforest. She got a little dog to keep her company while her husband was out. Then on August 10, 1915, she wrote, "Hunters found a body in the woods. They think he's been dead six months. Craig says it was a bear. Trooper Frank says it was murder. Six months ago—that was February. I don't want to think about it." The page for the next day was tear-stained, "When I look at him, I see a killer. But I love him."

I dropped the diary, tears pricking in my eyes. How would I feel if I suspected that the man I loved was a murderer? Poor Lucy!

I wiped my eyes on my sleeve. 'Cusin Cray' was our town founder, Craig Cornell. His loving wife fingered him as a killer in her diary. I didn't know of any evidence in the historical record of a murder in February 1915 or of Craig's involvement. Evidently Lucy kept her suspicions to herself and moved past them, as evidenced by the fact that the couple stayed married for the next thirty-nine years, during which time they had a son, Ryan, who gave them their granddaughter, Reba Cornell. Meanwhile, Craig rose to a position of prominence in Ptarmigan Port, to be lauded every summer on Founder's Day. No one was prouder of his legacy than Reba herself.

I gripped my head in my hands. Angus brought the other half of the Pastor's Confession Map to our town, with writing on the back that would expose Craig Cornell as a murderer. Was that enough of a threat to her family's reputation for Reba to kill to protect it?

Chapter Thirty

I raised my head, startled to find that Angus had not returned to our table. "I hope his mussels aren't giving him more trouble," I muttered, getting up to check the bathroom. The men's room was empty.

I spun around, trying to take in the entirety of the Historical Society in one long glance. The maze of metal bookshelves made this impossible. "Hey, Angus," I called out in a loud voice. "I've got something I want to show you."

I rounded a shelf laden with Ptarmigan Port High School yearbooks, then stopped short, stunned. Reba Cornell stood in my path, holding a double-barreled shotgun leveled straight at my chest. "March," she snapped.

I eyed the shotgun warily. It looked like it dated back to Craig and Lucy's newlywed days, and I didn't know if Reba had the upper body strength to hold it steady enough to fire it. It wasn't a question of aim, however. We were close enough together that she could do horrific damage to me no matter where the shells hit. I held up my hands where she could see them. "Where am I marching to?"

"Turn around, walk to the back door, and don't give me any trouble."

I could feel the shotgun barrels pressed into my back. I imagined a couple of quarter-sized circles imprinted between my shoulder blades. I guessed that the only reason Reba didn't shoot me right away was because she didn't want to deal with a dead body in her Historical Society. Too many questions.

"Open the door and walk straight to my car. Don't try anything stupid." The shotgun pressed harder into my back.

I shot a glance around. I didn't see anyone milling about in the alley behind the main drag. It seemed incredible that Reba could march me at gunpoint to her car in broad daylight without anyone noticing, but that's what was happening. "Where's Angus?"

She tsked. "You're the sleuth! You tell me."

I couldn't smell any gunpowder and I'm sure that, despite my absorption in Lucy Cornell's diary, I would have noticed the sound of a gunshot. "He's in your car." It wasn't a question.

"Open the back door and get in." I fumbled with the door handle, then ducked to one side instinctively as the butt of her shotgun caught me on the shoulder. I felt a searing pain. If I hadn't ducked it would have been the back of my head.

I fell forward onto the back seat, feigning unconsciousness. I felt her shove my feet inside and slam the door shut. I was just about to move around to explore the possibilities when the car door opened again. I lay motionless with my eyes closed, praying that she wouldn't want to mess up her car with my blood. She threw a heavy blanket over my body and slammed the car door again.

Under cover of the blanket, I opened my eyes. I lay sprawled on top of the inert body of Angus. I laid my fingers in the hollow of his throat, and almost sobbed at the feel of his pulse. I poked and prodded him. He was well and truly unconscious. Reba had tied his hands behind his back, presumably after whacking him on the head like she did to me. I struggled to untie his bonds, while periodically patting his cheeks, trying to bring him around.

The car was under way at this point. Reba had the radio blaring. It felt like she was driving very fast indeed. The rosy picture of Nels pulling her over for speeding flashed through my mind, though I didn't expect to be saved by my brother in that fashion. But maybe I could call him! I searched through my pockets, only to realize that I had left my phone plugged in on the table next to me in the Historical Society. I shoved Angus over to check his pockets and came up with his phone. It was no use to me without his password to open it. I groaned silently and continued my efforts to revive him before Reba got us to the remote location that she'd chosen to dispose of our bodies.

Finally, Angus stirred. I clapped a hand over his mouth to stifle his groan. I shoved his phone into his hand. Hoping the radio would cover my voice, I whispered, "Call 911. We're in Reba Cornell's car, headed to the beach." I didn't know if that was our destination. It was a good guess, anyway. I knew the tide was out. If she could avoid any low-tide harvesters, she could simply leave us unconscious at the water line and let the rising tide do the rest.

Angus stared at me, blinking rapidly. I lifted his hand holding the phone to his face. "Unlock it." I could take it from there.

Angus fumbled with the phone screen. His fingers shook so much that it literally took him ten tries to plug in his password.

I snatched the phone from his hand and dialed 911. I pressed the phone to my chest when the dispatcher came on the line with a hearty "What is your emergency?" I almost groaned out loud at the sound of her voice—it wasn't Stella, but a dispatcher from Juneau. "Shh," I hissed. "Hostage situation in Ptarmigan Port. Reba Cornell's car headed to the beach. Junetta Beale and Angus. Call local troopers. She's got a shotgun."

I could hear typing on the other end of the phone and prayed that she was putting me through to Stella and not just typing up a report. After an eternity of dead air, Stella's voice came on the line, "Junetta, honey...."

At that moment the car stopped, and I switched off the phone. Reba got out of the car, hefting the shotgun out with her. I whispered to Angus, "Pretend you're unconscious. When she takes me out, make a run for it." I pressed the phone into his hand.

Before he could react, I threw off the blanket and was frantically patting his face when Reba wrenched open the door. "I can't wake him up," I wailed.

"Get out."

I groaned and inched my way out of the car, moving as slowly as I could. A quick glance around showed me that my good guess was flat wrong. We were nowhere near the beach. Reba had driven out the road and stopped at a trailhead pull-out. I knew the short trail led to the abandoned entrance to the Lucky Mine. Rather than the hiding place for a murderer, it would be the perfect place to dispose of a couple of inconvenient dead bodies!

I shut the car door behind me and faced her. "Reba, you don't want to kill us. Think about it for a minute. There's no way you can get away with our murders. Nels will find our DNA in your car, on your blanket, even on the barrel of your gun." I leaned against the car door and rubbed my palms up and down on the wet metal. "He won't rest until he finds out what happened to his sister. You'll never be safe."

"Shut up!" Reba waved the shotgun at me. Thin strands of hair had escaped from her bun to blow wildly around her face. She looked like an evil witch about to strike us dead with a killing curse. I could almost hear her cackle.

I tried another tack. "Angus's map revealed that Craig Cornell was a murderer. But you already knew that, didn't you?"

She looked down the trail and back to the car where Angus lay, as if trying to figure out how to get rid of both of us. "Come on, walk." She swung the shotgun as an invitation for me to proceed down the trail to my death.

I had no choice. I walked. Shivering in the wind and rain, I limped along as slowly as I could, hoping to lull her into thinking I was too weak to resist. Maybe I could keep her off balance enough to make some desperate attempt at escape. "You didn't want anyone in town to know Craig's secret. Blake Rivers must have figured it out and confronted you while you were stealing the Pastor's Confession Map."

"Blake," she snarled. "Blake was there to steal the map himself. He wanted to hush up the story that part of the gold was gone from the sunken ship. He tried to cut me in on a deal. I knew he would never keep my secret. He would just have something else to hold over me, the little rat."

"He was a blackmailer," I said in a soothing tone, as if to validate her actions. Anything to keep her talking and distract her from blasting me with her shotgun. We were out of sight of the car now. I wondered if Angus had made a run for it. Oh, what were his chances, stunned and clearly a cheechako? Nels was probably on the way to the beach right now. If anyone was going to save me, it had to be me. "I suppose you stabbed Blake with Uncle Vance's knife on purpose, to pin the murder on him?"

"I didn't mean to kill Blake. He tried to grab the map and I pushed him over. He fell and hit his head on your bookshelf, and that was the end of him. Lucky for me, Vance leaves a pile of knives around." A note of gloating entered her voice. "I thought it was fitting to implicate him in the theft of the map, after he kept it out of my hands for all those years."

A few more halting steps, and I stood in front of the mine adit. It was nothing more than a cave entrance made of heavy beams of wood to form a massive doorway. A matching door used to guard the entrance to the mine, but it had been taken off its hinges and salvaged many years ago. These days, the entrance was covered by a series of two-by-fours nailed across the opening. Several of these were ripped off and strewn about the ground, just like Nels had said.

"Reba, Nels knows about the vandalism up here. This will be the first place he'll look. You won't get away with this."

"Inside!" Reba barked, pointing the shotgun barrel at the gaping hole in the wood which gave off a dank, musty smell.

I saw my chance, and I took it. While the barrel of the shotgun was pointing away from me, I caught up a broken two-by-four and swung it with all my might. I wasn't aiming for Reba so much as the gun. My board connected with her barrel with a crash that wrenched both items out of our hands. My two-by-four spun through the air to land somewhere behind Reba, and her shotgun skittered along the rocks at our feet. She swooped down to grab it. I was too quick for her. I rammed my shoulder into her chest, knocking her down. I don't normally go around tackling senior citizens to the ground, but there was nothing normal about this situation. I snatched up the shotgun and pointed it at her. "Stay down and don't move!"

She held a hand to her chest, whimpering. "What have you done to me?"

Oh, man, I hoped she wasn't going to have a heart attack. I shook the shotgun at her. "I'm taking control of the situation."

My arms trembled as I aimed the heavy shotgun at her. I had no idea how to fire it, and I surely wasn't going to hit her over the head with it. I swung around in a quick arc and threw the shotgun into the opening of the mine adit. It made a satisfying clatter as it bounced and fell down the deep hole into the maze of tunnels. Nobody was going to get shot today.

Reba scrambled to her feet while my back was turned. She hefted a big rock and held it over her head, menacing me. I grabbed my broken two-by-four and wielded it like a baseball bat. "Just try me," I shouted.

Into this picture of mutually assured destruction wandered Angus, his phone held to his ear. "Yeah, there's a broken-down doorway, and Junetta and Reba are both here." He held out his phone in my direction and mouthed, "Nels."

"We're at the Lucky Mine adit," I hollered. "Reba's gun is gone, but she's still dangerous. Hurry!"

Angus held the phone to his ear again. "He says he'll be right here," he called out to me, and hung up.

Reba saw that she was outnumbered, and the prospect of Nels's imminent arrival took all the wind out of her. She dropped her rock and plumped down on a boulder marking the end of the trail, rubbing her chest again as if I had seriously injured her.

Angus pulled off his belt and wrapped it around Reba's wrists, pulling her arms behind her back. Then he drew me aside and handed me his phone. "Call your brother," he whispered. "I wasn't able to connect with him."

My jaw fell open and I stared at this deceptive cheechako for a long beat. Then I grabbed the phone and punched in Nels's number. He picked up on the first ring.

"Which beach?" he barked, before I could even utter a word.

"I was wrong. We're at the Lucky Mine adit. We tied up Reba when she thought you were almost here. She might still give us trouble, even though I got rid of her gun."

"I'm on my way." I heard running feet, the slam of a car door, and the wail of sirens before I hung up the phone.

• • •

Reba didn't give us any more trouble. Good thing, because Angus was jelly-legged and most likely had a concussion, and I was trembling from reaction. Plus, my shoulder hurt something fierce. It had taken the blow from Reba's gun stock and then borne the impact of my flying tackle. "Football players wear shoulder pads for a reason," I muttered.

Angus heaved himself off the mine adit doorpost where he had been leaning. He tottered over and put both hands on my shoulders and began to gently massage my aches and pains away. "Not a football player," he whispered in my ear, keeping a watchful eye on Reba. "You're more like a superhero. I could almost see the words, 'biff,' 'bam,' and 'pow' hovering over your head when I showed up. You saved our lives."

My arms went around his neck, and I hugged him tight. "You showed up just in time. I didn't know what my next move was going to be."

"I'm sure you would have come up with something amazing." His hands slid up my neck to cup my face, and I closed my eyes for his kiss. For a man with a concussion, he was an excellent kisser.

Our first kiss, dramatic though it was, didn't last long. We were interrupted by my little brother.

Chapter Thirty-one

Nels came running at top speed into the clearing, gun drawn. For an instant I thought he was going to leap on Angus to get him away from me, but Nels was a more astute observer than I gave him credit for. He holstered his gun and caught up the handcuffs that dangled at his waist in one smooth motion. He snapped them on Reba's bound hands, then slipped off Angus's belt and handed it to him. "You all right, Sis?"

That minute or two that Nels took to apprehend his suspect gave Angus and me time to compose ourselves. While no longer locked in an embrace, I kept hold of Angus's hand as if it were an anchor in a stormy sea. "Reba is the killer. She killed Blake, and she tried to kill us."

Reba huffed like a cornered bear. Nobody paid her any mind. Nels struggled to follow my disjointed story of an unknown murder in 1915 that led to Blake Rivers's death one hundred years later.

"Blake had nothing to do with the map or its history. Why did he have to die?"

I glanced at Reba for an answer. She tossed her head and looked away, leaving me to fill in the blanks. "Blake showed up at the bookshop to steal the map to keep his customers from finding out that his shipwreck attraction contained less gold than he said. But Reba beat him to it. Blake saw her stealing the map, and she knew he would either blackmail her or turn her in. She pushed him off and he fell and hit his head and that's how he died. The knife was just to put the blame on Uncle Vance."

Nels stared at me, dumbfounded. "She killed him to cover up the story that her grandfather, Craig Cornell, was a killer? This was all about family loyalty?"

Reba sat up straight on her boulder. "My grandfather, Craig Cornell, was the founder of this town. We owe him everything. I won't have his name sullied in any way. I won't!"

Clearly, if she wasn't handcuffed by the law, she would happily kill all three of us and anyone else who came along to tarnish the sterling reputation of her esteemed grandfather. I was suddenly struck by the irony of the whole situation. In order to hide the fact that her grandfather was a murderer, Reba had become a killer herself. Our town historian strove to conceal history to protect her family's legacy.

Nels shook off any more attempts to try to understand Reba's motivations. "I'm going to get her behind bars before she tries anything else," he said. "I'll send Mark over to pick you up. Don't go anywhere or try anything foolish or heroic until he gets here."

I rubbed my aching shoulder. "I'm done with heroics for today."

Angus and I sat side by side on Reba's boulder, huddled under her blanket, until Trooper Mark showed up. We held hands and snuck in a kiss or two, but mostly we just sat. He whispered in my ear, "You'll always be my hero."

I whispered back, "Biff, bam, pow."

We both laughed.

• • •

Trooper Mark deposited the two of us at the Front Street Clinic, the closest thing to an emergency room in our small town. They diagnosed Angus with a concussion and tucked him up in bed overnight. Trooper Mark took me home to shower and rest, with the promise that Nels would fill me in on the case as soon as he could.

As it turned out, I didn't check back with Nels until the next day. I took Trooper Mark's words to heart and collapsed in bed after an hour-long shower that used up all my hot water. Cosmo came and curled up on the bed with me, for once curbing his boundless energy to allow me to sleep the sleep of exhaustion afforded to every superhero once the danger had passed.

It was well past time to open the Shipshape Bookshop by the time I roused myself and moseyed down the hill the next morning. I expected to face an anxious and harried Patrick. Instead, when I flung open the door, I saw Uncle Vance perched on his stool behind the counter, a knife in one hand and a whittling stick in the other. It was as if he had never left.

"Uncle Vance!" I ran to grab him in a hug, knife and all. He knew enough to sit motionless until I released him.

"What, you want to send me back to jail for accidentally stabbing you to death? 'Please, Trooper Nels, I'm innocent. There were numerous witnesses who saw her launch herself at me.'"

I laughed and let him go. "I'm so glad to have you back."

I was about to quiz him about his time in jail in Juneau when the bell on the front door jangled. Brenda Tarkington darted into the shop and ran straight to Uncle Vance to engulf him in a hug to rival my own. "I just heard they let you out. Thank goodness you're back!" She laid a hand on his cheek and gazed into his eyes with a huge sigh of relief. "You're safe!"

Uncle Vance drew her into a warm embrace. "What are you staring at?" he barked at me.

I threw out my hands, entranced. "The two of you. You've got no reason to hide. You're perfect for each other!"

Brenda's face flamed a deep red. "Who said anything about hiding?" she mumbled into Uncle Vance's shoulder.

"Now I get it, Brenda. My fatal mistake! You didn't care about Blake Rivers—you cared about Vance Peterman. All this time you were poking around, trying to prove him innocent." I gazed at her reproachfully. "You could have said something. We could've worked together."

"My private affairs are just that, private," Uncle Vance growled. He stroked Brenda's graying hair with a gentle hand.

I stared at that hand, fascinated. "Let me guess. You were with Brenda when Blake was killed, and you didn't want her to be your alibi. That's why you kept going on about your right to remain silent." I shook my head at the two of them. "You caused Nels a lot of unnecessary trouble, Uncle Vance."

"He caused me unnecessary time behind bars. I guess we're even."

Marcy ducked out from behind the beaded curtain, a full tray in her hands and a wide smile on her lips. "Coffee and scones to welcome you home, Vance."

• • •

After the excitement of Uncle Vance's return had subsided, everything slipped back to normal. Uncle Vance sat behind the counter, whittling a piece of wood no bigger than my thumb. Patrick took his time waiting on the rush of customers who flowed into the shop to escape the pouring rain. It was as if nothing bad had ever happened.

Angus showed up in time for one of Marcy's excellent scones. None the worse for being led to ingest potentially lethal shellfish and then bashed on the head by the woman he thought was helping him with his research, he sat in a corner of the café watching everything that was going on in both café and bookshop...or rather, he sat watching me. Whenever I caught his eye, his face lit up in a huge smile. I could feel that goofy smile on my own face every single time.

Nels strode into the bookshop late morning, a paper-wrapped parcel under one arm and a laptop under the other. Before he could say a word, Uncle Vance slid off his stool and stalked into the back room, slamming the door behind him.

Nels laid the parcel down on the counter with a sigh. "Guess I'm going to have to earn forgiveness. I wonder how long that'll take." He handed the laptop to Angus, who came to stand next to me. "When we searched Reba's house, we found this. She thought she could cover up history by erasing your research. But with no tech knowledge, she had no way to achieve that goal."

Angus cradled the laptop in his arms. "Everything was backed up, so she couldn't have destroyed my research. Even if it wasn't and I lost all my notes, I could have recreated them over time. Funny thing about history—you can't make it go away."

Nels turned to me. "Reba was the one who broke into your house as well. You showed her Betty Denton's diary, which she recognized as another piece of damning evidence. She searched through your things but didn't find anything before Cosmo scared her off. At this point she wasn't thinking that these break-ins would point a finger away from both Uncle Vance and Angus. She was a desperate woman."

I thought back to those boxes of documents, safely stowed in the bottom of my closet for the night. Thank goodness Reba didn't come into my room. In her state of desperation, as Nels put it, I could imagine her stabbing me in my sleep. I shuddered. Cosmo had very possibly saved my life!

Finally, Nels indicated the parcel on the counter. He pulled back the brown paper to reveal a small piece of paper sandwiched between two pieces of sturdy cardboard. "The Pastor's Confession Map. Reba had hidden it in her kitchen cupboard, but she couldn't bring herself to destroy it. It's priceless history, damning though it is."

Beside me, Angus held his breath, drinking in his first sight of our historical map as if he beheld a long-lost Shakespeare manuscript inscribed by the bard himself.

The familiar drawing looked small and vulnerable outside of its frame. I smoothed the paper with a gentle hand and turned it over.

Sure enough, there was writing on the back. Handwritten in pencil, the following lines were scrawled on the back of the map that had hung in my bookshop since before I was born:

Me and Bob filched the
Craig's house. He showed
gold. I made a map. But
a knife. Craig had a knife
left him there. I snuck
drew this new map. I

"There it is," I whispered. "'Craig had a knife.' When Reba saw that, she knew exactly who it meant. She must have read Lucy Cornell's diaries, where she suspected her husband Craig was a killer."

Angus rooted through his backpack and pulled out his own document holder. He eased his half of the map out of its envelope and laid it down next to ours. When he lined up the two halves correctly, we could read the full message:

Me and Bob filched the gold. We went to Cousin Craig's house. He showed us where to bury the gold. I made a map. But Bob was drunk and pulled a knife. Craig had a knife too. He killed Bob and we left him there. I snuck back and moved the gold and drew this new map. I can't trust anyone.

Angus, Nels, Patrick, and I clustered around this message in silence. I could feel Alexander Montgomery's fear stark on the page through his shaky handwriting and bald words. He had witnessed a murder by his cousin Craig, committed in the act of stashing stolen gold. He must have been afraid he would have to answer for the crime. Ultimately it didn't matter, because Alexander went down with the ship that very night. Cousin Craig rose to prominence in our young town, with no stain on his name until over sixty years after his death.

I narrowed my eyes at the message. "If your ancestor, Alexander Montgomery, wrote this message about his cousin Craig, Reba's grandfather, does that mean that you and Reba are related?"

Angus looked up, startled. "I suppose it's possible. I'll have to dive into some detailed genealogical research to sort that out. I don't like the thought that my distant cousin tried to kill me."

I patted him on the arm. "Statistically, more murders are committed by family members than by strangers. I read that online once."

Ignoring me and my foolishness, Nels carefully flipped both halves of the map over and adjusted them to form an intact treasure map. He leaned over and studied it avidly. "There it is," he whispered. "The missing clue." He turned to Patrick, who was drinking in the treasure map just as intently. "We all thought the 'tall tree' had to be in the stand of old-growth pines along the west side of the glacier. Here the map clearly shows it standing on the east bank of Seven Mile Creek."

Patrick leaned closer. "That's not Seven Mile Creek. There's a big bend in the creek on the map, but Seven Mile Creek flows straight out from the glacier with hardly any deviation at all."

"It does now." Nels could hardly contain his excitement. "There's a spot along the creek where you can see where the water used to flow, before that big flood in 1968 that brought down a lot of trees and changed the course of the river. Ask Uncle Vance about the big flood—he loves to talk about how the entire landscape along the Seven Mile Creek watershed was altered and the schoolhouse was completely inundated, and school was canceled for two weeks straight. Best two weeks of his life, to hear him tell it."

"Don't you forget it!" Uncle Vance moved out of the doorway to the back room, where he must have been lingering throughout this entire conversation. He stumped over to join the crowd of us bent over the map. "Looks like X marks the spot of Davey's favorite campsite, right there." He looked up to lock eyes with Nels.

"Come with me," Nels said. "Let's go find that gold!"

• • •

I left the two of them to plan their treasure hunt. I knew that Nels had realized his dream of becoming a trooper to serve his home community, but he had another lifelong dream. There was nothing more thrilling to him than the opportunity to find the lost treasure of the Pastor's Confession Map. As for me, I had a bookshop and a floating bookmobile to run. Or did I?

Connor Fisk barged into the bookshop. Ignoring the two halves of the map on the counter, he slapped down another piece of paper. "I've come for what's mine," he announced. "My Uncle Blake might have been happy to collect money from you on a weekly basis, Vance Peterman, but I want the whole thing. This bookshop is legally mine."

There it was in black and white, exactly as I had read on the yellow piece of legal paper in my ledger: "Vance Peterman attests that Blake Rivers won full ownership of the Shipshape Bookshop in a game of straight poker on this date of February 22, 2015." We could all see and recognize Uncle Vance's signature.

Uncle Vance stared at me in horror, his mouth hanging open. "Junetta..." he croaked. That's as far as he got.

Nels picked up the paper and flicked it with his fingertips. "What is this? A game of straight poker in February 2015? Were you all drunk?" He looked around at all of our blank stares and started to laugh. "Connor. Your uncle got cheated. Vance Peterman couldn't lose the Shipshape Bookshop in a game of poker in 2015. He didn't own the bookshop at the time. He legally transferred ownership to Junetta in November of 2014. This paper is less than worthless."

"What about all those weekly payments to keep things quiet?" Connor took the words right out of my mouth.

"Weekly payments?" Nels shook his head. "You should ease off on the whiskey, Uncle Vance. Looks like you were the one who got played, if Blake was collecting money from you to hide the fact that you lost the bookshop that you didn't have any ownership rights over anymore." He handed the paper back to Connor. "You can take it to court if you want. It would just be a waste of money."

Connor crumpled the paper in his fist and stalked out the door.

I don't often pronounce the words, "my hero," and "my little brother" in the same breath. This was definitely an exception to the rule. I threw my arms around him for a quick hug. "Thank you! I thought I was about to lose it all."

He just rolled his eyes in that annoying way of his. "Pay attention to what you read, Sis."

Chapter Thirty-two

Nels wanted to keep his treasure hunt quiet—just himself and Uncle Vance, if possible. I don't know what he was thinking. By the time he had photocopied the two halves of the map and laminated it to protect against rain, he faced a crowd of eager gold seekers gathered in the Last Chance Café. It was as if he'd called for a posse. Uncle Vance wore his weathered hiking boots that had taken him across the Chilkoot Trail in his younger years, following in the footsteps of the Yukon Gold Rush stampeders. Brenda Tarkington sat next to him, a smile not far from her lips as she gazed at her sweetie. Davey sat at the next table over, constantly ribbing Uncle Vance about following his young nephew into the woods on a search for buried treasure.

Nothing could keep Patrick away from the treasure hunt. "It's the chance of a lifetime," he said to me, his hands clasped together as if in a prayer of supplication. "But if you can't spare me, I'll understand. We need to keep the bookshop running."

"Are you kidding me? We're closing for the day. I wouldn't miss this adventure for the world, and neither will you." Patrick's beaming smile was worth more than any profits we would lose in one day.

Marcy elected to stay behind. Her lips trembled a bit as she served hot coffee all around. "Make a photo record," she said to me. "I want to see the exact moment when you hit gold."

I enveloped her in a hug. "I'll save a bit of gold for Baby Rain."

Angus was geared up for the treasure hunt in his still-new hiking boots, advertising himself as the cheechako that he was. He sat quietly at a café table, occasionally snapping a photo of the chattering crowd.

Even Kirk came along for the ride. He showed up at the trailhead when we were all assembling for our trek through the woods to Davey's favorite campsite, the probable spot of the hidden treasure. "This is it, babe," he called out to me with a huge grin. "History in the making. I can't wait to get my hands on that gold."

I waved at Kirk and took Angus's hand firmly in my own. I refrained from swinging our joined hands over my head, but if that's what Kirk needed to get the message, then that's what he'd get.

Nels organized the party, bringing Uncle Vance and Davey to the front of the line. Between the eight of us we had four spades, a pickaxe, and a Vietnam War era machete, not to mention Uncle Vance's ornately carved walking stick. We looked like we were storming the castle to confront the dragon.

The trail was narrow and rooty, hardly more than a deer track through the thick underbrush. The spiny leaves of devil's club scratched against my arms. I was glad I'd worn my windbreaker, even though there wasn't any rain, only mist swirling through the understory, creating the perfect mood of mystery for a treasure hunt for gold.

After a bit, Nels dropped back to walk next to me and Angus. "Reba Cornell is having conniptions about this treasure hunt taking place without her." He assumed a falsetto, "'You mustn't allow this historical moment to go undocumented.' She's livid at being left out."

I rolled my eyes. "Serves her right for resorting to murder to suppress history. Good thing we brought along a different historian to do the honors."

Angus held up his phone. "I'm ready." His eyes sparkled in anticipation.

It wasn't a long walk to Davey's favorite campsite on what used to be the east bank of Seven Mile Creek. There were a number of tall trees shading the little clearing. After a spirited argument about the orientation of the map and the choice of tree, Uncle Vance broke ground for the dig. Soon every spade was in play as dirt and clods of moss flew everywhere.

In a surprisingly short time, Patrick let out the cry, "Eureka!" He was nearly bowled over by half a dozen eager hands all reaching into the hole and scrabbling for the prize. Brenda was the one who came up victorious. She pulled out a leather drawstring bag small enough to fit in one hand. In a quick motion, she loosened the string and tipped the bag to reveal the bright glint of gold.

Angus fired off a series of photos as, one after another, we all got a chance to touch the gold. Holding that heavy little bag in my hand was a moment of pure magic, as if an eagle were to swoop down and land on my finger. I could hardly believe it was real.

Angus put an arm around my shoulder. "Our moment of intersection comes full circle. I brought half a treasure map to Ptarmigan Port, and now we're holding my great-grandfather's gold in our hands. Too bad we won't get to keep it."

"Wait, what?" I cried, my voice nearly drowned out by Brenda's loud screech, "What?" She folded her arms on her chest and faced Angus. "Who do you say this gold belongs to, then?"

He shook his head sheepishly, stroking the gold with a gentle finger. "The gold was stolen from the SS *Fortunate* by my ancestor, Alexander Montgomery. I can't profit from his crime. The gold originally belonged to the passengers returning from the Yukon gold fields who went down with the ship. They probably have descendants that a good historian could find. Failing that, I suppose a local museum would welcome a new exhibit, right?" He eased the bag out of my grasp and handed it to Nels.

Nels clasped the bag tightly in one fist. "You're right, doggone it. This gold, which could be worth thousands of dollars, by the way, is not ours to keep, by law." He shook his head sadly. "Take a picture of it now—that's all you're going to get." Then his face brightened. "We found it! After all these years, all those expeditions into the woods, we finally found it!"

We spent the next half hour lining up and posing with the shovels, pickaxe, and bag of gold, snapping photo after photo for posterity as if we were at a beach wedding. I planned to frame the one of me and Nels with Uncle Vance to hang on the bookshop wall next to the reassembled Pastor's Confession Map. It was our family's story, after all.

Nels cornered me at the tail end of the photo shoot. "Your new boyfriend can be a very annoying stickler for the rules," he grumbled, glancing sideways at Angus posing with the bag of gold.

I felt a rush of warmth that had nothing to do with the sun breaking out from its cloud cover to bathe our group with rays of light. My new boyfriend. I kinda liked the sound of that. "Come on, Nels, you would have done the right thing with the gold even without Angus."

He laughed. "Maybe. Maybe not. We'll never know now, will we?"

Chapter Thirty-three

It couldn't be put off any longer. The ferry waits for no one.

I went on board with Angus to accompany him to Juneau for his flight back to New York. I spouted some story about shopping in town. I'm sure nobody believed me. I just wanted to see him off properly.

The ferry ride from Ptarmigan Port to Juneau took about four hours. It was smooth sailing the whole way. I didn't have to save Angus's life even one time.

We stood together on the bow rail, savoring the fresh breeze and the sight of a pod of Dall's porpoises frisking alongside. Their black and white markings gave them a look of tiny orcas as they raced the ferry.

Angus braced himself against the rail to take a picture of the porpoises. "Let me guess—you see these porpoises on a weekly basis, right?"

"I live in paradise." I slid along the rail until I was snuggled up next to him. "You could too, you know. Reba's off to prison for murder, which leaves the Ptarmigan Port Historical Society without a director. Who better to fill her shoes than a grad student in History whose great-grandfather authored the most prized historical document of our little town?"

He pocketed his phone and slid an arm around me, drawing me close to his side. "Paradise...I love the sound of that."

Epilogue

Baby Rain was born on June 26, a beautiful baby girl that Marcy and Rob named Lisa, in honor of her great-grandmother. It was a long, hard labor. Thank goodness Rob was able to take time off to be there.

"Poor Rob, I nearly broke all the bones in his hand for squeezing it so hard," Marcy told me when it was all over. "I hollered every swear word I know, and a couple I just made up on the spot. I hope Lisa didn't hear any of that."

I looked at the tiny pink bundle I was cradling in my arms. "If she did, she won't hold it against you." I leaned down to breathe in the sweet scent of her newborn head. "She's perfect."

Marcy held out her arms and settled Lisa close to her chest. "In every way."

"I don't have any gold to give her, but I've got this." I handed her the balloon-covered bag I had brought. Nestled inside was the nicest collection of board books that the Shipshape Bookshop could boast. "I picked these out seven and a half months ago, the very first day you told me you were pregnant." I fished around in the bag and pulled out a slip of paper—the form I used to sign kids up for their library card for the floating bookmobile. "Then when she's ready, here's her library card."

Marcy laughed while wiping away a tear. "Thanks, Auntie Junetta. It's perfect."

About the Author

Photo by Mike Barnhill

Greta McKennan is a wife, mother, and author, living her dream in the boreal rainforest of Juneau, Alaska. She is the author of the *Stitch in Time* Mystery series. She enjoys a long walk in the woods on that rare sunny day and reading cozy mysteries when it rains. Her author heroines include Louisa May Alcott, Mary Stewart, and M.M. Kaye, among many, many others.

Greta's six-word biography is titled Creation: "Three children, three books, and counting." Be on the lookout for the fourth book!

www.ingramcontent.com/pod-product-compliance
Lightning Source LLC
Chambersburg PA
CBHW011515100726
47899CB00010BD/3379